Saint-Malo Murder

Sandrine Perrot – Brittany Mystery Series
Book 2

Christophe Villain

The Rue de la Cloche

Sandrine opened the glass door that led from her cottage out onto the terrace and into the garden. Although she had only lived here for a few weeks, she already felt at home in the old stone house which had previously been used as a sheepfold. Her Aunt Celine had lovingly restored the little building as a guest house in the years before her death. The kitchen-cum-living room occupied almost the entire ground floor; on the crowded upper floor was her bedroom, a study and a tiny bathroom. After her aunt's death, Sandrine had rented the main house to Rosalie Simonas, a very successful writer. When she moved into the neighbouring building, Rosalie had immediately asked if Sandrine was planning to end her lease, but she had everything she needed here, especially compared to an apartment she could hardly afford on her police salary in Paris.

In one hand she held a cup of hot coffee, and seated herself on the varnished, red-brown acacia wood garden lounger which she had put on the terrace. In her pockets were a paperback, her phone and a handy Bluetooth speaker. She inhaled the fresh sea air, filling her lungs with the smell of salt and seaweed, but also the scent of pine trees that grew on the border of her property

1

and from whose branches a blackbird watched her curiously. She ran her bare feet over the cold stone slabs and shivered in the light breeze that swept in from the bay. It was the end of May; the days were quite warm, but the nights cooled down considerably. The sun was already well above the horizon, but it would still take a while for it to prevail. The woollen blanket lay on one of the garden chairs; she would need it.

She made herself comfortable on the lounge chair, pulled the blanket over her stomach and warmed her hands on the cup. From her cottage, the flat lawn stretched out to a knee-high wall that bounded the property on the sea-side. Behind it lay a hiking trail and a slope falling steeply towards the sea. She loved the view over the bay. On a clear day she could make out Mont-Saint-Michel and the Normandy coastline beyond. So far she hadn't managed to visit the tidal island. Maybe she'd go in the next few days, if the dry weather held up. It was a nice trip by motorcycle. From June at the latest, tourists overran Mont-Saint-Michel and crowded the narrow path that led up the hill to the abbey, a sight only the owners of restaurants and souvenir shops enjoyed.

This weekend, she was free from all standby police duty; she'd decided to enjoy this Sunday by spending most of the time lazing on the lounger in the garden. She glanced at the cover of the paperback. *Oyster Killer*. It was the latest crime novel by Rosalie which she had dropped off a while ago, but the investigation into the case of a dead woman on the Brittany coastal path had kept Sandrine busy.

Today she would take the time to finally read the story of Commissiare Hugo Delacroix. Rosalie was becoming impatient and wanted to hear Sandrine's professional opinion as an investigator.

She put the book on the blanket, turned on the speaker and picked up the phone on which she had put together a playlist during breakfast for a lazy morning. Suddenly, her cell phone began to vibrate.

The name *Adel* came up on the caller ID and Sandrine cursed. When her assistant, Brigadier Chief of Police Adel Azarou, called on her day off it didn't bode well for her weekend plans. A premonition came over her that Rosalie's crime novel would remain unread today.

"Hello, Adel. Why are you disturbing my richly deserved weekend off?"

She listened intently, then her face darkened.

"Are the forensic technicians already at the scene? I'm about to leave." She looked at her watch. "Give me thirty minutes."

She ended the call and tossed her cell phone onto the blanket. Her dream of a cosy morning in the garden had just burst like a soap bubble. Why couldn't people die on weekdays or at other, more convenient times? Sandrine sat up and gathered her belongings. She looked at the cloudless sky and decided to leave the lounge chair where it was. With any luck, this would be a natural death and she could make it back to the garden by noon.

She went inside to put on her black leather motorcycle trousers and sturdy ankle boots. She fastened her shoulder holster, took the SIG Sauer SP 2022, the standard weapon of the national police, from the mini-safe in her bedroom and pulled her motorcycle jacket over it. Her helmet hung on the wardrobe hook next to the door. Since it was Sunday morning and low season, the streets would be relatively traffic-free. In twenty minutes, she could make the distance from her house in Cancale to Saint-Malo without exceeding the speed limit too much.

* * *

The Rue de la Cloche was part of a well-known street, located in the old town, near the Place du Québec and right next to the historic city wall. The address belonged to a building which overlooked the seaside fortress wall and could be plainly seen on any panoramic picture of the former Corsair city.

Sandrine drove slowly towards the house and looked around for a parking space. A policeman recognized her, waved and lifted the barrier tape behind which were several police and an ambulance. She parked the motorcycle next to the old Citroën owned by Jean-Claude Mazet, head of forensics. Adel had said on the phone that the forensics staff had been in the victim's home for more than an hour. The team worked very meticulously, so it could take a while before they left until she'd be allowed to look unhindered at the crime scene, assuming it even was a crime. Adel had spoken quite vaguely, which was not like him.

She packed her leather jacket into one of the side cases, took out a light wind and rain-proof jacket and slipped it on. A T-shirt would have sufficed on this nice warm day, but she didn't want to scare passers-by with the sight of her gun.

"Hello, Sandrine." Adel Azarou approached her; he must have noticed her arrival right away. As usual, the slender man was groomed to perfection. His beard was neatly trimmed and the fresh breeze did not disturb his carefully arranged hair. The apricot cashmere sweater looked expensive and perfectly matched his designer jeans and dark leather shoes. Even though Adel definitely put a lot of time into his appearance, he always seemed effortlessly dapper.

"Thank you for messing up my Sunday."

"It couldn't be helped. I had other plans, too." What, exactly, he didn't say. Sandrine appreciated that. They were a good investigative team but not close friends who shared details about their private lives.

"We can pity each other afterwards," she said, laughing softly. "Where's the crime scene?"

"On the top floor." He pointed at the long stone house with four floors. The open attic covered by a slate roof had been converted into more living space, with walls, insulation and dormers. Something that was certainly worth it in this area. The view of the sea and the mouth of the Rance to Dinard from the upper windows must be fantastic, and for which both local owners and renters would pay handsomely.

"Shall I get you up to speed?"

"No, thanks. I want to get my own impression first, as unbiased as possible. Then you can fill in the gaps."

"I would need an excavator to fill in these gaps. We don't know much yet, except that there is a person who most definitely did not die a natural death."

Two of Mazet's men were standing in front of the building, smoking. One of the technicians held the massive front door open, threw his cigarette on the ground then followed them into the stairwell. On the ground floor there were garages and storage rooms, above that was a dentist's office and the office of a tax consultant, then came rental apartments. Two occupied the top floor. The door to the right was slightly ajar and Sandrine entered.

"Bonjour, Monsieur Mazet," she greeted the forensic technician. "How far along are you?"

"It'll take us a while, but you can come in and look around as long as you don't disturb the crime scene." He put overalls, disposable gloves and shoe covers into her and Adel's hands.

The apartment wasn't large, but the sparse stark white décor throughout made it seem much more spacious. The parquet floor reflected the light in a slight shade of red, like acacia honey. Right in the middle of the room was a thick rug. A sofa and a chaise lounge stood opposite a floor-to-ceiling closed wall unit with frosted glass doors. Between two windows hung a nearly two-metre-wide art print of a wave breaking on the quay wall of Saint-Malo.

"A pretty sterile apartment. Elegant, expensive design in white and easy to clean. No dust on the ground. Even the magazines on the table are neatly aligned, parallel to the edge." Sandrine shuddered at the thought of living in such an environment.

"The kitchen is similar. Very expensive appliances which seem as though they've been barely utilised. From the look of it, you would get the impression that nobody lived here. I can't find anything personal, no photos or souvenirs, not even a used coffee cup. Whoever lived here did not want to reveal too much about themselves," said Adel. "A very introverted person."

"Where is the body?"

He pointed to a spiral staircase leading to the attic.

At the top of the stairs, Sandrine stopped and looked at the scene in front of her: the forensic technicians were taking fingerprints and putting evidence in transparent bags. The photographer was packing his camera in a padded aluminium box. Doctor Hervé, the medical examiner, closed his doctor's bag and greeted her with a quick nod.

Monsieur Mazet, would it be possible to have the crime scene to myself for a moment? I promise not to touch anything.

He looked at his people. A woman who had put markings on the floor looked up at him and straightened her mask. "We're through here. I need to go downstairs and continue there anyway," she said.

"That's fine by me, I'll give you five minutes. After all, we all want to go home."

Sandrine stepped aside and let the forensic technicians

descend the stairs. Doctor Hervé stopped in front of her and raised his hands in defence. He knew what she wanted from him.

"At least a rough estimate of the time and cause of death."

"I can give you exact results as soon as I have the woman on my table. Don't hold me to it, but I would guess she died last night sometime between ten o'clock and midnight. There are a few possible causes of death and I won't commit myself, but suffocation is at the top of the list."

"That's enough for now. Thank you very much, Doctor."

"Have a pleasant Sunday." He glanced at the body. "Though now, that's rather unlikely." At the sight of the victim, Sandrine had instantly buried the hope that this might be a natural death.

A naked woman lay on a massive wooden table topped by a transparent lacquered slab. Sandrine estimated the woman to be in her mid-twenties. Her arms and legs were fastened to the four table legs with cable ties. She would hardly have been able to move if she had been alive. Long, red curly hair hung over the edge of the table, the ends touching the wooden floor. A camera and microphone were mounted on a tripod and aligned with the crime scene. Two light fixtures commonly used in photo studios stood beside it. Someone, probably the perpetrator, had professionally illuminated and recorded the scene. A kind of trophy?

"A whole new kind of still life," Adel muttered behind her. "I guess there's little chance that we'll find the shot in the camera. I'm sure the son of a bitch is calmly gazing at his work from home. Like a junkie who always needs his fix."

"It's staged, that's for sure. The question is for whom: the perpetrator or for us? Perhaps this was commissioned. We can't exclude any possibilities."

"Mazet's people couldn't detect any evidence of forced entry. She must have opened the door for him or her, assuming there was only one perpetrator."

The woman was petite. Sandrine estimated her height to be around five feet, five inches, maximum; she could hardly weigh more than a hundred and ten pounds. Her breasts and belly were painted with Asian characters. The black paint stood out clearly on her pale skin. A few characters were smeared, but most looked razor sharp. The killer had probably started his work of art, then stopped when his victim began to move. Her eyes were wide open, staring at the exposed beams on the ceiling. Blood had dripped from a wound on the back of her head, forming a small pool on the floor. The skin on her slim hands looked red and irritated as if she had been working unusually hard or cleaning the entire apartment without gloves using harsh products. Bloody saliva and vomit oozed from her mouth; scraps of paper stuck to her skin and hair.

Though curious about what was on the paper, Sandrine left the scraps on the corpse. Dr. Hervé and Jean-Claude Mazet would take care of it. Instead, she knelt beside the table. The otherwise pristine floor was speckled with similar vestiges. She picked up a strip of paper. It looked like part of a page someone had ripped from a book and crumpled. She smoothed the paper on her knee and glanced at it before handing it to Adel.

"Looks like it's from a novel," she said.

She looked around. On a table in a corner stood a square, collapsible plastic box, the front of which was open. An illuminated space for commercial advertising shots. Someone would place products there, adjust the lighting and photograph them against a white background. A simple but effective assembly for taking professional photos and displaying promotional products or incorporating them into any image.

"Maybe we'll find something there."

Next to the box was a shelf on which lipsticks, creams and small electrical appliances were arranged alongside several books.

"The paper probably came from the pages of this," said Sandrine as she held a book up.

"*Icy Death*," she read. "The beginning of a new series by Pierre Salazar." The name was not familiar to her.

She barely found time to read Rosalie's thrillers, not to mention other writers. But her friend would surely have something to say about the author, since she knew every crime novelist in the wider area. She opened the book. Someone had roughly torn out the first few pages. Scraps were still hanging from the intact binding. She put it in an evidence bag. A YA book written by an author she didn't know and an English-language thriller, *Deadly Sins Will Hunt You*, were undamaged.

Strange collection, she thought.

"Look at this," she heard Adel say.

Sandrine walked over to him. The attic consisted of one room in which the dead woman had her studio, but it was also her bedroom. Only the semi-transparent curtain pulled aside by Adel created a touch of privacy. The victim obviously hadn't separated her private life from her professional life. As in the rest of the apartment, white prevailed. Bed linens, lamps and pillows. Just over the head of the bed hung a life-size portrait of the dead woman, a nude photo. Arms crossed over her breasts, head thrown back, the photo ended with a flood of curly red hair flowing freely like a waterfall to her waist.

"She was very attractive," Adel said.

"And she had an excellent photographer. This is not the work of somebody who takes photos of children's birthdays, weddings and company parties. The person who shot this was an artist." She stepped closer to the picture that the photographer had created in the style of a fine painting.

"You're a photographer yourself, aren't you?"

"I am. But mostly landscapes that hold so beautifully still." She gave the victim a look. She was also held still. This thought cut her like a knife. "I've seen enough, let's go and you can fill me in on any background information."

She didn't look back again, but the image of the young woman was seared into her memory.

Sandrine bought two cups of coffee in a bakery. Next to the victim's house, a gate opened through the mediaeval wall which led to the Bon-Secours beach. The sun had intensified in the last hour, luring the city's residents to the water. The sea had ebbed slightly from its peak. The rocky islands of Grand Bé and Petit Bé with the 17th century fortress, built by Marquis de Vauban glistened in the sunlight. During low tide, it was reachable by foot in a few hours. A handful of windsurfers with their colourful sails cruised off the coast, but most were waiting on the beach for stronger winds. The ferry to Portsmouth had already left the harbour, heading for the English Channel.

"That would be too icy for me," said Sandrine, pointing to the swimmers in the walled man-made pool, filled at high tide with fresh but cold seawater.

"I feel the same way. Hard to believe the pool is over ninety years old."

"Really? You can't see the masonry at all."

"Inès told me, she knows all about the history of the city. The builder ran a beach bath here. With the walled, man-made natural pool, swimming was even possible during low tide, unlike the baths of his competitors. The man was also the first to introduce showers and sun umbrellas to the loungers. Extremely innovative for his time."

Sandrine didn't ask on what occasion Inès had given him a

lecture on the history of the local bathing establishments. It was obvious that the office manager and her assistant liked each other, but that they met in their spare time had escaped her notice.

They sat down on a rounded rock that protruded from the sand and were pleasantly warmed by the sun.

"Give me the background story," she asked Adel.

"The dead woman's name is Aimée Vilette, twenty-seven and she lived in the apartment on Rue de la Cloche for four years. She was born in a village near Saint-Brieuc; her mother and stepfather still live there. High school, then art studies in Paris. Now she runs a blog." He leafed through his notes. "Here it is: '*Savoir vivre avec Aimée*. Art, culture and the trivial.'"

"A blogger," Sandrine muttered thoughtfully. "The woman must have been successful. Her equipment seems professional; a hobby blogger couldn't afford it. An apartment in this location is also no bargain."

"What kind of money can you earn talking about art and culture? I bet we'll find some other lucrative source of income, probably something not totally legal which financed her lifestyle."

"You're thinking about the portrait? The woman was extremely attractive and didn't seem shy about presenting herself nude."

"That's pretty obvious. She was young, stunning and could express herself in any way she wanted to. Somebody like her would be highly sought after by any escort service."

"We can ask vice but I suspect they won't have anything on her. Put Inès on the blog tomorrow morning and have her look into her personal life and finances."

"I bet she's already sitting at the Commissariat, looking through the documents."

"On the weekend?"

Adel nodded. "For a murder case, she'll drop everything. As soon as we're back at the office, we'll find her working at her desk."

He was probably right. At their first meeting, she'd asked herself whether the woman was even old enough to have finished school; she looked so young, yet she managed the office quite efficiently. Inès had grown up in Saint-Malo and seemed to know every single resident personally, and in addition she was pre-eminently involved in the network of office managers in other departments. Her direct manner was not for everybody, but for Sandrine a priceless treasure. Especially since she herself had lived in Brittany for such a short time and hardly knew anyone.

"Who found the body?" asked Sandrine.

"Her business partner. Dominique Petitjean. A freelance photographer. No criminal record whatsoever. Nothing out of the ordinary, just a handful of parking tickets and a few complaints of nocturnal disturbances, so we let him go," Adel informed her. "He also happens to live here in the old town, just a few hundred yards from here."

"What was he doing in the apartment on a Sunday morning? Did they have a relationship?" Sandrine inquired.

"Hard to imagine. The victim and Petitjean don't play in the same league," said the brigadier. "But often there's no explanation for what women see in some men. He claimed they wanted to shoot some advertising photos and prepare a couple of videos for next week."

"Do you think he's capable of committing such a crime?" Sandrine asked.

"I've been with the police long enough not to rule anything out. However ..." Adel hesitated briefly. "He seems to have a fierce temper. I believe he could be violent if he thought he could get away with it. But this was a planned act."

"I agree. We can rule out a crime of passion. The perpetrator carefully prepared this in advance, staged the crime scene and the victim, then went through with a cold-blooded murder," Sandrine stated decisively.

"What do you think about the cable ties?" Adel asked.

"Nobody brings something like this when you come for a visit or a business meeting. In addition to the characters drawn on her skin," Sandrine said. "They look like they've been drawn with a marker but Mazet and his team couldn't find anything in the apartment. The perpetrator must have taken the thing with them."

"Just like her clothes," Adel said, nodding his head thoughtfully.

"They were stolen?" she asked.

"Jean-Claude found fibres and fabric scraps in the studio. Her attacker must have hit her from behind and tied her unconscious body to the table. Afterward her clothes were removed," said Adel. "It could be that they were afraid she would wake up too soon and fight back. I'm guessing the perpetrator probably isn't very strong, possibly a woman."

"The only way to have taken off her clothes without untying her," said Sandrine, "would have been with scissors or a very sharp knife."

"We'll search garbage cans in the area," Adel said, touching his lower lip thoughtfully.

Sandrine took a sip of coffee and looked out over the water. Plenty of room there to make things disappear forever. "Let's start with the neighbours," she decided.

* * *

In the stairwell, two men came in to transport the body to

forensic medicine. In the next few days Doctor Hervé would hopefully be able to report more on the cause of death.

Sandrine rang the doorbell at the opposite apartment. An old lady in a gold-coloured dressing gown opened the door a crack, the safety chain still engaged. She squinted at both of the police officers.

Disapproval flowed from every pore of her body.

"Madame Drouet?" Sandrine asked.

"Yes." The old lady's gaze shifted towards the open door of the neighbouring apartment; the wrinkles on her forehead became even more prominent.

Sandrine showed her ID. "I'm Lieutenant Perrot and this is my colleague, Brigadier Chief of Police Azarou. We'd like to ask you some questions."

"I can assure you that I haven't seen or heard anything. You better go ask the guy one floor down, I wouldn't put it past him."

"Even small things can be valuable, sometimes things that seem insignificant at first glance can help us," Adel said.

His charm bounced off her without effect. The lady continued to stare at him distrustfully and her hand clung tighter around the door handle. She seemed to be wondering how to brush them both off.

"Who's at the door, Mamie?" cried someone from inside the apartment.

She turned around. "The police, Geneviève. A woman and a foreigner. Because of the weird tenant across from us."

"Then please let them in. Since when are you so rude as to leave people standing at the door?"

"Whatever you think," she murmured and closed the door. It took a little while before Sandrine heard the jingle of the safety chain, then the door opened again. "Come in, but I can't tell you anything."

A woman, maybe late twenties, in a simple bright dress and

a blue silk scarf, stepped out of the room and walked towards them. "My name is Geneviève, I'm Georgine's granddaughter," she said. "Please come in."

The old lady took her arm and they both slowly shuffled into the living room.

"Have a seat, please." Geneviève pointed at an old-fashioned sofa with a red velvet cover, probably from around the time of Toulouse-Lautrec, just like the rest of the furnishings. Compared to Aimée Vilette's stark white design, Madame Drouet's apartment looked like a cluttered and slightly dusty museum. Pictures including some yellowed black-and-white photos covered the walls, kitschy porcelain figures crowded the dresser and the dainty side tables, on which lace doilies lay.

"May we offer you coffee or tea?" asked the granddaughter. Madame Drouet shot her a look of disapproval. She clearly didn't like letting police in the apartment.

"That's not necessary," Adel declined. The friendly smile that he sent the young woman did not escape Sandrine's attention.

"What has the tenant next door done?" Madame Drouet came back to the purpose of their visit. "It's not proper for a respectable household to have the police come and go." She pulled down the spectacles from her head, put them on her nose and gazed at Sandrine. "That didn't happen in my day: women at the police station." Her eyes went to Adel.

"Mamie!" Her granddaughter slowed her down before she could give her opinion about *foreigners* in the police department.

"She lived here four years and never bothered to introduce herself to me or invite me to her place. A miracle that she greeted other tenants in the stairwell," said the old lady.

"With so many police here now, something must have

happened to the poor woman." Geneviève laid her hand on her grandmother's arm.

"Madame Vilette died last night," Adel informed her in his usual calm tone.

"I knew she would be trouble," growled the old woman.

"And how did you come to that conclusion?" Sandrine asked.

"She was home all day; she almost never left her apartment. There's something wrong with that. In addition, she had so many visitors. Mostly men." She turned to her granddaughter. "A tramp, if you ask me."

Geneviève Drouet rolled her eyes.

"Had she given you any grounds for such a suspicion?" asked Adel.

"How was she able to pay for an apartment here? She never went to a regular job."

Geneviève stood up. "I need to get something to drink." She nodded at Sandrine, who followed her in short order.

"My grandmother thinks like she did when she was young. She struggled with the way Aimée lived," she said, as Sandrine walked alongside her into the kitchen.

"And exactly how did your neighbour live?"

"She ran a lifestyle blog, a YouTube channel and her own show on the local radio. They all seemed pretty successful. Obviously she had no money problems, she paid her rent on time. I only knew her from seeing and chatting with her occasionally in the stairwell. One time I helped her carry up some lamps and she invited me to her place for tea. To me, Aimée seemed very nice and calm."

"Do you know who in this building is behind in their rent?"

"Yes, it belongs to Grandmother. I help her with the bookkeeping now and then."

"Were you here last night?"

"Yes. She went to bed early, around nine o'clock. I stayed for a while and worked on my doctorate. I have more peace here than at home among my siblings." She winked at Sandrine.

"Noisy girls and all names starting with G. A familial quirk. The boys' names all start with H." She laughed melodically. "I suppose there are worse familial lunacies."

"Absolutely. When did you leave?"

"A little before midnight. I checked on my grandmother. She was sleeping so I set off."

"Did you notice anything?"

"Has the woman been killed?"

Sandrine nodded. There was no use lying about it since it would be in the morning papers.

Geneviève shook her head sadly. "I heard someone walk down the stairs just ahead of me. Do you think that was the murderer?"

"It's possible."

" Then I almost encountered him. Maybe ..."

"It's highly unlikely that you or your grandmother were in any danger."

"How did she die? Have you caught the killer?"

"I can't say anything about that since we're right at the beginning of our investigation." Sandrine sat down at the kitchen table.

"Grandmother will be ninety next month and she's not as sprightly as she used to be though she refuses to admit it. In the evening she falls asleep in front of the television or when I'm here, I take care that she goes to bed, like yesterday."

"And what about you? Did you notice anything? Maybe a fight?"

"Unfortunately not. The walls in this building are massively thick and that's a good thing. Grandmother doesn't hear very well and turns the television up pretty loud. And like I said, I was working."

"On your doctoral thesis?"

"French literature of the Middle Ages. My subject is the correspondence between the philosopher Abaelard and his lover, Heloise." She laughed lightly. "I'm a total romantic. I normally put on my headphones and type away for hours. Sometimes I get emotional and cry a little."

"Well, it's the one big unfulfilled love story of the Middle Ages as far as I know. A few tears are totally appropriate."

"Do you know the story?"

"Only that it was a romantic one."

"That's right. The two loved each other but were separated by Heloise's influential father. He locked him in a monastery and had Abelard emasculated. After Abelard's death, Heloise had his body buried nearby. When she died, they were buried next to each other. Bound in death."

Sandrine leaned forward slightly. "Really romantic, but also tragic."

Geneviève nodded. "I probably won't get a decent job with my choice of doctoral thesis and my romantic streak, but I just couldn't resist choosing the topic."

"And did you have your headphones on yesterday evening?"

"As usual," she replied. "Aimée had added more insulation to the attic. She probably needed it for her video recordings. She could have had a party in her studio and nobody would have noticed."

"You didn't convert the attic above your apartment?"

"No, we used to hang the laundry up there but my grandmother couldn't make it up the stairs any more. Now she gives me the laundry and I throw everything in the dryer."

"Thank you very much. If anything comes to mind, call me or Brigadier Azarou." Sandrine handed her a card.

"Do you have one from your colleague?" A slight blush crept over her cheeks. "Just in case I can't reach you."

"Excellent idea. He'll give you his." Sandrine stood up and went back into the hallway. She gave Adel a sign and both left the apartment, but not without Adel leaving a business card behind.

The neighbour in the apartment below, a certain Aubert Pascale, opened the door. He wore a wrinkled T-shirt that stretched over his biceps and colourful sweatpants. The man seemed to spend a lot of time on a weight bench. He had ruffled hair and stubble on his face; apparently they'd woken him up.

They introduced themselves and he studied Sandrine's police ID for a while.

"Police. So that's the noise. I wanted to go upstairs and complain."

"So sorry for disturbing you," Adel said.

"It's alright. But I didn't get to bed until half past seven. I work nights."

"When did you leave the building yesterday?"

"Around six o'clock. The party started at ten and ended at sunrise."

"I would hardly call that work," Azarou remarked.

"When you're the organiser, it is. It's a tough job, not exactly a fun evening with friends."

"And this party took place where?"

"In a club called the Équinoxe." He gazed at Sandrine for a moment. "Perhaps you know the venue. I wouldn't be surprised if you did."

"Witnesses?" she asked without responding to his remark. In fact, she did know the club. The victim in her last case visited the club regularly. As it turned out, Léon, the owner, trained in the same martial arts studio that she did.

"My employees, club managers and about five hundred paying guests. I'm sure you'll find plenty of witnesses who can attest they saw me there the entire night."

"Then you didn't notice anything unusual yesterday?"

"A small, excited guy slipped in through the door as I left. But I didn't run into anybody else."

"And you simply let him into the building?" she asked.

"He was just a half-pint. A puny guy. What could he do: steal the flowerpots in the stairwell? About this tall." He held his hand in front of him around chest level. This visitor must have been wearing children's clothing. "Besides, I know him. He's been here several times as of late."

"Who did the man visit?"

Monsieur Pascale pointed upstairs. "He was an acquaintance of our blogger. Not a friend though. The guy had a shrill little voice. Normally it's dead quiet in that apartment but the dwarf's hysterical bickering got through to me."

"Were they fighting?"

"Hell, yes."

"Could you understand what was going on?"

"I'm sorry. I just turned up the radio; other people's dirty laundry does not interest me. I get enough of that crap in clubs. That's enough for me."

"Did you know Mademoiselle Vilette?"

"Hard to say. It never got any further than a *hello* on the stairs, not that I ever intended any more than that. She wasn't my type, too pale, if you know what I mean?"

"If you think of anything else, call us." Sandrine handed the man her card.

"Sure. Will do." He pointed at the apartment across from him. "You don't even need to try ringing it. They're on holiday for two weeks." He shook his head. "Living here directly by the sea and going somewhere else to relax. Unbelievable."

"True," Adel agreed.

They were already on the stairs when Monsieur Pascale called out behind them. "There was maybe something else."

Sandrine stopped and turned to face him.

"The woman was a perfect neighbour. Always calm. Only in the last few weeks were there loud arguments. Didn't fit the little mouse at all."

"With the man you held the door for?"

"Not only. Others. I would recognize the little fellow's voice in my sleep. There was someone else. If I heard it, it meant things had got really heated. It certainly didn't sound friendly." Then he turned around and disappeared into his apartment. The door slammed shut.

"The number of suspects is increasing. It would be nice if we had names to go with them," said Adel as he went down the stairs.

Jean-Claude's group would need a little while longer in the apartment. Maybe later in the day they could take a better look inside.

"We should talk to the man who found the corpse. What's his name again?"

"Dominique Petitjean," Adel answered. "Mademoiselle Vilette's business partner. He lives a couple hundred yards away."

"Let's talk to him before we go back to the police station."

The photographer lived just a few minutes by foot from the crime scene. They went through an archway into the building's courtyard and found his name on a door plaque. Adel had to ring two times before someone stirred in the ground floor apartment.

"Coming," the man called from inside. They could hear the sound of a woman's bright voice coming from within. Sandrine couldn't understand what they were talking about, but she didn't sound pleased to have been disturbed.

"Seems as though our witness is busy," Adel remarked.

A man opened the door and gazed at them with annoyance. He was medium-sized, lean, with prominent cheekbones and deep dark circles under his eyes. His streaky blond hair reached to his shoulders. His wrinkled black shirt fell over his jeans. There had clearly been no time for socks or shoes.

"What do you want?"

Sandrine dug out her ID and held it up to the man. "Lieutenant Perrot and Brigadier Chief Azarou. I'm sorry to disturb you."

"Police? Yeah, of course. Because of Aimée, right?"

"For what other reason would the police pay you a visit?" asked Adel, scrutinising him intently.

Cigarette smoke clung to the man's clothes but did not hide the strong smell of alcohol.

"No, no reason. I'm just kind of in shock. The sight ..." he stammered.

"May we come in?" she asked and stepped forward. Surprised, Dominique Petitjean made room and let them in.

"Just go straight ahead." He tried to push past but Adel discreetly blocked his way. He seemed bent on putting something aside before the police came inside his apartment.

Adel let Sandrine go ahead and she entered the room at the end of the short hallway. She found herself in a photography studio. However, the man seemed to use half the room as a living room. A half-naked woman sat on the sofa, nervously sucking on a cigarette then emitting a large cloud of smoke in Petitjean's direction.

"I've been working. That's distracting." He picked a sweater off the floor and tossed it to the woman. "Put that on, we'll continue tomorrow morning."

"You promised we'd finish today," she grumbled and held the fabric in front of her breasts.

"My agent needs new pictures. He's got inquiries."

"Come back tomorrow. The people from the police have some questions." He stressed the word *police* and she looked at them both with a mixture of fear and distrust.

"All right. Tomorrow morning." She quickly put on the sweater, grabbed the rest of her clothes that were on the floor and ran out of the room. She probably wanted to dress in the hallway rather than in front of the police. *Photos probably for an escort service or a pimp,* Sandrine guessed. She looked around. At the head of the high-ceilinged room was a red velvet sofa, like the one Madame Drouet owned. Photos of half-naked women covered the side walls, probably intended as an inspiration for his models. Some fabric backgrounds hung from the ceiling; cameras and lenses sat on a nearby table. Other than that, the room looked bare, cold and lifeless.

"Please sit," Petitjean asked them. "Something to drink?"

"No, thanks," Azarou declined.

Sandrine wondered how devout her Muslim assistant really was. She knew he drank alcohol on special occasions but only really expensive brands. So far, religion had not been an issue between them and she had no intention of changing that.

"Well, I need one." He poured Pastis in a half-full glass of water, drank it and poured another. The second one was left untouched on the table and the smell of anise wafted into Sandrine's nostrils. She couldn't imagine what made a woman like Aimée Vilette work with this unctuous guy. It was hard enough to even imagine this unkempt-looking man in the meticulously clean apartment.

"You found the body." The brigadier returned to the purpose of their visit.

"Yes. What a sight. Poor Aimée." His voice trembled then finally broke. The second Pastis followed the first one. But this time he didn't refill.

"Tell us exactly what happened," Adel asked Petitjean.

"I have already told all this to your colleagues."

"Then please tell us again. Maybe you have thought of something in the meantime that you left out."

"I came to her apartment early in the morning. The lower floor was empty and she didn't respond when I called her name. I assumed she was already working on her podcast for next week – she always wore headphones – and I went up to her studio. She was on the table. I barely made it to the bathroom and threw my guts up."

"That's understandable. It was an ugly sight, even if you didn't know the woman personally." If it had been Sandrine's first corpse, she probably would have reacted the same way.

"Did you touch anything?"

"Just in the bathroom, otherwise no."

"How did you get into the apartment? Do you have a key?"

"No. I rang the doorbell several times. The guy downstairs yelled at me because he needed his sleep. I knocked on the door and it just opened. The lock was faulty, no idea what the problem was but it didn't close right. Anyway, it opened up."

"Mechanical unlocking," the brigadier told him.

"Did Mademoiselle Vilette leave the door unlocked often?" Sandrine asked.

"Never. That wasn't like her, so I wondered about it. Maybe an oversight or she had been expecting a visitor."

"How was your relationship with the victim?"

"We worked together," Petitjean said. "Actually, Aimée and I were partners, so to speak. I did everything related to photography and video. She was responsible for the texts and the presentation. She was pretty, and very smart on top of that. She could really express herself."

"Did your relationship go beyond business?" Sandrine noted Adel's sceptical gaze.

"No. We didn't have anything to do with each other like that. She wasn't my type. Too intellectual, hard-headed ... kind of complicated as a human being." He sniffed. "I have no idea how to continue the business alone," he whispered thoughtfully.

Sandrine suspected that the thought of how he could profit from her death had just come to him.

"Was she in a solid relationship?"

"There was some guy but she kept her private life to herself. I got the impression that things weren't going so well between the two of them any more and she was a little afraid of him. Maybe there was a fight and he did this to her. Or maybe the macho man in the apartment below. He made a pass at her, so I wouldn't put it past him."

"We'll look into that," the brigadier assured him. The photographer was already the second person that pointed in the direction of Aubert Pascale.

Petitjean reached for the Pastis bottle. Sandrine pulled the glass away. "There's time for that when we're gone."

"All right." He held out his right hand. "I'm still shivering. It's the shock." She suspected it had more to do with his consumption of alcohol. In any case, the shock of finding the corpse didn't hinder him from shooting photos, which he probably found erotic. She stood up and went over to one of the large-format nudes that hung on the wall.

"Is this your work?"

"Of course. All of this is my work."

"Did you photograph Mademoiselle Vilette?"

"That's how we earned our money. Obviously."

"The portrait in her bedroom is yours?"

Petitjean paused then nodded. "She wouldn't let anyone else photograph her."

Old VHS videos, DVDs and cheap-looking girlie magazines were stacked on an open shelf. "Do you collect these things?"

"Some of them have been here since time immemorial, others I got from a customer who wasn't liquid, so now I sell this stuff at a flea market or on the Internet to earn money."

Sandrine turned back to the man she was becoming less and less sympathetic to.

"What were you both working on? Was there any project that would have made somebody angry enough that he would want to silence her?"

He thought for a moment. Sandrine asked herself whether he was perhaps already too drunk to remember, then he looked up at her. "She didn't mince words. If Aimée cared about something, she would go through with it. Of course, that didn't suit everyone. Surely you'll be able to find mail with insults and threats located in the studio. I'd be happy to search for you, if she hasn't already thrown the crap away."

"We'll find them. The apartment and studio are crime scenes, therefore locked up until the forensic team releases them." She noticed his look of disappointment. Did he want to go to the apartment to look for something specific? Or was it really about the business? The idea that this guy could talk about art and culture seemed absurd to her.

"What project was Mademoiselle Vilette currently working on?"

"To be honest, I don't know. She'd been acting pretty secretive but claimed it was personal. It seemed very important to her, something appeared to be eating at her more than usual. I have no idea how many shots she normally took to be halfway satisfied."

"She was a perfectionist?" asked Sandrine.

"You bet. We would photograph for hours until she gave her okay. I really had a hard time earning money with her."

"Fussy clients like her can really get on your nerves," she said.

Petitjean nodded thoughtfully. "But she was the same way with her own projects, maybe even worse." He raised his head and looked at Sandrine. "That's how you have to be to be successful."

"We need access to the unpublished recordings that Mademoiselle Vilette made in the last few weeks," Adel said.

"She kept them under wraps." He shrugged. "Aimée had a crypto ... an encrypted directory in the cloud. You can't crack it. She always called it her Swiss bank vault." He laughed bitterly. "It's going to be difficult to continue without these things." Petitjean stood up and picked up a new glass from the shelf. "Are we done?"

"For now," said the brigadier. "Stay at our disposal and don't leave the city."

Petitjean looked around theatrically. "Do I look like a travel photographer? No, I'm definitely not leaving Saint-Malo. I have to concentrate on the business. Aimée would have wanted me to continue." He poured himself a hefty shot of Pastis, held the glass under the tap and let water run into it.

"We'll find our own way out," Sandrine said as a good-bye. The man was no longer paying any attention to her.

She stopped in the courtyard. "The guy is lying through his teeth."

"He never was Mademoiselle Vilette's partner, at the most

he was a mere employee. For the life of me, I can't imagine him in the apartment, where it was so immaculately clean. In contrast, he stank like an ashtray in a cheap drinking hole."

"I agree. What do you think about the unidentified lover?"

"The one he conjured up out of thin air?" Adel laughed softly. "He doesn't exist, just a distraction to get us off his back. Looking for him would be a waste of time. Presenting us with a possible perpetrator that he's never met personally made Petitjean look quite suspicious."

"I'm not sure. The most important thing right now is to find out who took the photo hanging in Aimée's bedroom."

"He claims it was him."

"I looked at his work. The guy has enough ability to take a few snapshots for advertising prostitutes on the Internet but a portrait like that is way out of his league. The post-processing was excellent, one of the best photographs that I've seen in a long time."

"Well you should know, since it's your hobby."

"I'm pretty good but the one who took that picture was a real artist. Moreover, Aimée Vilette trusted whoever took that photo. She looked so relaxed. Can you imagine that, with Petitjean staring at you lustfully? I can't."

"No, he's disgusting. What does that mean for the case?"

"I don't know yet but I'd really like to talk to the photographer. There's something connecting them. Maybe the unknown lover isn't so false after all. But I ask myself, why did Petitjean lie to us?"

The brigadier laughed. "They all do that. At least at the beginning of an investigation, as long as they think they can get away with their shenanigans."

"That's true."

They slowly strolled through the streets of the old town back to the victim's apartment.

The last forensic technicians were leaving the crime scene, stowing away their equipment and securing evidence, as Sandrine and Adel reached the building on Rue de la Cloche.

"Are you done?" she asked Jean-Claude Mazet.

"We don't have anything left to do here. I've seldom seen an apartment as clean as this one."

"Do you have any clues that could move us forward?"

"Not a lot but what we have found is guaranteed to be from the evening the woman was murdered. It had been thoroughly cleaned and dusted beforehand. There was hardly a speck of dust on the furniture."

"What do you have for me?"

"I can say that this was no burglary. The lock is fine, the windows are intact and also locked. The victim must have let the murderer in."

"So they knew each other?" Adel asked.

"That's possible, but they may have gained access under some kind of pretext: most people open the door for couriers, mail or parcel carriers. From what I saw in the studio, I suspect that the woman regularly received promotional materials. Probably also unsolicited material sent randomly."

"That doesn't particularly shrink the circle of suspects."

"Maybe this will help you. We've already secured evidence that was on this." The forensic technician handed her a small, leather-bound notebook. "The woman wrote down her appointments on paper. That's pretty rare these days."

Sandrine took it and leafed through the most recent pages. "Local radio on Friday evening, Doctor Leriche at noon on Saturday. And a To-Do list without appointments. Chardon and Pascale, double underlined."

She handed Adel the notebook. "Can you go through the appointments of the last few weeks? Maybe you'll notice something unusual. Any entry that stands out from the normal routine."

"We met Pascale but a Chardon hasn't come up in connection to her," said the brigadier, pocketing the diary. "Will do."

"I need the key to the apartment," she asked the forensic technician.

"No problem. I don't believe we overlooked anything. Try not to trash or burn down the apartment." Sandrine smiled wryly. He was referring to the barn that she'd recently paid a late-night visit to. Somebody shot at her then the old wooden barn was locked from outside and set on fire. She had been lucky enough to escape the flames but afterwards all that was left of the crime scene was a pile of burnt logs.

"I'll do my best," she promised. The man rummaged through his pocket until he pulled out a bunch of keys and handed one of them to her. "The one with the yellow ring belongs to the front door, the others are mainly for the filing cabinets and desk. The woman kept the really expensive equipment under wraps."

"I'm going to look around the crime scene for a while later." She needed quiet in the apartment, to get a feel for the occupant. A bathroom reveals a lot about a person's character, preferences and habits. Aimée Vilette was still a stranger to Sandrine. She wanted to change that. The more she learned about her, the closer she would get to her killer.

"Do that, but please lock it and use crime tape to seal the door afterwards," Jean-Claude Mazet said.

"I'll pick up some tape from the police station."

"The majority of the team have already driven up and are working in the lab. We should have the first results by tomorrow morning."

"I'm sure you will." Sandrine assured him of her confidence in his work.

He nodded and said good-bye. She saw him get into an old Citroën, which gave under his weight and drove away. At first glance, the head of forensics seemed quite sedate but that was deceptive. From what she knew about the man, he would spend the rest of the day and probably a good part of the night in the lab. In her first criminal case here, she had found him to be extremely competent and cooperative. He was also popular with the people on the team, which said a lot about him.

"I'll leave the motorcycle here and ride with you to the police station," she said to Adel. "Or would you prefer the other way around?"

"Riding on the back of the motorcycle with you?" The brigadier shook his head vehemently. "Never ever. I'm not tired of living. You should get a decent vehicle. You're entitled to an official car, you know that."

"When the weather's good, I take my BMW or my trusty Citroën 2VC. It takes me everywhere." Sandrine smiled, knowing full well that the somewhat vain Adel was shy about being seen in her 2CV, which was often affectionately referred to by many owners, including Sandrine and other classic car enthusiasts as 'ugly duckling' or 'duck' for short.

Adel unlocked his white Peugeot 306 and she got in. It was only a few minutes' drive to the police station. On the way back, she would go by foot to enjoy the lovely Sunday weather. She wouldn't see her lounge chair waiting for her in the garden before sunset, she was sure of that.

Adel Azarou was right: Inès Boni sat behind her desk, typing on her keyboard at breakneck speed.

Sandrine stepped into her field of vision, which made her flinch. She took off her headphones, laid them on the desk; the music from her playlist could be heard playing quietly. As usual she wore a garishly coloured top which fell to her hips and faded jeans.

"You startled me. I wasn't expecting you both so soon."

"I was hoping to spend Sunday in my garden, too."

"You would think a person would feel safe and unafraid in a police station. Unless you've done something illegal?" Adel picked up the headphones and held it to one of his ears. "Oh, yeah." He made a face and lay them back on the desk. "If I had to listen to that for more than ten minutes, I would be a nervous wreck, too."

"Funny, my grandfather says the same thing. You would get along well with him since you have so much in common. Come over here and let's have a chat," she replied.

Sandrine smiled. The two liked each other but definitely did not have the same taste in music. The brigadier had little use for the fast, hard beats the energetic Inès preferred while she concentrated on her work.

"Forensics has already left and sealed up the apartment on Rue de la Cloche," Sandrine interrupted the two friends. "I'd like to learn more about the victim's background before I take my time to look around the apartment again or scrutinise the woman's surroundings."

"Is the deceased really Aimée Vilette?" Inès sounded sad and shaken.

"You knew her?" Adel asked.

"Of course. The woman was a local celebrity. I subscribed to her social media channel and listened regularly to her Midnight Chats. That is what she called her program on local radio, which runs every Friday from 10 p.m. to midnight."

"You liked her. I'm so sorry."

"She summed up the problems of the local area quite

precisely. Of course, not everyone liked it but to kill her because of it?" She shook her head in disbelief.

"We still don't know the motive for the attack. Perhaps it had nothing to do with her job," Sandrine said.

"We'll get the guy, right?" Inès gazed at Sandrine with a pleading look. She seemed completely convinced in her abilities as an investigator.

"I can promise that we'll try our very best to arrest the perpetrator, whether male or female. But we barely have anything to go on right now."

"You can count on me," the office manager assured her. "In this case I won't even write down my overtime."

She suspected that the woman only did this in a very limited way. Inès Boni loved being involved in on-going investigations separate from her pure office work, something that had never happened under her old boss. She had never been allowed to contribute more than making coffee, archiving minutes and some background research, let alone being allowed to partici-pate in team meetings. That had all changed since Sandrine took over.

"First, we need information about her finances. Her apart-ment is in the best location, undoubtedly expensive, decorated with the finest furnishings and best studio equipment, things a young blogger could not easily afford," said Adel. "Who knows, maybe she had a couple of not totally legal sources of income," he said, continuing his train of thought.

"I'll do it, but I think it's a waste of time," replied Inès. "She has some hundred thousand subscribers and I guarantee you she earned top dollar."

"That doesn't seem like so much when it comes to bloggers my little sister follows. They claim to have millions of follow-ers." He sounded pretty sceptical.

"That's not really comparable. Aimée had another target audience. She reports on life by the sea. Maritime Lifestyle is what she called it. Her focus was on trendy cultural events and a healthier and more sustainable way to exist in harmony with yourself and nature. She did not discuss fast food outlets or cheap clothing stores, but multi-star restaurants and newcomers with potential, concerts, museums, expensive tech toys, designer products and so forth."

"How did she make money? With advertisements, I guess?"

"Yes. But not with lipsticks that you could get for a few Euros in a supermarket. Her products were top of the line, no animal testing, often sustainable, traditional and locally made, little to no chemicals and hypoallergenic. Do you know what I'm talking about?" She turned to Sandrine.

"Exactly what a hip and wealthy clientele wants and can easily afford," she answered.

"Accordingly, companies look deep into their pockets to reach the women in their target demographics." That explained the chic apartment and expensive equipment. "Did she discuss books?"

"Yes. Here and there. Local authors but she also talked about socially relevant themes and those that affected Brittany. Is that important?"

"It could play a role. The woman was knocked down from behind. The perpetrator had draped her on the table like a professionally illuminated promotional product. He probably thought that setting up the scene by suffocating her with the ripped-out pages of a book was a good embellishment." She thought about the book the pages came from. There must be a connection between the victim and the crime novel. The perpetrator had taken the time to wait until the woman regained consciousness before he crammed the crumpled pages in her mouth, otherwise she wouldn't have vomited, perhaps several times. In addition, she fought back fiercely, hence the bloody saliva and the cuts as she struggled against the ties on her wrists and ankles.

Inès grimaced. "Disgusting. Who would do something like that?"

"Someone who had a personal motive for the crime and wanted the woman to suffer." Images of Aimée Vilette appeared in her mind. The blood on the white lacquered table, the wide-open eyes and the saliva-soaked pages that oozed from her mouth. "A cruel death," she murmured. "As yet, they haven't been able to find what the victim was hit with," she continued. "Until Jean-Claude's team finds the murder weapon in the apartment or in the surrounding area, we can assume that he brought it with him like the cable ties with which he tied his victim onto the table legs. The marker with which he drew the characters on her belly is also missing."

"Likewise the clothes she was wearing," Adel added.

"Maybe when she resisted the perpetrator felt there would be traces of evidence left behind. Why else would he have taken them? We need to find them."

"What do you think about the book?" Adel asked. "Coincidence or a message?"

"Nothing about the crime scene seems random to me. Either the novel was already in the apartment or the perpetrator brought it with him. It would be best to talk with the author, Pierre Salazar. There must be a relationship between him and the victim."

"Noted," said Inès. "You will receive the data as soon as I get the publisher on the phone. In the imprint, there's only the address of the publisher, and the author's name could also be a pseudonym."

"There are two other people we need to talk to. In her notebook she has an appointment with a Dr. Leriche. I have no idea whether it's a man or a woman, but I'm guessing they're some sort of medical doctor. Secondly, we only have the name Chardon, nothing else. Besides that, I would like to talk with the people at the local radio station, at least with someone that had something to do with her program."

"That's no problem, one of my cousins works there. I'll call him right away. Are there relatives we need to inform?"

Sandrine wrote down a name and nodded. "She grew up near Saint-Brieuc. Her father died when she was eleven. Her mother and stepfather still live there. She had a brother who moved to Paris. A chef, so far as I know. The local authorities have already informed the family before her death got in the news."

"Then we'll question them tomorrow."

Inès picked up the telephone handset. "Should I call Dubois and Poutin? You must need reinforcements."

"Not necessary," Sandrine said dismissively. "Let them enjoy a quiet Sunday. From tomorrow on, they'll have their hands full and nobody will be thinking about an early end of the day." Collaborating with Luc Poutin, the older brigadier, was no pleasure. She excused his laziness but his constant nagging really got on her nerves. He was one of those employees who would have wished for a different department head. She suspected that he would enjoy seeing her fail and even perhaps contribute to that end. She didn't know how far the man would go to get her in trouble, and she didn't trust him.

"Matisse called me. He's on a weekend trip in Paris." Inès grinned mischievously. "Second honeymoon."

"How fun."

"He wanted to jump into his car and drive here but I slowed him down; I hope that's all right."

Commissaire Jean Matisse was the head of Sandrine's department and her direct superior. In her first case there had been no problems whatsoever working with one another.

"That's best. If he calls again, tell him we have everything under control and it's okay for him to just be here tomorrow. Let's set the department briefing at nine a.m."

"Will do." Inès typed the conference room reservation into her computer's organiser. The notification of the meeting time was probably already on its way.

"Anything else?" Sandrine asked.

"Yes. Deborah Binet from the editorial office of *Ouest-France* called and she wanted to speak with you."

"The journalist?" She had helped in the last case with inside information which Sandrine had thanked her for. She hoped the woman wasn't expecting any special treatment. "Did she say what she wanted? The state of the investigation will be announced at a press conference Monday afternoon." It shouldn't be too difficult to persuade Matisse to lead the meeting with the pack of journalists. The man was only forty and motivated to climb the career ladder a good deal further. He wouldn't refuse the publicity and nor would the state prosecutor, Lagarde.

"In fact, she claims to have important information on the case."

"From where?" Sandrine said, then stopped. Saint-Malo was a small town where nothing stayed secret for long. "Did she say what it was?"

"No. She was pretty buttoned up."

"If she calls again, make an appointment for tomorrow morning, somewhere in a café in the old town. I don't want the woman in the police station and certainly not anywhere near the team of investigators." She knew only too well that the journalist was new at her job and wanted to prove herself to her editor. She would use every opportunity to gather inside information by snooping around the police station.

"Sure thing."

"I want to take a closer look around the deceased's apartment."

"Should I come with you?" Adel asked.

"That's unnecessary. I would rather you read through her latest articles and watch her videos from the last few weeks."

"There must be several hours of videos alone, not including her radio show and podcasts." He sighed deeply. His off-duty time was a long way off.

"I can call Poutin to support you," she suggested jokingly. Inès giggled and Adel held his hands up defensively.

"I'm afraid Mademoiselle Vilette's views on maritime life, art and healthy sustainable nutrition are incompatible with Poutin's philosophy of life. He wouldn't be much help to me."

"I can take over part of it," Inès offered. "I'm familiar with most of the things anyway."

"Thanks, Inès. I'll be on my way now."

"Should I drive you?" Adel offered. He didn't seem to be too motivated to watch hours of videos. He obviously didn't share Inès' enthusiasm for Aimée Vilette.

"No, it's all right. It's a short walk to the old town and a little exercise would do me good." Above all, it helped her think. When she was confronted by a puzzle on whose solution she was gnawing on, she would usually go out for a run or a hike. And in this case, she lacked any tangible evidence on which to build her investigation. Maybe along the way she would remember something she'd overlooked.

* * *

Sandrine decided to walk on the beach promenade which led to the old town. It was a bit further but it offered a magnificent view of the coast and sea. For the end of May it was pleasantly warm. The Plage du Sillon, the longest and, in her opinion, the most lovely beach in the city, was bustling with life which did not surprise her on a Sunday. The breeze had subsided and surfboards were leaning against vertical logs, dug deep into the sand as breakwaters.

It was lunchtime and tourists occupied restaurants and cafés in the old town. She postponed her meal, finding no respite to be able to enjoy food right now. Before tomorrow's team meeting, she desperately needed more information and evidence. She hoped Inès and Adel would discover something useful when viewing the videos and articles.

Her phone buzzed: a message from Inès. She had reached Dr. Leriche. She was a female psychotherapist. She had time for a chat and would be waiting for Sandrine next to the victim's apartment building, at the Porte des Champs-Vauverts. It had to be the gate through the city wall, through which she had walked with Adel that morning to drink coffee on the beach and talk undisturbed for a moment. A strange place to meet with the police for an interview.

It took a little more than twenty minutes to arrive at the victim's apartment. She made sure that her motorcycle she'd parked there that morning was in place and her helmet hadn't been stolen. It was only a few steps to the gate. She looked around. There appeared to be nobody waiting for her.

"Madame Perrot?" said somebody from behind her in a melodic voice.

She turned around. In front of her stood a woman only a few years older than herself, late thirties.

She was dressed casually, wearing beige jeans, a light, long-sleeved rose-pink sweater and high-top white sneakers. A chain with a shell-shaped pendant hung around her neck. Her wavy blond hair fell well below her shoulders. The woman smiled and held out her hand to greet Sandrine.

"Are you Dr. Leriche?"

"You don't have to call me 'doctor'. You can call me Suzanne."

"As you wish. Is 'policewoman' written so clearly over my face that you were able to single me out among all these people?"

"Don't we psychologists have the reputation of having especially good perception?" Laugh lines deepened around the woman's blue eyes and pearly white teeth flashed out between her lips.

"You are the first psychologist I've ever spoken to so I can't afford to make a general judgment."

"It's always wise to avoid jumping to conclusions, especially in your line of work," said Suzanne Leriche with a wide smile. "I have to admit finding you wasn't especially difficult. Who other than a police officer wears a shoulder holster under their jacket? The detailed description that I got from Mademoiselle Boni, your assistant, also helped. So you see, I had a clear advantage."

Sandrine smiled back. The psychologist seemed to have a good sense of humour. "I was pleased that you had time for a conversation," she said, quickly coming right to the point of the meeting.

"It fit perfectly into my daily routine," the woman replied. "On my lunch break I walk along the fortress walls once around the old city. You can accompany me."

"If I can ask questions during this time, please?"

"Of course. I often go outside with my clients, so I'm used to talking as we go. A nice sea breeze clears the mind and new thoughts can develop more easily. Let's go."

The slim woman walked toward the gate at the wall, which at this location was almost ten feet tall.

The narrow passageway offered a view of the beach and the shimmering green sea. On the left, stairs led to the old fortress wall. Suzanne Leriche climbed up the steps quickly.

"I can't stand sitting in my office all day. Jogging in the evening and daily walks are my own personal method of relaxing and grounding myself," she explained. "Your assistant said you wanted to see me with regards to an investigation."

"That's right. Your name was in Mademoiselle Vilette's appointment calendar, so I'm guessing she was one of your patients."

"Client," the woman corrected.

"What's the difference?"

"Patients are people that, because of some illness, go to a doctor to be cured by him or her. They give the responsibility of getting better to the practitioner. My clients retain responsibility for their lives and wellness, they are not incapacitated. I help my clients to develop and learn to handle their crises independently." She laughed suddenly. "This is a topic that could be debated for quite a while."

"So, she was one of your clients?"

"This being a case of medical confidentiality, so I can neither confirm nor deny. Bring me a court order or a non-disclosure of the person concerned and we are welcome to discuss it. As long as you're unable to show me the correct papers, we'll have to be satisfied with a nice walk in beautiful weather, which is never a waste of time." She paused and looked at Sandrine with a serious expression. "What happened?"

"Mademoiselle Vilette died yesterday."

Her eyes widened in surprise. "She was killed?"

She was savvy enough to know the police wouldn't want to talk to her if the young woman had fallen off a ladder while cleaning windows. Sandrine did not reply.

"Since there was an appointment in her calendar for yesterday, I assumed that Aimée Vilette was your client."

"A murder? Here in Saint-Malo?" She shook her head in disbelief. "I believe I knew her well enough to know that she would definitely have wanted me to cooperate with the police to catch her murderer. But let's take a few steps first, I have to sort out my thoughts." The news seemed to have shaken her.

Unless the psychologist was a gifted actress it was apparent that she had not known of her client's death.

"I'm happy to take the time."

The woman turned south and walked in a leisurely pace. Sandrine noticed Suzanne looking at the upper windows of the building on Rue de la Cloche. At least she knew where the victim lived; Sandrine shot her a knowing glance to acknowledge that fact.

"We sometimes met here at the wall and talked while we walked," said Suzanne. "She loved this view of the beach and the sea. She was particularly taken with the white sailboats. She would tell me how she would often sit for hours at her window and think about the world."

For a while they walked side by side, past the Plage de Bon-Secours and the tidal pools until the fortress wall changed direction at a right angle to the east.

"Was she in therapy?" Sandrine said, breaking the silence.

"When she was fourteen she found her dead father, who had hanged himself in the barn. Something like that is pretty traumatic."

"Didn't she live in Saint-Brieuc at that time? That's a long way from Saint-Malo."

"That's right. She visited a colleague of mine to deal with the suicide. However ..."

"Yes?"

"She ended the therapy relatively quickly and her condition worsened dramatically afterwards. Two years later she stood in front of my practice. Aimée suffered from an obsessive compulsive cleaning disorder and emetophobia."

"What exactly is that?"

"An anxiety disorder. The irrational fear of vomiting. Aimée's phobia was exacerbated by panic attacks. She was afraid of dying from vomiting."

"Did she have a pre-existing condition or a diagnosis meaning that the possibility existed?"

"She was a healthy young woman, who conscientiously looked after her body and nutrition. Her fears were completely irrational. There was never any danger of death by vomiting. But the effects of panic attacks are very real."

"And how would the panic attack present itself?"

"Sweating, racing pulse, nausea, tightness in the chest, laboured breathing. Many who have experienced an attack have the feeling that it is a real physical phenomenon with symptoms similar to a heart attack. But in fact, it's simply a mental disorder."

"How do such phobias and anxiety attacks develop?" Sandrine asked.

"Emetophobia can often be traced to a certain experience in the past. The causes of Aimée's panic attacks are similar in this respect. Here, too, it is found that the clients had been burdened by a period of stress, often accompanied by a traumatic event which triggered the first attack. This prepares the ground for further ones."

"What would be the underlying cause?"

"A psychological wound. Often these have more dramatic long-term effects than physical injuries."

"Did she talk about what it was? Her father's suicide?"

"That would not be unlikely. My suspicion, though I can't prove it, is that something bad must have happened after that and probably before she withdrew from therapy. She was a teenager when she first came into my practice, and refused to talk to me about it. So I could only poke around in the dark and that did nothing to bring us forward."

"That was almost ten years ago. Why was she still in treatment?"

"She came to my practice when she finished high school. She got her problems under control to such an extent that she was able to finish her studies in Paris. We stayed in loose contact until she moved to Saint-Malo. Since then, she's come to me but less frequently, maybe one time per month or quarter."

"Did she tell you anything that depressed or frightened her?"

"Her cleaning and washing compulsion focused on her hands." Suzanne Leriche stopped and leaned her hips on the granite blocks of the wall. "She recently suffered a relapse. I noticed the red, damaged skin. Something happened and she withdrew from therapy. In her Saturday session, Aimée went into a highly emotional monologue and talked about wanting to expose a bombshell. I supported her so she could let it out, but before she got to the details, she jumped up and stormed out of my office. After that, I wasn't able to reach her. Her mobile phone was switched off. She doesn't have a landline and I received no answer to emails."

Sandrine had noticed the redness on the victim's hands but she hadn't made sense of it. At least on that point she had gotten a little more information. Aimée had planned to publish something explosive, so her death seemed somehow connected to her profession. Whatever she was planning must have affected her deeply, as it had led to a relapse to her old, self-harming behaviour. Sandrine suspected that her intention seemed so dangerous to a third party that they had decided to silence her.

"Too bad. It would have helped if we knew what it might have been. Maybe we can find a reference to her plans in her diaries or other records."

"I hope so." Suzanne Leriche looked out thoughtfully over the harbour where sailboats were moored on the jetties, floating quietly over the smooth surface of the water. "How did she die?" she asked after a while.

Sandrine wasn't in the habit of giving details about an ongoing investigation but maybe the woman's professional assessment could help her. She was willing to take the risk. Her instinct told her that the woman had honestly cared for the victim. Mentally, she ruled out the psychologist as the perpetrator.

"She was tied up and someone stuffed paper in her mouth until she choked to death."

"Did she vomit?"

Sandrine nodded.

"Then it must have been something personal. The male or female perpetrator knew her well enough to know about her phobia and chose this type of death with the intent of making it as gruesome as possible." Suzanne turned to her. "I can hardly imagine a more terrible death for Aimée." Tears glistened in the corner of her eyes and she gulped. This woman heard day after day about the gruesome things her clients had experienced, but the death of this young woman obviously touched her deeply. "It won't bring Aimée back, but I hope you find whoever did this to her," she said in a voice choked with emotion.

"We'll do what we can," Sandrine assured her.

"No one can expect any more than that." Suzanne took a step forward. "May I?" she asked and opened her arms wide.

"Of course."

The woman embraced Sandrine. It seemed she needed someone to hold onto, even if only for a few seconds.

"Thank you." She took a step back. "Is it alright with you if I walk the rest of the way alone, or do you have further questions? I fear I would be a sad companion and the little I know, I've already told you. If anything comes to mind, I'll call you."

"I understand. I have one last question. Who treated her in

Saint-Brieuc? Maybe we can find something more about her trauma there."

"A colleague of mine: Philippe Chardon. But it's not necessary to go to Saint-Brieuc as he has recently settled here in the city."

That was the name Aimée had underlined in her notebook calendar. She must have contacted this man. But for what reason? Maybe there was something that she couldn't talk about with Suzanne Leriche and she'd decided to contact her former therapist.

They said good-bye and Sandrine watched her for a while until she disappeared from her field of vision. The surprise and the sadness over the death of her client seemed real. In her mind, she struck her off the list of possible suspects. Then she made her way back to the apartment building on Rue de la Cloche.

Sandrine cut through the police seal with her Opinel pocketknife and opened the apartment door. Without a thought, she automatically took her shoes off on the doormat before she entered and closed the door behind her. She stopped for a moment and listened. Silence. There wasn't any noise coming from the other tenants. A quiet building, just like Geneviève Drouet had claimed. She looked out the window. The view extended over the sea to Dinard. Apparently Aimée Vilette would often sit in her high back armchair and watch the world. She could easily put herself in the woman's shoes, spending hours looking out and watching the changing tides. During autumn storms, waves would break against the wall and the wind would clap against the glass window panes, and a person could sit in the warmth, sipping on a hot latte and feel safe and secure. Aimée Vilette must have felt comfortable here.

She ran her fingertips across the window sill. No dust whatsoever. The woman genuinely seemed to have detested dirt and disorder. From what she had learned from Inès, the blogger had committed herself to environmental and animal protection, sustainability and good nutrition. All the things that, in a broader context, fell under the concept of a clean environment. This required a straightforward and uncompromising attitude, which had certainly created more than one enemy. In her investigations, Sandrine often despaired of having too few suspects. A thought came to her: in this case, it would be the other way around.

The kitchen seemed so pristine, as if it had never been used before. It could have easily been on display in a furniture store. There were no cookbooks or a pinboard like in her own kitchen which was littered with paper, notes and delivery menus; there wasn't even one obligatory magnet on the refrigerator. The chrome of the espresso machine reflected the glare from the overhead lights. The meticulously clean kitchen didn't match the woman who had waved the flag for healthy cooking. Sandrine opened some drawers, and each one appeared the same: perfectly assorted cutlery and utensils. Even the garbage can was empty. She wasn't going to find anything here and decided she would continue her search in the living room.

She pulled out a bright fleece blanket from a chest and laid it over the white designer sofa, before she sat down. Aimée Vilette surely wouldn't have appreciated her sitting here with her leather trousers. *My gun would especially bother you, wouldn't it?* Weapons would have undoubtedly been something the victim would have seen as repellant.

Her furnishings were straightforward and functional; decorative items had no place here. Every object in this apartment appeared to have a useful purpose. The only exception was a narrow glass vase in which a rose was in full bloom as it sat on the windowsill. *Where did the flower come from? Perhaps from the unknown friend Petitjean mentioned.*

On the opposite side of the sofa was a closet. Sandrine rose and went over to it. The front side consisted of four offset sliding doors. She pushed the two middle ones aside.

Well, what do you know? Behind the door appeared a television, several speakers, an expensive-looking music system, some high-end headphones and other technical gadgets. She lifted the transparent cover. There was a vinyl record on the turntable. Dave Brubeck. The woman had liked classic jazz. Sandrine crouched in front of the equipment. She found a black VHS cassette recorder under the Blu-Ray player. The rest of the equipment was chrome. The recorder didn't match the colour of any of the other gadgets. Aimée Vilette would never have committed such a design mistake without a good reason.

"What are you doing here?" Sandrine murmured. She turned the recorder around. On the backside was a converter which enabled a VHS-cassette to be played on the television. The power light indicator was on. The victim must have used it right before she died. She pressed the eject button. The mechanics started but no cassette came out. Someone had taken it with them. *What were you watching?* Sandrine thought.

She pushed the other doors open. Shelves with records, a CD stand and technical accessories appeared but no VHS cassette, not even an empty sleeve. Something had been recorded that was worth stealing, maybe even worth killing for. Only a few people could have stolen it. The culprit, or possibly Petitjean when he discovered the body. But there also could have been a trivial reason. Maybe she borrowed the cassette and returned it yesterday evening. No. What she had learned about the woman with the obsessive sense of order told her that she would certainly have switched off the recorder and probably would have even removed it completely from the apartment. The device had only been used for one single occasion.

Maybe it's somewhere in the studio or forensics took it as evidence. Her gut feeling was that the cassette was significant, but not important enough to fully focus on and ignore other evidence.

She climbed up the spiral staircase, turned on the light and moved the dimmers to half power. The table on which the perpetrator had tortured, murdered and displayed the victim captured her attention for a moment and her stomach contracted painfully. After the conversation with Suzanne Leriche, she had become more aware of the cruelty with which the murderer had proceeded and also how much he knew about the victim. It was hard for her to imagine that Aimée Vilette would be the type of person who would share her fears carelessly with others. But Inès and Adel might find out about that as they worked through the articles and videos. She looked at her wristwatch. They might have already looked through documents from the last couple of weeks. Sandrine relied on the duo's knowledge of human nature and quick comprehension. If the victim's behaviour, language or topics changed, they would notice.

The technicians had taken most of them but some scraps of paper coated in blood and vomit still stuck to the polished wooden floor. She could imagine the agony the young woman suffered, whose greatest fear was death by vomiting. The murderer had relentlessly stuffed her mouth with crumpled pages of the book until she bled and vomited over and over again, and suffocated slowly and painfully. Did he take his time and rejoice in her suffering? Of course. He had begun to paint her stomach with strange characters to dehumanise her while she was still alive. He wanted to humiliate and torture her. But for what reason? Who could have been so hurt or threatened by this woman that he felt this kind of death was justified? This was supported by the fact that it looked as if he had meticulously recorded the act. What could he want with the recording? Was he at home calmly watching it repeatedly and enjoying it, like Adel suspected? Maybe it gave him a sense of superiority that he desperately needed. *We'll know as soon as we catch him.*

Sandrine dropped to her knees. Blood had dripped onto the floor from the wounds created by the cable ties. The woman had resisted with all her might but it had done her no good. She must have trusted the perpetrator otherwise she wouldn't have let him in the apartment and turned her back on him. The blow that had stunned her had been carried out from behind. But where had it happened, in the living room or here in her studio? If it were downstairs, Jean-Claude Mazet would have found blood there.

The table on which the victim was found was used for her video recordings. She had been working on another desk which was pushed up against the wall. Forensics had taken the laptop with them but they had left behind the external monitor and the two keyboards. This was where she had written articles, edited videos and recorded the podcast. On the table lay a small black box, a bit bigger than a matchbox out of which a cable protruded. She had no idea what it was used for. Sandrine took her phone out of her pocket and shot a photo then sent it to forensics. Marie, the Mistress of Bits and Bytes as Jean-Claude Mazet called her, would know. *It's probably something totally trivial.*

Her eyes fell upon a white shelf.

"Now what do we have here?" A VHS cassette sat between some illustrated books. She pulled it out. "*Sinful Sisters,*" she read quietly. On the cover, a naked, cow-eyed brunette stared at her lustfully. This thing had to be from the nineties. What was somebody like Aimée Vilette doing with third-rate porn? Sandrine couldn't imagine how the woman could watch a film like this without feeling tarnished. She placed the tape in an evidence bag. There would be little left for her to do except wait for what was discovered, after the forensic technician came back with his results.

She stood up and went to the sleeping area and looked for a while at the nude portrait above the bed. The red curls fell down her back like waves on the sea. The subtle lighting cast a gentle glimmer on her skin, her eyes glistened with life and radiated a sense of self-assurance in her nakedness that amazed Sandrine considering the woman's troubled background. She must have trusted the photographer completely otherwise this kind of art could not have been created. This was the kind of artistic eroticism that she could reconcile with Aimée Vilette's lifestyle. But who had shot this photo? She had taken a close look at the pictures in Petitjean's studio. Uninspiring and cheap poses with the focus on tits and ass. Such an artistically demanding image as this was way beyond his abilities. Why had he lied and said it was his work?

The apartment door opened. Someone stepped inside, then shortly after the door closed again. Her hand went to her gun but she hesitated to take it out.

"Aimée!" someone shouted.

A burglar wouldn't behave so conspicuously. She left her pistol in her holster and went downstairs.

"Who are you and what are you doing in this apartment? What does the seal on the door mean?" A man stood in the living room, looking at her in irritation. She guessed his age: around mid-thirties. Short hair, a three-day beard and in good shape. His clothes were casual but he was well-groomed. An attractive man. In his hands he held a folder, like the ones used for drawing and architectural plans. He took his phone out of the back pocket of his jeans. "Get out or I'll call the police."

"That won't be necessary," she answered and showed him her badge.

"What are you doing here? Was there a break-in?" His eyes rushed around the apartment. The folder fell from his hands and clapped on the floor. Large format photographs slipped out but he ignored them. "Where is Aimée? Did something happen to her?"

"Come with me." Sandrine led the man into the kitchen and ushered him onto one of the stools at the table. He didn't let her out of his sight for even a second. The panic in his eyes revealed that he knew what she was going to tell him even though he resisted what his intuition was telling him.

"What ...?" he tried to ask but his voice failed him.

"Mademoiselle Vilette died yesterday evening and the police have already started the investigation." It was always her policy to state the truth in as few words as possible. Most people could tolerate clear and concise information better than euphemisms and empty phrases. And sooner or later they would find out what happened anyway. If she lied to him now he would never trust her again and she didn't want to risk it. He seemed to know the victim well if he had a key to her apartment and could tell her a lot about Aimée's private life.

"An accident?"

"No. She was murdered."

His eyes widened and he stared at Sandrine in disbelief. "Murdered? But who would want to do that? She was a wonderful and peace-loving person."

"We'll do everything in our power to find out."

He shook his head and stared at his hands as he rubbed them together.

"Do you live with Mademoiselle Villete?"

"Not really. I have my own place. But I'm here with her a lot."

"So you know this place?"

"Yes, of course."

Sandrine pointed at the espresso machine. "Would you be so kind as to make us an espresso? We could both use one."

The man looked at her in amazement. Then he nodded hesitantly.

"Yes, of course. Whatever you want."

He stood up and turned the machine on. From a cabinet he pulled out two espresso cups, and from a drawer two tiny spoons and several packets of sugar. As if in a trance he moved slowly but unerringly about the kitchen. It was obvious that he was familiar with the apartment, better than someone who only visited the victim occasionally. She wasn't particularly in need of a shot of caffeine but she wanted to pull the man out of his shock and nothing worked as efficiently as physical activity. She watched him put the cups in the machine. The grinder started and Sandrine used the opportunity to go into the living room to pick up the folder with the photographs.

The man brought over the two cups full of coffee and she sat down with him.

"May I ask your name and what your relationship with Mademoiselle Vilette is?" She avoided calling the woman a victim as well as using the past tense.

"Sébastien Duval," he said. "We loved each other. No idea how else to classify it."

"Love is enough for me," she replied. "You stayed in the apartment overnight?"

"Of course. When we do stay together, it's usually here. Aimée seldom separated work from her private life. It was not uncommon for her to get up in the middle of the night to write down a thought that had come to her and formulate an article about it."

Sandrine nodded thoughtfully. Her studio and bedroom were the same room, only separated by a privacy screen.

"She hated it when I called what she loved to do 'her work'. It was an important part of her life; she was so successful at it that she was able to get paid for it. But she wouldn't have done anything else even if she hadn't made any money."

"You intended to move in together?"

"No. Each of us had our own domain and we preferred it that way. We're both workaholics and need to concentrate. I travel a lot and so I live in Saint-Lunaire. A small town west of Dinard." She knew the area. A tranquil little town with several wide sandy beaches which are not over-crowded, even in summer.

"You're a photographer?" Sandrine lay the photos that she had picked up in the living room on the table.

"Yes. That's how we met. I've taken some pictures for her lately."

"The photo from the bedroom?"

"That's from me."

"An excellent portrait."

A gentle smile slid across his face. "It was impossible to take a bad picture of Aimée."

"We assumed that it was Dominique Petitjean." She didn't want to beat around the bush to see if they knew each other.

His smile instantly vanished and his voice became quite sharp. "You've caught me off guard. That guy would have made even a unique person like Aimée look cheap and slutty in a photograph. The man is third rate, if that."

"Seems you have a dim view of him."

He grimaced. "How can anybody like a man like that? He takes very young girls out of the countryside, hopeful for a modelling career, so that he can get them into bed. With the photos he leaves them with, they can only imagine themselves at a brothel at best."

"But your girlfriend worked with him."

He ripped open a sugar packet and tipped the contents into the espresso. The white mountain sank slowly in the foam and he stirred it in.

"Aimée returned to Saint-Malo from Paris four years ago. She had finished her studies and begun to build her social media presence. At the beginning she shot pictures herself. They weren't bad at all but didn't meet her own standards. The little money she had she put into her articles, voice training and video equipment. An acquaintance brought her into contact with Petitjean. She needed acceptable pictures and he was the only one she could afford at the time."

"Forgive me for asking: how close were they?"

He lifted his eyebrows and his forehead became covered with wrinkles.

"That's not really what you're driving at, is it?"

"Just a question."

He shook his head. "Have you met this guy?"

"Yes," she answered, concealing the fact that he was the one who found the body.

"Aimée had some psychological ..." he thought for a moment, "... restrictions."

"I talked with Suzanne Leriche."

"You are thorough. That is good," he said slowly, emphasising every syllable. "Then you know about her problems?"

"Roughly speaking."

"With Suzanne's help she got her washing compulsion under control but she attached great importance to cleanliness in other parts of her life."

"One look at this apartment is enough to get a good idea."

"The idea that she even entered Petitjean's studio frequently, if you can call that place a real studio, is absurd. That place stank of cigarettes, booze and cheap sex. All the filth stuck to you. Aimée went over there when she had to but then spent an hour in the shower to feel halfway clean again. She almost never invited that man into her own apartment; they mostly met somewhere outside or he left things at the door."

"That must have hurt someone like Petitjean."

"Of course, but the man blamed it on Aimée's problems. He's like a Teflon pan, nothing sticks to him. Photographing naked skin is pretty boring in the long run, but he needed the money." Sébastien Duval took a sip of espresso. "As you may know, he liked to brag about taking photos for local celebrities."

"Had anything changed recently in their business relationship?"

"You mean, since we met?" He laughed bitterly. "She was gradually separating from him. He probably sees me as the main reason he was thrown out but that wasn't it. On one hand Aimée had evolved as a photographer and I proudly take some responsibility for that. On the other it was becoming clearer to her what a bastard that man is. Last week she realised that he was trying to blackmail some girls with the photos he had taken of them. So she kicked Petitjean out of her life." He looked up towards the office. "Somewhere up there must be a copy of the termination letter."

She made a mental note to ask Jean-Claude Mazet if he had found it.

"When did it happen?" he asked suddenly.

"Yesterday night between ten p.m. and midnight," Sandrine answered. "Unfortunately, it is my duty to ask ..."

"Where was I and whether I have an alibi?" he interrupted her. "That must certainly be one of the unpleasant things your job entails: not being able to trust anybody. I was in Paris and I drove directly here this morning. Working with a few old friends. I'm involved in an exhibition about traditional but dying crafts and trades, and yesterday was the opening. It was quite late and I decided to stay in Paris overnight." He pulled his wallet out of his jacket pocket and dug out some receipts. "Hotel, fuel receipts and here's my agent's business card. He'll be able to confirm that I was in Paris at midnight. Just like a half dozen of my colleagues."

"Thanks, that's enough for me."

"It's your job, I get it. Even though it hurts like hell to even be suspected of having anything to do with her death." His voice sounded strained, and his pain could not be ignored.

"Had anything changed lately in your relationship? Did she receive threats or was she afraid of anyone?"

He massaged his chin with his right hand while he thought it over. "Threatening emails and insults came no more than usual, nothing that Aimée considered especially important. She dealt with polarising topics, where verbal gaffes and insults over Twitter or email were just part of daily business. But you're right, something was burdening her and throwing her off track. She started washing her hands excessively again. I noticed some red spots and she withdrew as far as physical intimacy was concerned. I don't know if she was afraid of anyone but some-thing must have happened recently. I asked her to go and see Suzanne and Aimée agreed. Conversations with that woman really helped her."

"And you had no idea what the situation might have been?"

"Not in the slightest. Even though it almost tore me apart to see her in that condition without being allowed to help her, I didn't push her to tell me anything. As long as she was brooding over a problem, she clammed up, not only in her private life but also professionally. Only when she was absolutely satisfied with an article or a video was I allowed to see it and talk to her about it."

"Where did she keep her notes and work results? Maybe we can find a clue there about what she was currently working on."

"Not a chance," said the man decisively. "She took pride in working one hundred percent paper free. Aimée owned a ridiculously expensive cloud storage account with an encryption that cannot be cracked by traditional means. Like a Swiss bank account. For security and secrecy. And before you ask: no, I do not know any of her passwords."

"That doesn't make our work any easier. One last question. We found a VHS tape. Do you have any idea what she was doing with it or where it came from?"

"She called me in Paris and asked whether she could borrow my recorder. I had no objections though I was unsure whether that old thing even worked or not."

Sandrine laid the cassette tape on the table and turned it so he could read the title.

"Absolutely no way," he said immediately. "Aimée had no reservations about erotic films, but she would not have endured this garbage voluntarily."

"But in order to watch this garbage, she took the trouble to drive to your house in Saint-Lunaire to pick up the recorder. Not to mention connecting a converter to play it on her television."

"Certainly not to watch such porn. There must have been something on it that she needed for her research otherwise she would have waited till I could bring the machine to her personally. Getting into a taxi with a stranger and leaving Saint-Malo wasn't exactly easy for her."

"I see." Sandrine pulled the evidence bag towards her. Adel would have to look at it.

"I'm very sorry. I wish for nothing more than to help you

catch this guy." He looked at the clock. "I need to get home now. I can't stay in this apartment."

Of course that would be impossible, but Sandrine didn't say that aloud.

"I can take you to Saint-Lunaire. You probably shouldn't drive in your condition."

"It's all right. I want to be by myself for now." He stood up, took the photos and went to the window. Sébastien reach out to the rose, hesitated and turned to Sandrine.

"May I?"

"Sure. I'll take responsibility for this." The flower would only wither unseen in this apartment. She saw no reason to deny him the rose.

She remained seated until the door closed then she picked up the phone and called Adel, to keep him informed. From the background, she heard Inès cry out. Deborah Binet had called again. Sandrine looked at the kitchen clock. Lunch time was almost over, and she hadn't had anything to eat.

"I can't give the woman special treatment but I'd be glad to speak with her tomorrow if she wants to make a statement," she said to Adel. "I'm hungry and need to find a snack."

"Try the Crêperie Papillon Rouge on the Grand Rue, it's only a five-minute walk from where you are. I highly recommend the quiche, it's almost as good as my mother's," she heard Inès say when she got on the line.

"I don't think that's a good idea," said Adel to Inès. Sandrine didn't know why he would complain about the recommendation, but something seemed to be bothering him.

"I'll give it a try. The restaurant is just around the corner and I haven't had a quiche in a long time."

"I've spoken with my cousin from the local radio station," said Inès. "You can come around any time during the day;

they're waiting for you. The sound engineer responsible for Aimée Vilette's radio show is Rajiv Bhamra."

"Also an acquaintance or some kind of relative?" Sandrine asked.

"More like a friend of a friend. Like you hear about so often. Anyway, he worked with the victim on Friday night. If something unusual happened, he would remember."

"Thank you. I'll drive over after lunch."

"Will we still see each other sometime today?" asked Adel.

"Rather unlikely." She was planning to check into Pascale's alibi, the muscly man who lived downstairs from Aimée. She also wanted to find out a little more about Pierre Salazar, the author of the crime novel whose pages had been used as a murder weapon. She knew just the right person for that.

"See you in the morning, then. If I were you, I would also try the tarte au citron, which is excellent. And the service is also very nice."

"Inès!" Adel interrupted. "We still have a lot of work to do."

Sandrine ended the conversation and left the apartment, restoring the police seal on the door behind her.

Sandrine took the path that went by the Cathedral of Saint Vincent and turned into the cobbled Grand Rue, which led to the main gate dating back to the middle-ages. The restaurant was impossible to miss, with a dark red facade which could be seen from afar. Two little tables stood under a tiny veranda which had been built over a narrow sidewalk. A couple of seats in front of the crêperie were unoccupied and she decided to take advantage of the wonderful weather and eat outside. There were no menus, only a tall board with the day's specials listed, leaning against the facade.

A waitress came to her table as soon as she sat down.

Sandrine guessed her age to be around sixteen or seventeen, probably a student trying to earn extra money. She wore vintage earrings with a North African motif, and horn-rimmed glasses in the shape of butterfly wings apropos to the crêperie's name, which perfectly complemented her slim and pretty face. The girl had excellent taste.

"Are you ready to order?"

"I'll take the vegetable quiche and a Badoit."

"Good choice, people love that and it's really delicious."

The waitress paused and looked at her curiously.

"Can I help you, Mademoiselle?" Sandrine asked.

"You're the lady cop, aren't you?"

"Is it that obvious?"

A light blush spread over the waitress's cheeks.

"No, not at all. I'm sorry, I don't want to be intrusive." She made to turn around but Sandrine gestured for her to stay.

"Mademoiselle, it's my job to help others, so sit down and talk to me."

The girl pulled out a chair with some hesitation then stopped.

"I happened to see you this morning with my brother. That's how I know who you are."

"And your brother is?"

"My name is Jamila Azarou. By the way, you don't have to address me formally, it makes me feel so old. Just call me Jamila."

Sandrine nodded thoughtfully and looked at the girl. A certain similarity was definitely clear. "You should sit down."

"Let me get your order in first." She disappeared inside the restaurant.

"Lieutenant Perrot, what a coincidence," she heard a female voice say. It was Deborah Binet, the journalist from *Ouest-France* newspaper, accompanied by her younger sister, Carine

Fortier, the blogger who had obstructed her last investigation into the murder of Isabelle Deschamps. She sighed noiselessly. She didn't believe in coincidence any more than she believed in Santa Claus. *How did the woman track me down?*

"Saint-Malo is a very small town. People run into each other all the time," she answered and nodded at the two of them. Deborah looked chic, as always. She asked herself how this woman with such high heels was able to walk on the cobblestone Grand Rue and yet still look so elegant. In those shoes, she herself would have certainly broken an ankle after only a few feet. "Did Mademoiselle Boni reach you and make an appointment for tomorrow?" She tried to avert the inevitable without much hope of success.

"That effort is unnecessary now that we've met by chance. You seem to have time right now and we're not in a hurry." She turned to her younger sister, who shot Sandrine a dark look. "Why don't we all just sit down and have the conversation now?"

Before she could raise an objection, Deborah Binet pulled out a chair, sat down and waved at her sister to do the same, which she did reluctantly. She certainly must have vivid memories of how Sandrine had arrested her after finding her in bed with her neighbour and holding her in a jail cell overnight.

The journalist ended the polite chatter and came right to the point. "Aimée Vilette was killed, wasn't she?"

"Even if that were so, I couldn't reveal anything about it since it's an ongoing case. As you know."

"Everybody is already shouting it from the rooftops. There is no point in denying it. Let's just assume that everybody in Saint-Malo already knows about it." She pulled out a small notepad and started reading. "Police have been standing in front of the building at Rue de la Cloche since this morning at nine. Dominique Petitjean found the body; he confirmed it to me on the telephone and is ready to talk to me." She looked up from her notes. "Do you think he murdered Aimée Vilette?"

"Madame Binet," Sandrine admonished her.

"You arrived around half past eleven," the journalist continued. "Long after forensics and your handsome assistant entered the scene. Of course I spoke to Aubert Pascale. He assured me this was a murder investigation." She clapped her notebook closed. "What more do you need before you're willing to admit that a murder has been committed in our town?"

The waitress came with Sandrine's order and saved her from further pressing questions from the woman.

"What will it be for the ladies?"

"Two café au lait," Deborah Binet ordered without first asking her sister.

The quiche looked delicious but at the moment she lacked the tranquillity to enjoy it. The bottle cap on the mineral water bottle cracked when she opened it then poured herself some.

"There will be a press conference tomorrow afternoon. You can ask all your questions there."

"I assume that Commissaire Matisse will be there to manage the press?" She scowled. "Of course he will, after all, he wants to advance his career. Saint-Malo is definitely not his last post. He probably has his eyes on Rennes or maybe even Paris."

"You should ask him yourself."

"From Matisse you only get *blah blah blah* and a few vague generalities. He would be a first-class politician. But since you know the dirty details, don't turn over the playing field to that man."

"Press conferences are not my thing," Sandrine admitted. She lacked the diplomatic flair crucial when dealing with the press.

"Nonsense. We women must not allow ourselves to be pushed into the second row."

"I'd rather solve cases than let journalists eat me alive." Besides, she had written off a long prestigious career with the police some time ago. At the end of last year she had made a substantial mistake and had been demoted from the rank of capitaine to lieutenant by the Paris police prefect. She was still unsure whether she would be fired or if she would quit the police service on her own accord, but that was none of this woman's business.

"As you wish."

"Honestly, I can't say very much. Aimée Vilette died in unnatural circumstances sometime between Saturday night and early Sunday morning. But you already know that."

"Suspects?"

"We just started the investigation. I can't perform miracles."

"What do you think?" The journalist leaned forward slightly and looked at her with excitement.

"I believe what Mademoiselle Boni told me is that you knew something that could help clarify the case."

"One hand washes the other." Deborah Binet brushed a strand of her blond hair from her forehead and looked at Sandrine defiantly. The woman assumed that she could negotiate with her on an equal footing. She had to put an end to this as quickly as possible.

"You claimed to have relevant information. Not sharing it with us can have dire consequences." She looked at Carine Fortier who avoided her gaze. "Your sister also tried to trick us for her own benefit resulting in an embarrassing situation and a night in jail."

"As a journalist, I make my living from knowing or finding out things."

"I understand that," Sandrine said calmly. She stuck a fork into her quiche that she wanted to eat while it was still warm.

"You need to do your job, that's clear. But I need to do my job, too."

"I'm glad to hear that." A smile appeared on her lips; the woman thought she had won.

Sandrine ate with great relish. Inès wasn't exaggerating when she said the quiche tasted much better than she would have expected from a Saint-Milo tourist district. She wiped her mouth with the napkin and laid it on the table. "Commissaire Matisse is very interested in a smooth interaction with the press," she said.

The woman's face brightened further.

"However, he gets the best press when his staff solve current cases and at the moment I'm the head of the department. He's probably taking a gamble supporting me in my investigations."

"What are you getting at?" The smile vanished from Deborah Binet's lips, giving way to a thoughtful expression.

"You give me the information that you claim to have and I will be extremely grateful. Otherwise, I will eat my quiche in peace which is slowly getting cold. Then I will ask Mademoiselle Boni to call the editor of your newspaper and make it clear that the lead investigator will no longer answer questions from his employees in the future. Your choice."

"You can't do that," she stammered in astonishment.

"You can roll the dice."

"I will file a complaint against you."

"Do you really believe that your threats scare me?" Sandrine grinned broadly. "In winter I heat my home with all the complaints I receive during the course of the year." For a moment, there was silence at the table, that she used to eat another bite of quiche.

"All right, you win."

"If your findings help the investigation, we both win," Sandrine said reassuringly.

"Fair enough." The journalist had ventured too far and gotten a bloody nose but now was not the time to enjoy the victory.

"Last week, Aimée called my sister," said Deborah.

"And what did she want?"

Carine Fortier sighed deeply. Sandrine could see how uncomfortable she was in front of her. "We knew each other from some past events."

"Are you both bloggers?"

"Not at all. We're influencers," replied Carine Fortier indignantly. "Michelangelo wasn't just some guy who painted church ceilings."

"Explain the difference to me."

"A blog is a simple diary that's kept online. These days, every schoolgirl has one. Influencers like Aimée and me publish on all media channels, whether a blog, video, podcasts, live radio and internet stations. We have a knack of discovering and initiating new trends, and presenting them to a broad expectant audience. We make our followers reflect on their habits and change them for the better."

"And earn money from advertising."

"Of course. The days of the starving artist are over."

"At least for those who are able to market themselves skillfully," Sandrine replied.

"Correct. That's the essence of art," agreed Carine Fortier. "And Aimée mastered those skills perfectly."

"But she was your competitor. Weren't you jealous of her?"

"Jealous?" she repeated thoughtfully. Then she nodded firmly. "I certainly was, the woman was in a class of her own, but I was never resentful. Her success only spurred my ambition to develop and improve. In fact, we worked together on interesting projects from time to time. I liked her even though we were very different."

"When and why did she call you?"

"Thursday. After midnight. Not an unusual time for her. It didn't bother me though because I also enjoy working at night." Jamila Azarou brought the two café au lait and put them on the table. Carine put some sugar in her cup. "But she sounded quite agitated. That was pretty unusual for her. Aimée was more of an introvert, so far as I knew. In any case, she claimed she had a bombshell that she was about to drop."

"A bombshell? Did she give you any details?" The same words that Suzanne Leriche, the therapist had used. This gave Carine Fortier's statement some credibility which Sandrine had not anticipated from this woman.

"No, she was very vague, but she did tell me it would happen on Sunday. On local radio. It would get nasty and she needed the backing of the community."

"And? Would she have received this support?"

"Of course. We stick together."

"Did she offer some kind of compensation?" Sandrine was sceptical that Carine Fortier would do something without receiving personal benefit, especially if there could be headwinds. What had Aimée lured the woman with? She sought eye contact but Carine looked at her coffee and stirred in the sugar.

"She offered to share the details with us," said Deborah quickly. "If it was solid, we could have put the story in the newspaper." The answer came quickly, almost hastily. Sandrine suspected that the journalist was hiding something.

"Did she send you any documents?"

Deborah shook her head. "She promised to bring a dossier after the broadcast. But that obviously didn't happen. The person she wanted to drag into the spotlight beat her to it. I bet the evidence for her allegations has disappeared and ended up in a shredder."

If her death is related to the broadcast, Sandrine thought.

Maybe it was a coincidence or a deliberate deflection. She wasn't far enough into the investigation to rule out any leads. "Did she give any hints about this bombshell? Do you have any idea who or what it might have been about?"

"Not in the slightest," Carine Fortier answered. "She was more than just a little mysterious about her projects. I don't know any person that she would have shared this information with. And certainly not with Petitjean, whom she worked with off and on. I don't know what she saw in that guy. He is disgusting." She sipped her coffee.

"Rumour has it that she had a lover."

"Nobody's ever even seen the mysterious man, if he's even a man. Maybe it was a love tragedy that cost Aimée her life."

At least on this point she was ahead of the two women. Her knowledge of human nature told her that Sébastien was out of the question. Nevertheless, she would check his alibi carefully in case her gut feeling wasn't enough.

"Thank you for the information you've shared with me." She kept up the appearance of kindness even though she had put pressure on the women.

"And what can you tell us about the circumstances of the death?" Deborah Binet tried her luck again.

"I heard your newspaper was the first to report the arrest of the murderess in the case of Isabelle Deschamps. My congratulations." Sandrine had given a tip to the journalist at that time, about when the perpetrator would be taken to the police station. Deborah Binet only had to wait on the street until the patrol car drove by so she could be the first to report the news.

"I hope I will succeed again."

"I'm hopeful, too. After all, you are quite an ambitious journalist."

Deborah Binet nodded approvingly. Sandrine assumed that

the woman saw herself as a rising star in the editorial department of her newspaper.

The sisters said good-bye and left her on the veranda.

Both women had ruined her lunch break. Instead of enjoying the excellent quiche, Sandrine's thoughts circled around this bombshell which Aimée Vilette had spoken about to two people who were not connected to each other. In the apartment she'd found no clues as to what it might have been, and even Sébastien Duval, the victim's partner, couldn't tell her anything about it. At the moment, the content of an ancient porn video or the ripped pages of a crime novel seemed a bit too obscure to be a bombshell. After what she had learned about the encryption of her on-line storage, it was difficult for her to be optimistic about being able to look at the influencer's projects anytime in the foreseeable future.

Jamila poked her head out of the door and Sandrine waved her over.

"Did you enjoy your food?"

"Very much."

"Should I bring the bill?"

"You wanted to talk to me but then we got interrupted."

"It's not so urgent."

"I have a couple of spare minutes before I have to leave. Sit down. I'm totally harmless even if Adel may have claimed otherwise." She pushed a chair toward the girl.

Jamila took a look around the restaurant. There wasn't much going on and she sat down hesitantly.

"It was nothing important, I just wanted to take a closer look at my brother's boss."

Sandrine didn't believe her. Something more must be behind this otherwise she wouldn't have spoken up to begin with. "Boss is an exaggeration. We're partners and I just happen to have a higher rank, which ultimately means that I get in trouble when one of us steps on somebody's toes."

The girl looked at her then smiled shyly. "I've never met a policewoman like you. Adel often talks about you. He never used to talk about work. Sometimes it seemed to me that he regretted joining the police force. That's changed now."

"Oh. I hope he didn't say too many bad things about me."

"Not at all. Is it true that you can crack open door locks like a professional and that you stay fit by doing martial arts?" Curiosity suddenly shone in her eyes and she looked at Sandrine expectantly.

"I'm pretty good at one but in the other I usually get my butt kicked," Sandrine said modestly. Her Uncle Thomas had taught her how to pick a lock when she was twelve. He'd said she had a natural talent which she had bragged about at the time. A year later he had allowed her not only to be a lookout but to open a lock on an old villa, which they entered. At fifteen there was hardly an alarm or vault that was safe from her. In hindsight, nothing to be particularly proud of, but you never know when it might be beneficial to have a talent to fall back on.

"You are a cool cop," she said with conviction in her voice. "I hope you can get my brother to loosen up a little bit."

"I think your brother is quite cool in a slightly different way." They had only been working together for a few weeks but she had quickly come to appreciate and rely on the quiet man.

"But he doesn't send you to bed at eleven or complain about your clothes which he finds way too revealing." She sighed in irritation and rolled her eyes.

"Isn't that a big brother's job?"

"Adel has three older sisters that aren't nearly that stuffy. Not even my mother is so strict."

"That's the disadvantage of working in the police department. We always see evil happening around us, which often makes us overprotective. I'm absolutely sure he loves you."

She remained silent for a while before she nodded. "Of course he does, but he's still annoying."

"I'm sure you didn't want to talk about your brother. What's on your mind?"

"Is Aimée really the victim?"

"Does everyone in this city know that now?"

"It's like living in a tiny village here." Jamilla pulled her cell phone from her back pocket and tapped on the display. "Fifty-three texts and two dozen voice mails. Yes, this is the talk of the town here in Saint-Malo. And since my brother works at the police department, everybody asks me for the latest news."

"Then I won't be telling you any secrets. Mademoiselle Vilette is indeed dead. Did you know her?"

"Knowing her would be an exaggeration. I watched her videos sometimes if it was a topic I was interested in, but I always listened to her broadcasts on local radio. Mostly recordings when I had the time."

"And do you know something that could help us?"

"It's probably not important but I saw her fighting with a man."

"Here in the crêperie or somewhere else?"

"No, on the street, right in front. It got pretty heated. I looked out to see what was going on, but in that moment she turned, left the man standing and stormed past me in the restaurant. She perched herself at a table in the far corner and even ordered a quiche. Then she sat there for half an hour and didn't eat one bite. She was shaking, and I have no idea whether it was from anger or fear. When she calmed down, she disappeared. Without eating."

"And the man?"

"He looked for her but didn't come in. I saw him going towards Grand Porte."

"What did he look like?"

"Mid-fifties, I would guess. White, some grey hair but still halfway attractive. He wore square glasses and an expensive suit."

"You must make a formal report, maybe look over a couple of photos or sit down with our artist."

"At the police station?"

"Does that bother you?"

"Me not so much, but I imagine Adel won't like my getting involved with a murder case."

"It's not as if you are some kind of criminal. He would definitely be proud that his sister trusted the police enough to want to help us. These days this it's no longer a matter of course."

"Sure, I can do it. But only after school."

"All right. Tomorrow afternoon. We'll drive you home, too."

A guest waved and Jamila stood up. "It was so nice to talk to you. Maybe the police aren't as bad as people think." Without waiting for an answer, she picked up the money and disappeared into the restaurant. Sandrine smiled. The girl definitely won't let her brother boss her around so easily. She had no doubt that Inès Boni recommended the Papillon Rouge not just because of the food but also to meet Adel's sister. She just didn't know what was behind it. She couldn't have known that Jamila had observed something about the case.

She stood up and went back to the Rue de la Cloche where her motorcycle was parked. On the way to the radio station she decided to leave the cassette at the police department.

"I have informed Monsieur Bhamra and he'll be meeting with you soon. You can wait there." The man behind the reception desk pointed at a typical sitting area with black leather sofas that stood in front of a window. The radio station was located in a redesigned industrial building on the outskirts of Saint-Malo. In the foyer hung a sign with logos from various companies that were located here, most of them small advertising or software companies. She had barely had time to check the messages on her cell phone when a young man in knee-length shorts, sandals and a loose T-shirt which was supposed to conceal his thick waist, headed towards her.

"Lieutenant Perrot?"

She stood up and showed him her police ID.

"Inès already made me aware of your coming. Tragic. I can hardly believe what happened. Poor Aimée." He sounded very upset.

"That's why I have to talk with you, Monsieur Bhamra."

"Call me Rajiv, we're not very formal here."

"Gladly."

"Come with me, I've reserved a conference room."

She followed him through an open office. Only a few of the desks were occupied and the employees' eyes stuck to them as they walked by. She guessed that everybody knew why she was visiting.

A glass cubicle served as their meeting room. The décor was simple but functional. On the table were glasses, water bottles and an open can of Sablés Bretones, a popular brand of butter cookies. She pulled out a chair and sat down. Rajiv got two café creams from a fully automatic coffee machine. He placed one cup in front of Sandrine and the other on the opposite side of the table. He himself had a Coke and a cookie.

"We only have these when we have a visitor," he said and took a bite. "Arianne is coming, too." He ignored her quizzical look and took another cookie from the can.

"Are you the producer of Mademoiselle Vilette's broadcast?"

"The 'Midnight Chats', yes. But the title of producer is probably a bit exaggerated. Sound engineer and recording director is probably more accurate. Aimée was an absolute professional. She was always perfectly prepared and left nothing to chance." He leaned forward slightly and sighed. "Not all hosts around here are alike, I can tell you that."

A woman with a bulging folder marched through the open plan office and towards the cubical. Asian-looking tattoos covered her arms and her coloured hair was shaved on both sides. Silver piercings glittered in the light of the desk lamps as she went by. The woman was probably only a couple years older than Rajiv. Everyone over thirty in the office must feel ancient.

"Arianne," she introduced herself and pressed Sandrine's hand in greeting. "I'm the program director. You've already met Rajiv. He probably knew Aimée best of all. They were a super team." She sat down, grabbing the café cream as if it were natural for him to have put it there for her. She opened the folder. "Can you tell us when and how she was killed?"

Sandrine shook her head. The woman was outwardly dissimilar to the elegant Deborah Binet but as similar as possible in nature, as if they were twins. Always looking for a story to sell to their audience.

"You have probably misjudged the reason for our meeting. You are not interviewing me. On the contrary, this is a police investigation." *And I'm the one asking the questions.* She didn't have to say it aloud, it was clear enough.

"But of course. Fire away." The woman lay down her pen and leaned back in her seat.

"Madame Vilette died late yesterday evening. We assume it was a deliberate act. That's all the information that I can give you. Tomorrow afternoon there will be a press conference at the police station." She pulled two business cards out of her pocket and slid them over the table. Rajiv took one and looked at it. Arianne left hers untouched and kept eye contact with Sandrine.

"Her last public appearance was on Friday night. Did you notice anything unusual? Did she seem nervous, anxious or act strange in any way?" She looked at Rajiv who must have been in the control room with the victim.

"No." He tugged thoughtfully on his lower lip. "Actually, she acted the same as ever. A real professional, which I've already told you. Maybe a little less patient than usual. She was quick to counter some callers with particularly skewed views."

"Was that unusual?"

"By her standards, yes. Most of the time she let people talk until they'd made enough rope to hang themselves or contradicted themselves. But Friday she was a little more aggressive."

"Were there any threats?"

"Not at all. Heated discussions, of course, but nothing more."

"What was the topic of the evening?"

"Somewhat boring actually. To what extent is it legitimate for an author to separate his or her personal views from their work," said Rajiv.

"Can a real asshole write good literature that you should read or do you generally have to reject it?" Arianne said succinctly.

"And the conversations got heated?"

"Well, on the one hand there are those listeners who scream for political correctness and quickly become indignant. On the other there are listeners who equate any form of criticism with cancel culture and believe that it's nothing less than a culture war in which there can only be one winner. Those conversations rarely stay moderate. But Friday night was not particularly

Christophe Villain

disturbing. Literature heats up the spirits in Saint-Malo a lot less than in Paris." The woman drank her coffee and grinned broadly. She seemed to be having a lot of fun.

"And what topics seem to heat up the spirits in this area?"

The program director pulled print-outs from her folder. "Immigration is a red flag for some right-wing politicians. Over-fishing and factory farming. A goose farmer talked about Aimée's views on animal cruelty in the traditional production of foie gras. Farming and environmental issues are generally very emotional topics. And so forth." She pushed the folder to Sandrine. "These are some of the threats and insults we have received in the last few weeks. About a dozen, so it's still within normal range. I imagine some might slash tires or throw a bunch of crap over a car but murder? I just can't imagine it. Who would kill someone only because they believe the stuffing of geese is animal cruelty? That's what almost the whole world believes now anyway."

Sandrine took a look at the pages. Most were blunt insults, often with a bunch of spelling mistakes, but nowhere were any threats of violence.

"She announced the special Sunday broadcast. She promised it would be very interesting. And very personal."

"Why did she get a special slot?" Sandrine turned to the program director. "What did the host who gave up his time slot think about that? Was he upset? Were there any problems with other station employees?"

"It seemed important to her. There was something on her mind that she wanted to share with her listeners. Aimée was one of our most popular hosts and I saw no reason to turn her down. But you're off the mark about one thing: Albert, who would have had to relinquish his time spot, had been bugging me for weeks about his need for a vacation. So, I killed two birds with one stone. I hadn't heard about any jealousy or quarrels. Half the people at this station were secretly in love with Aimée, and not just men." Arianne smiled mischievously and Rajiv bowed his head in embarrassment.

"Are you one of them?" Sandrine asked the woman.

She laughed. "She was extremely attractive, I must admit. But she was also rather complicated. Not a partner for me, I lack the interpersonal sensitivity that a person like Aimée needs. Besides, I'm in a solid relationship."

"Any idea what she wanted to share with her fans?"

"Not in the least," Rajiv answered. "I asked her about it but she clammed up completely. She only indicated that it was something personal. I don't know anything more than that. She was a person I trusted which is not very common. If she said it was going to be an exciting evening, I had no reason to doubt her. This morning I brought out a bottle of wine, cancelled my appointments and was ready to be surprised. Do you believe that broadcast had something to do with her death? Did somebody want to silence Aimée?"

"We're still at the beginning of our investigation, so I can't rule out anything." But it seemed to Sandrine to be the most promising approach so far.

"Can we report it that way?" the woman asked.

"That we're investigating all possibilities? Of course."

"We're sorry that we're unable to help you more."

"I hope you get the guy," said Rajiv. "It sounds terribly trite but we're actually one big family here, and losing our Aimée has broken our hearts."

"If you need help to find the perpetrator, we're here to help you," Arianne assured her.

"Thank you. I'll be back."

"Do you have any further questions for us?"

"Not at the moment but I'm sure something will come up in the course of the investigation."

"I don't want to appear irreverent," the program director said, "but would you be interested in an interview?"

"The press conference is tomorrow. That's all I can say about the case."

"I'm not talking about that. We regularly invite strong women who have established themselves in a male-dominated world and can be an example to others. This Thursday, Odette Marchal will be talking about her new book."

"I'm no role model," Sandrine said.

"Tough policewoman who has solved a high-profile murder in the area and runs a crime-fighting unit in Saint-Malo after clashing with the Paris police prefect. A motorcycle rider with BMW F 750 GS and a martial artist. Our audience would love you."

"How do you know so much about me?"

"This radio station is too small for me to just sit on my ass all day in front of my desk. I'm a journalist at heart and naturally I reported on your first case: the dead female from the beach path in Cancale. Getting your biography wasn't very hard. Your motorcycle is parked underneath my office window and I saw you in the martial arts studio when I interviewed Lilou Lanvers." The woman was astoundingly perceptive and clearly took action when the opportunity presented itself. Sandrine warned herself to be careful about what she said in her presence.

"Understood." She had already gotten to know Lilou better. After a really bad day she'd wanted to fight, provoked the woman and got in the ring with her when she was slightly drunk. The inevitable had happened.

"We can talk about this case when it's solved," Sandrine said. A public appearance was foreign to her. Technically she had been suspended from police service and lent temporarily to the Saint-Malo police department until the internal affairs investigation was closed.

"In any case, it would make our listeners very happy." Arianne clapped her folder shut. "I have to go back to work."

"Me, too."

They said good-bye and Rajiv escorted her to the door.

* * *

She circled the main house and found Rosalie on her terrace talking with a woman that she didn't know.

"I'm sorry, I didn't mean to disturb you," she apologised.

"Nonsense, come here, we were talking about you anyway and now you can listen in." Rosalie smiled and waved her over. "This is Sandrine, my landlady and proper investigator for the police," she introduced her to the visitor.

"Odette Marchal." The woman with the charisma of a prematurely aging diva held out her hand. Sandrine estimated her to be in her mid-fifties with a blond hair colour that nature did not produce in this intensity.

She wore a ring on almost every finger and a heavy gold chain over the blouse which concealed her small padding. She must have been quite attractive in her youth. But now a thick layer of makeup covered her face and the penetrating smell of strong perfume hung in the air. She reminded Sandrine of Catherine Deneuve, but without her class and timeless Parisian chic.

She sat down with the two women. Rosalie gave her a cup and poured her some tea.

"Too late for coffee for me, otherwise I won't be able to close my eyes tonight. Odette is also an author." She looked over at her. "And a very successful one, too."

"Crime novels?" Sandrine asked.

"Oh no, I can't bear anything to do with death and violence." She shuddered theatrically. "Young adult and children's books are my passion."

"Girls who have to struggle in a society dominated by men?"

The woman paused for a moment. "You've read something of mine? Now I'm really amazed. I would have thought that you would be a fan of heavy thrillers."

"Not at all. I have enough of that in my job. I read for relaxation. But I must confess, I'm not familiar with any of your books."

"So how do you know which topics I write about in my stories?"

"Arianne Briand mentioned that you were going to be in her show about strong women. I guessed the rest."

"And right on target." She tapped Rosalie lightly on her arm. "Just like you said, a really clever detective. If I ever commit a crime which I've certainly done before, I'm sure that you would catch me." The woman laughed, a trace too affected.

"Odette's new book will be published next week. She is on tour through newspaper editorial offices, radio stations and countless literary blogs which have sprouted up like mushrooms."

"I heard about poor Aimée," said Madame Marchal in a restrained voice.

The news of the woman's death had made waves beyond Saint-Malo's city limits; they were even talking about it in the quaint town of Cancale. Almost everybody Sandrine had talked to today seemed to know about it.

"Did you want to present your book on Aimée's social media channel?" asked Sandrine.

"I don't think so. We didn't talk about it explicitly. Grégoire, my publisher, will know more."

"But she discussed literature."

"As interesting as she might have been as a human being, she was completely uninteresting to me in terms of marketing."

"How am I to understand that? Didn't the woman have a hundred thousand subscribers?"

"Aimée speaks … spoke to high-income people, mostly singles from mid-twenties to forties, who have the time and money for exclusive events and high-tech gadgets. Her followers don't buy my books. What I need are parents, better yet, grand-parents who want to buy a gift for their children or grandchil-dren. Therefore, very little mutual interest existed."

A car honked in front of the house. She looked at her black Rado watch.

"It's already late. That must be Grégoire; we have yet another appointment with some newspaper. I'll be glad when the circus is over and I can sit down and write again." She stood up and gave Rosalie a kiss on the cheek. Her gold chains clinked with every move. Sandrine shook her hand in good-bye. Swaying slightly, she walked over the gravel path that led around the house in her elegant but impractical high heels.

"Interesting woman," said Sandrine thoughtfully.

"For sure. When we were both young, Odette never missed a party. She was game for everything: men, alcohol and anything you could swallow, smoke or sniff. Then the inevitable crash happened for her in the late nineties. But she got back on her feet again and emerged a new person: sober and a rising star among young adult and children's books authors. Although, her writing might be a touch too moralistic for my own tastes. A good long-time friend, even though she's a couple of years older than I am."

"Her wild times are written all over her face."

"No woman should be ashamed of the vestiges of the life she displays. The heavy make-up highlights it even more, but she needs to find that out for herself."

Sandrine took a sip of her tea which was already lukewarm.

"A hard day?" asked Rosalie.

"It's always a hard day when you have to look closely at a dead body."

"I know who it is."

"I can't tell you much more about this case."

"She was an extremely pleasant person, with a host of problems, but I had the impression she could handle them."

"You knew her?"

"As opposed to Odette's books, her followers loved mine. I always sent her a signed copy and she introduced her followers to every one of my novels."

"Praise or disgust?"

"I don't know if she personally liked my books but she recommended them so I can't complain."

"Are you familiar with an author named Pierre Salazar?"

Rosalie moaned softly. "All too well. His crime novels are also published by Grégoire's publishing house."

"Did Aimée recommend his books as well?"

She sucked the air between her teeth, making a hissing sound as if she were in physical pain. "Total garbage. She regularly and publicly humiliated him as a writer."

"Rightly so?"

"Completely. The man doesn't have one shred of imagination, his characters are one-dimensional, his plots are bland and the sex is mind-numbingly boring. After the first quarter of the book at the latest, it's evident to all readers who the murderer is."

"So, not a bestselling author."

"I can only guess why Grégoire holds onto him. Probably an old male friendship. Although ..."

"Yes?"

"It's rumoured that his brand-new novel could be quite

good. Which would surprise me, personally. Writers who haven't developed a compelling style after two dozen books generally never succeed. But ..." she held up her hands theatrically, "he could be the exception."

"We found his novel in Aimée's apartment along with an English language crime novel. From the blurb, it's set somewhere in Cornwall."

"That must be an extraordinary story since she never discussed foreign publications."

Sandrine thought for a moment. She didn't see the connection between the novel and the death of the young woman. Maybe with her expert knowledge, Rosalie could give her some advice.

"It's not exactly a secret but it should remain between us."

"Of course."

"*Dead Sins Will Hunt You* from a certain Sarah Mason."

Rosalie shrugged. "Never heard of it." She picked up her cell phone from the table and tapped the title into it.

"Found it." She scrolled over the site and read the description. "The blurb sounds exciting. However, the book hasn't been translated. If it was an actual bestseller in the UK, like my *Oyster Murder* that's probably on your night-table, I would have heard about it."

Sandrine got the unmistakable hint and held her hand up in defence. "I'm sorry, I wanted to start it this morning but then Adel called. Now I won't be able to for a few more days."

"As soon as you solve the case, I'll lock you in the library and won't let you out until you've read the whole thing and given me a proper review," Rosalie threatened.

"I promise. But now I have to get going, run one more lap and then go to the Équinoxe."

"To that exceedingly handsome man who stayed overnight with you?"

"On the sofa."

"Of course on the sofa, where else?" Her tone indicated that she didn't believe one word of Sandrine's story. "Who knows if he's working there today?"

"It's about an alibi I need to check on."

"A suspect?"

"So far only a witness and I doubt that will change."

"Commissaire Hugo Delacroix would have been satisfied with a call."

"I'm more thorough than he is." She stood up and said good-bye.

"Send my greetings to him," Rosalie called out. "Tell him he should come by again."

Sandrine did not turn around and went into her cottage. Her friend had read too much into a casual acquaintance.

Since she wouldn't need her weapon any more today, she hung her shoulder holster on the wardrobe, put her pistol into the gun safe in her bedroom then took off her leather outfit and placed her motorcycle boots in the closet. After quickly putting on her jogging clothes and running shoes, she left the cottage, crossed over the lawn and descended the stone steps to the hiking trail where she ran most often. It was half past five.

It was a little over three and a half miles from her cottage to the Pointe du Grouin. That would be enough for her today. She had to go to the club and check into Aubert Pascale's alibi, the tenant who lived under Aimée Vilette's apartment. Sandine pulled up her wind-breaker's zipper and trotted off slowly.

* * *

It was early, so most of the seats in the club were unoccupied and the volume of the music was still acceptable to her. Both would change drastically during the course of the night. A fog machine emitted a powerful cloud and the lighting system bathed the dance floor in a poisonous-looking green. The air conditioner was working hard against the stale smell of beer and sweat. She saw Léon behind the bar and sauntered over. He was her age, mid-thirties and quite attractive. She knew he was muscular and fit, after all, they trained in the same fitness studio. As always he was dressed rather casually: a white shirt with the sleeves rolled up above the elbows, jeans and sneakers. As soon as she sat down, he saw her and smiled. She waved at him. Léon served some guests at the other end of the bar then came over to her.

"The dangerous woman has come back?" he greeted her. "You left your gun at home?"

"Do I need a weapon here?"

The man looked around dramatically then shook his head. "I don't see anybody that you couldn't handle."

"Thanks for the compliment."

"I watch you when you're training and I'd think twice before messing with you."

Léon had a pretty good punch and a decent arm reach but she was more nimble. She would hardly have a chance with him in the ring, but she could keep up with him for a few rounds as well as annoy the hell out of him every now and then.

"So what will it be? We have some new cocktails which I can highly recommend."

"Just water."

"Are you trying to ruin an honest businessman?"

"I'm here on business."

"What a pity, I thought you'd come here to accept my invitation. I'm going fishing on Friday and whatever I catch – or buy from Carrefour – goes right on the grill."

"We have a case. I can't plan anything in the next few days but I will gladly take you up on your invitation another time."

"I'll take your word for it."

"Do you know an Aubert Pascale?"

His smile disappeared. "I thought this was just an excuse to chat with me, but you really are here on business. What has that guy done now?"

"Probably nothing. I just wanted to check his alibi. He claims to have been here at the club on Friday night from six to early in the morning."

"Aubert organises parties. Lots of alcohol, half-naked girls and heavy beats. Not necessarily my taste but he's acquired a solid base of guests over the years. He rented the Équinoxe on Friday. It was packed and by sunrise we were escorting the last few guests out the door, at least the ones that could still walk. The man is a control freak, constantly afraid that his employees are going to rip him off. As stingy as he is with paying his staff, that's probably true. He was at the club. He wouldn't dream of keeping his eyes off the cash register."

"Constantly or was he gone for a while?"

"I wasn't here the whole time. Why? But if I were I would have seen him squatting right where you're sitting now. Sure, he could have stepped away for a moment, but in the hustle and bustle it would hardly have been noticed. But I don't think so. Especially not for an hour or more."

"Then the man has an alibi, albeit a rather shaky one."

"Disappointed?"

"No. On the contrary, in this case I'm afraid we won't be short of suspects."

"What happened?"

"Apparently you are the only one in Saint-Malo that hasn't heard. In the building where Aubert Pascale lives, a woman was murdered."

"The third murder in a month." Léon scrutinised Sandrine closely. "It appears that living in your proximity is hazardous to people's health. Before you showed up, this was a peaceful community. It won't be boring with you around."

"I'm not going to kill anyone. At most I'll just be putting murderers in prison."

"I remember the evening of the last grilling party – that you ruined in the most spectacular way by having a shoot-out with a suspect who then burned down the barn you were hiding in. It will undoubtedly take a lot of persuasion to make Alain feel comfortable in your presence again." He was grinning from ear-to-ear exactly like Jean-Claude Mazet who'd made similar allusions this morning. The story of the burning barn would haunt her for a long time. Anyway, Léon hadn't been laughing that night, when he'd found her in the field and had had to patch her up. Poor Alain Thibaud, Léons friend and the farmer on whose land the barn had stood, had stumbled across a decomposing corpse in his cauliflower field, which had not done his stomach any good. He, too, would remember that night for a long time.

"I'll make it right to you both," she promised. "Honestly."

"That's appropriate. I just happen to know how."

"How about a case of wine?" she offered.

"That would be too cheap. You burned down an entire barn along with a dozen ancient oak trees and left a corpse in Alain's cauliflower field."

She sighed deeply. The way he put it made it sound pretty gruesome. Whatever he was thinking, she knew she wouldn't like it.

"Spit it out! What do you have in mind?"

"Lilou is a friend of Alain and me. She has a problem."

"The way she behaves, she has more than just one."

"Agreed. But you're not so different."

"Nonsense."

"Marie, her sparring partner, broke her leg and is out of training for a month. The championships are coming up and ..."

"Oh, no."

"It would only be once a week and it will keep you fit. And you could learn a lot from her."

She had dug herself a hole with her promise and it was going to be difficult to get out of. If she had known what he was up to, she probably wouldn't have showed up but instead have asked Adel to call on him.

"One time a week?"

"At the most."

"She must ask me personally." No way would Sandrine go to her. The woman had to come and ask.

Léon drew his lower lip between his teeth thoughtfully.

"We can make that happen," he said finally, though he didn't sound too convincing. "Then we'll see each other tomorrow evening."

"I have a case and can't promise, but I'll try."

"Good. I'll tell Lilou that we'll meet in the studio. I've got to go now, otherwise the other customers will get jealous."

She sat for a while and watched him as he expertly mixed cocktails. She didn't take much pleasure in that kind of drink but his guests seemed to like them. She waved at Léon, then left. Sandrine imagined a cosy evening with fresh fish and a crisp white wine. Perhaps life in Brittany had some advantages that she hadn't thought about when she moved here.

An Unexpected Offer

The wind that whistled loudly around the corners of her house and shook the shutters woke Sandrine. She pulled on her thick socks that lay on her bed, reluctantly got up and took a pair of cotton sweatpants out of her closet before going down to the ground floor, stacking wood into the wood stove and lighting it.

For a moment she gazed at the flames rising from the fireplace licking the bark of the logs. She put her hands in front of the glass but the fire was too weak to warm them up.

After showering and getting dressed, she came out of her tiny bedroom. She poured fresh coffee into a cup and turned on the milk frother. As usual there wasn't much in her fridge, except for an open package of madeleines which she dipped into the foam of her café au lait.

The branches of the trees in her yard shook violently and low-lying dark clouds raced across the sky. Rain began to fall, tapping softly on the windowpanes. She would have preferred to crawl back into bed.

"It's definitely good for the lawn," she muttered, as she usually did when it rained. She couldn't change the weather, but she could try to find something positive about it. Sandrine wished she could do the same at work, but the murder of Aimée Vilette seemed exceptionally tragic and pointless. As much as she tried, she'd so far failed to discover a tangible and understandable motive for the gruesome act. Neither could she find anyone who could have profited enough from her death to risk going to prison for a very long time. She pushed the last of the madeleines to the side. She had lost her appetite.

Distant thunder rolled across the bay. Today she planned to leave the motorcycle in the garage and instead take her ancient Citroën. She had to be at the nine o'clock meeting at the police station, but she wouldn't spend the rest of the day there. Phillipe Chardon and Pierre Salazar were on her list and she wanted to speak to both of them personally as quickly as possible. If the motive for the murder lay in Aimée's past, the psychiatrist might be able to give her some clues … unless he entrenched himself behind the obligation of confidentiality, then she'd have no choice but to come up with a court order.

* * *

Sandrine was one of the last to step into the conference room. Inès set a tray with coffee and cookies on the table. Jean-Claude, who looked as though he'd spent the night in the lab and Luc Poutin availed themselves generously.

Sandrine smiled; they were the same butter cookies that had been offered at the local radio station. Renard Dubois was reading a file and gave her a brief nod when she entered.

She sat down next to Adel.

"Late night?" asked Sandrine.

"Pretty much. I watched Aimée Villette's videos until after midnight, now I'm on the cutting edge of what is expected of a single man my age who wants to be eligible."

"So now you're ready for the marriage market here," joked Sandrine.

"Don't start with that, you sound like my mother," replied Adel. "There are still some traditional marriage markets in Morocco and she would love to drag me to one, next time we go back to visit our relatives. She is afraid I will end up an old and lonesome single man." He rolled his eyes and shook his head.

"Your sister said you sound like your mother too. A really likable girl, by the way."

"I can vividly imagine what she complained about."

At that moment, Commissaire Matisse came into the conference room. In his Armani suit, he looked more like a successful local politician than a cop. But appearance aside, he led the national police office very efficiently, and above all let the team get on with its job. She had seen many bosses that immediately blamed their subordinates for any failed activities. She trusted Matisse not to behave like that.

He greeted everyone present with a handshake.

He stopped beside Sandrine. "I'd like to speak with you personally afterwards," he said.

"I'll stop by your office."

"I don't want to distract you from your case, it won't take long," he promised her, as he sat down in a chair at the perimeter of the room. In doing so, he made it clear who was in charge of the investigation, namely, Sandrine.

With a brief summary of the findings thus far, she updated the team on the situation. Inès had printed photos that lay at the head of the table.

"The victim." She pinned Aimée Vilette's picture to the bulletin board.

"A beautiful woman," Brigadier Dubois muttered. "Maybe a crime of passion? A jealous lover? Or a rejected suitor?"

"There's no proof of that." She wrote Sébastien Duval on a

card and pinned it next to Aimée's photo. "Her partner didn't strike me as a violent person. But you never know. Have we been able to check his alibi?"

"Everything he said checked out," said Inès. "The man has a tendency to understate things. The exhibition he talked about wasn't in some ordinary gallery. It was at the Centre Pompidou. Witnesses include the director of exhibitions, the minister of culture, and our beloved prosecutor, Antoine de Chezac." Inès rolled her eyes. She couldn't stand that arrogant man. Sandrine felt the same way. They'd worked together on several cases in Paris and de Chezac had been put in charge of her disciplinary case.

"So Sébastien Duval is just a witness. However, one that hasn't helped us very much so far. Same for Aubert Pascale, the neighbour. He was at the Club Équinoxe all night, which his staff and a bunch of his guests can attest to."

"It's different for Dominique Petitjean, the photographer. He was at home at the time of the murders but there are no witnesses. The man didn't report any possible motives or personal animosities," Adel added. "He found the body but I don't see any concrete evidence of a crime."

"I don't see it that way," Jean-Claude Mazet interjected.

"You're right, first we should let forensics bring us up to date on the latest findings before we jump to conclusions on any potential suspects," Sandrine told him.

"It's okay, there wasn't much to report. The apartment was absolutely clean," Mazet reported. "I wish my cleaning lady was even remotely so thorough. However, we found Dominique Petitjean's fingerprints on the victim's desk and laptop."

"That was quick," Dubois remarked.

"We took his prints at the scene of the crime so we could rule him out. He didn't object."

Adel leafed through his note pad. "According to what he said, he found the body and didn't touch anything."

"Mademoiselle Vilette dusted the furniture in the loft thoroughly, so we could only find her and Petitjean's prints on the desk."

"So he lied. I'm curious as to what he was looking for there." Adel pulled his eyebrows a little closer together. Being lied to was one of those things he had difficulty tolerating. The next interrogation would be much less pleasant for Petitjean.

"Mademoiselle Vilette's partner claimed she had ended her collaboration with that man. There should be a letter terminating his services. Maybe that's what he was looking for. When we questioned him, it seemed he intended to hijack the business."

"That sleazy guy would never ever manage that business," Inès blurted out indignantly. "Sorry, but the idea of someone like that replacing Aimée Vilette is just preposterous."

"It's okay, I agree," said Sandrine.

"Then I'll go on," Jean-Claude Mazet continued. "There were scraps in the paper shredder. They're in the lab but I can't promise much. The shredder is top notch like the rest of the victim's equipment. But we found the woman's cut-up clothes in a garbage can a few blocks from the crime scene and this here." He picked up a pipe.

It looked metallic, about 20-inches long, covered in a layer of dirt and a little thicker than a thumb. "There was blood and bits of tissue on it that probably came from the victim, but Dr. Hervé has yet to check. I assume that it was used to knock her out."

"I guarantee that filthy thing didn't come from her apartment," said Sandrine. "The perpetrator must have brought it with him."

"In addition to blood and saliva, we also found traces of fat and animal feed, both on the outside and inside. We're in the process of finding out exactly what it is. But I agree the victim would have never kept anything like this in her apartment."

"So, you don't have any idea what it is?" Luc Poutin mumbled, his mouth full and all eyes on him. The man made everyone wait until he washed down the rest of the butter cookies with a sip of coffee. "It's a darning pipe."

"A what?" asked Adel.

"The tube is pushed into the goose's mouth and into the stomach. Then you press a load of corn with lots of goose fat through it, which is the only way to get a decent fatty liver to make a traditional foie gras."

"That's disgusting," said Inès. "Animal cruelty."

"There was something," Sandrine muttered as she leafed through her files. "Here. From the local radio." She pulled out a piece of paper. "Among the insults received by the victim, some came from a certain Marc Bergier, a goose farmer out of Saint-Coulomb, a village between here and Cancale. I drove through there this morning."

"Hopefully your ugly duckling didn't frighten the geese." Brigadier Dubois hadn't been able to resist the joke. No wonder Adel refused to ride with her in her old but mint condition classic Citroën. He wanted to avoid the ridicule of his colleagues.

"The car was designed for farmers, so the geese should be used to its sight and sound by now," she replied curtly. Her Uncle Thomas had been happy to tell her that the French government had commissioned Citroën to design a car that would hold two farmers with rubber boots, a 50kg sack of potatoes and a barrel of wine. In addition, the suspension had to ensure that a basket of eggs could be driven undamaged over a potholed dirt road.

"It would fit, the initials M and B are on the pipe," said Jean-Claude Mazet, ignoring Dubois' and Sandrine's comments.

"Inès, find out what is known about this man. Criminal records, reports and so on," said Sandrine.

"Will do."

"Back to forensics," she decided, looking at Jean-Claude Mazet, who nodded his thanks. "The evidence shows that the victim was knocked down on the upper floor. Therefore the perpetrator could also have been a woman. The cable ties she was tied up with can be bought in any hardware store, so that doesn't help us any further. In addition they were either wiped clean or the perpetrator wore gloves. There were also no prints on the camera, the tripod or the lamps. I have no doubt the crime was recorded. In any case he also took the memory card with him. The camera has the option of recording directly to the network via W-Lan. Marie is checking whether this function had been activated."

"And the cassette tape I brought over?" Sandrine asked.

"A standard VHS tape from the nineties. With the converter the woman was able to play them on the television without any problem, but apparently that wasn't enough for her. This is what is known as a video-grabber," Mazet explained. "This digitises and stores the film that was on the cassette. Mademoiselle Vilette obviously needed the content in digital form."

"Did she want to use it in one of her videos?" Adel looked at Sandrine questioningly. "It could mean anything from a report about sexual exploitation of women to a potential motive for murder."

"She went to great lengths to get the contents of the cassette. It must have been about that one film specifically, not about sex work in general. But why?" wondered Sandrine.

"We haven't had time to look at it yet," Jean-Claude defended his team.

"That's more our job," Sandrine reassured the man and looked around. "Volunteers?"

"I'll do it," Brigadier Dubois offered.

"Too boring at home," Poutin laughed.

"I'm not like you," he countered. Sandrine didn't intervene; the two men had been working as a team for a long time. As far as she knew, they were friends outside of work and went fishing together.

"I was with the vice squad for ten years, I'll know what to look for. If there's anything odd, I'll notice it," said Dubois.

"Make it happen," she said decisively.

"The sharpie used to draw the marks on her probably didn't come from the deceased's household. In any case, we couldn't find any other markers of this brand," Mazet continued. "At least we were able to clarify that these were Japanese characters. Marie took Japanese at university."

"Do we also know what they mean?" asked Sandrine. *Because that would really help us.*

"'The mouth is the root of misfortune'. It's supposed to be a well-known saying."

"The perpetrator is playing with us. Either he intended to mislead us or he left a clue to the motive on purpose, because he's assumed he's too smart for us to catch. If it's a clue it has to be something that Aimée Vilette wanted to cover on Sunday: the bombshell that she said she was going to drop."

"No one has been able to give us any clue as to what it is." Adel Azarou sounded frustrated.

"We've been unable to access her cloud storage or hard drive yet," Mazet remarked. "The woman's partner wasn't exaggerating, the security and encryption are rock solid. Marie gave up, which I've seldom seen. It can't be cracked with our equipment."

"Then the only hope is to find a clue to the password."

Sandrine picked up her coffee cup from the tray and took a sip. She wondered where to look for it. She didn't believe the woman would have used one of the common ones, like her birthday. Maybe her partner could be of some help. They would probably notice as soon as the case was solved and then wonder how they could have overlooked it. But these thoughts weren't going to get her anywhere.

"Any other forensic findings?" she asked Mazet.

"Nothing new," Adel said. He ran a finger along the lines of the report as he scanned it. "Dr. Hervé is still staying with the time of death between ten o'clock and midnight. She was smothered to death. A front tooth was broken off." Adel looked up. "The perpetrator probably used the darning tube to stuff the paper deep down her throat hence the saliva residue on the metal. He not only tormented her, he dehumanised her, presumably because of how vehemently outspoken she was about animal cruelty and factory farming."

The more details they uncovered, the more sadistic the perpetrator seemed to Sandrine.

"I'm assuming we're all on the same page now. Adel and I will pay a visit to Chardon the psychiatrist, Salazar the author and our goose farmer, Bergier. Inès will comb through the background information of the suspects." She pointed at the two brigadiers. "Dubois will watch television at state expense. Poutin, will you go through the writers of the rest of the threatening letters we received from the station and check their alibis?"

Both men nodded.

"Then get to work. Hopefully we'll be able to make a productive step forward today." She closed the file and put the coffee cup back on the tray.

Commissaire Matisse stood up, nodded at her and left the conference room behind Jean-Claude Mazet.

She stayed in the room and pinned index cards with the names of possible suspects on the wall, which still looked very empty. *Hopefully that will change in the coming days.* What was missing was a convincing motive.

Perhaps Dubois will find something interesting amid the naked flesh.

Inès closed the lid of the cookie tin that she would then lock away in one of her cabinets until the next meeting.

"I'll bring the dishes to the kitchen as it's on the way to the boss's office," Sandrine offered. "I would rather you do research than tidy up. I need addresses and backgrounds from the men that we're planning to visit."

"You go talk to the boss and I'll take over the kitchen duty. It'll be faster as we have a full schedule." Adel picked up the tray and disappeared. Sandrine sighed. She would have liked to postpone the conversation for a few minutes longer. It would hardly be pleasant after Matisse had spent a week in Paris. It was hard for the man, even on his second honeymoon, to keep from making a few unofficial visits to the police prefecture or the Ministry of Interior.

The office door of Commissaire Matisse was open. He was leafing through a folder when Sandrine knocked on the door frame.

"Come on in and close the door." He motioned to her and pulled a folder of signatures toward him. She sat down on one of the two chairs in front of the desk.

"We don't have much yet, but the direction of the investigation is beginning to emerge," she began but Matisse waved her off.

"I received enough information during the meeting. I'm

well-prepared for this afternoon's press conference but I would prefer that you participate. Apart from that, I'm confident the investigation is in capable hands."

"The team works extremely well together."

"I spent the last week in Paris," Matisse began. "I had promised this holiday to my wife for a long time. A wonderful city."

"I'm so happy for you both." She looked conspicuously at her watch. "You more than deserved this break."

"I happened to bump into the police prefect and we used that opportunity for a brief chat." She didn't believe in this coincidence for one second. It was quite difficult to get an appointment with the prefect. Matisse must have planned this meeting long ago. Or he was far better connected than she had guessed.

"I'm sorry to hear that."

"Why?" Her superior looked at her with irritation. Apparently, a private meeting with the police prefect seemed to have been one of the advantages of his stay in Paris.

"Your wife must have been looking forward to not having to share you with your work for once."

"I think she was quite content to be able to stroll through the Galeries Lafayette without my company. A half day at the Louvre is exhausting enough but more than thirty thousand square feet of women's shoes is quite beyond my endurance." He stroked the lapels of his Armani suit. "Of course, I was there to carry the bags."

At least the man didn't have to pay the bills. It was known that Madame Matisse was not only an exceptionally kind and intelligent woman, but also a lawyer with a prosperous firm.

"I would have loved to give you some tips for evening entertainment, after all, I grew up in Paris."

"Next time," he said dismissively. He was probably right that their ideas of what a nice evening looked like were vastly different. Although, she could have given him some advice about the Louvre. Her father liked to tell her often that some of his paintings hung there although nobody knew anything about them. *Purely showing off.* Or so she assumed. As a police officer she was reluctant to believe that his forgeries had made it to the Louvre.

"You spoke to the police prefect," she urged. Adel was waiting and they had a lot to do.

"How do you want the facts: in nice words or in a nutshell?"

"I'd prefer the latter, I've got a murder to solve." She took a deep breath and readied herself for a few hard hits.

"He thinks you're an excellent investigator ..." Matisse began. Sandrine's eyebrows rose in disbelief and she let her breath out loudly between her lips. "But a miserable policewoman."

"Isn't that a contradiction?"

"Not in the least. You solve cases extremely efficiently but you ignore official channels and instructions from your superiors. In addition you operate in legal grey areas when you want to bring down a perpetrator. The police prefect despises cops like you."

"The feeling is mutual because—"

"I really don't want to know," he interrupted her. "The man wants to get rid of you and won't hesitate to throw you out of the police force."

"I've been expecting that for a long time."

"I know. You're thinking of giving up your career."

"Then it's time to hand in my resignation."

"Don't talk nonsense," he said with a surly tone. "You love what you do. Assessing criminal behaviour and pursuing perpetrators is not just your job, it's your calling. You just don't throw something like that away."

"You said he wanted to get rid of me. What choice do I have but to beat him to the punch?"

"Exactly. You are a problem that he wants to get rid of. Preferably with as little fuss as possible."

"And that means?"

"Honestly?"

"I'd appreciate that."

"It means, I kill two birds with one stone. On the one hand I get points in Paris if I can get a problem off his hands, on the other hand, I get an excellent detective."

"How do you plan to get his problem, meaning me, off his hands?"

"That's easy. You apply for a permanent position in Saint-Malo, which the police prefect and I will accept, and the disciplinary proceedings will be immediately dismissed."

"My demotion?" she asked.

Commissaire Matisse pulled a letter from the application folder. "This was the hard part, but I predicted that it might be a requirement. In the end, he agreed. You will regain the rank of Capitaine de police upon signing and submitting the application."

She whistled softly. "He's willing to pay that high of a price to get rid of me?" She hadn't guessed her exit was so important to the man.

"Oddly enough, unlike the prefect, you seem to be extremely popular with the capital's press. Your demotion caused a great uproar. He wants to avoid more attention at all costs. Anyway, that was my impression."

"How long do I have to decide?"

"He'll give you a few days. Mademoiselle Boni has the application for a transfer ready for you to sign."

"Let me solve this case then I'll have a clearer head with which to make to a decision."

"That's the reason I want to keep you here in Saint-Malo."

She shot him a puzzled look.

"Because of your firm belief that you can solve any case."

"Keep your fingers crossed that the team succeeds. But now I have to go, I don't want to keep my suspects waiting."

She said good-bye and shut the door behind her.

"Where are we going first?" Sandrine got in the car with Adel.

"I want to start with the writer first," he suggested. "The man is a teacher at a local high school. Inès said he didn't have any classes this morning and his home is on the way to our goose farmer."

"Agreed." The wind that had rattled her car this morning had died down to a light breeze, but low clouds covered the sky. Sandrine gave up hope for sunshine today. *Never mind. We'll probably spend most of the day in the car.*

It took them about fifteen minutes to get to Pierre Salazar's address. Adel pulled in front of an old house, that was a little more than a half mile from Rothéneuf. It only had one floor and judging by the new-looking dormers, a converted attic. Ivy covered the natural stone facade leaving only the front door and narrow windows exposed.

"We're expected." Adel looked in the direction of the open front entry. A short man stepped out and stood on the gravel path that led to the garden wall. At the sight of the cigarette in his mouth and the beret on his head, Adel murmured, "Artistic type. Hopefully not the annoyingly pompous kind."

"I especially like arresting that kind," Sandrine joked. "In any case he bears a remarkable resemblance to the visitor described by the neighbour."

Adel pulled up to the side of the road and they got out.

"Monsieur Salazar?" Sandrine asked.

"Your secretary informed me of your visit," he replied, radiating hostility. There could be no misunderstanding – they were not welcome here.

"We'd like to ask you a few questions, if that's okay."

"I have no idea what information I can give people like you. But in this jurisdiction, I have no other choice but to bow down to police brutality."

"No. You can of course refuse, that is your right. Then we'd go and summon you to the police station, if you'd prefer."

"Ask," he said through gritted teeth.

"Wouldn't it be better if we went inside?" Sandrine suggested.

"It probably won't take that long," Salazar snarled. "Who likes having the police in their house?" He was beginning to sound like Madame Drouet, except he refrained from being overly sexist or racist. She looked over to the house next door. An elderly woman opened a window and put a narrow bucket on the sill.

"As you wish." She held out her police badge then gave a friendly smile to the neighbour, who began washing the window. "I'm Lieutenant Perrot, and this is my colleague Brigadier Chief Azarou. We're from the national police, investigating the death of Mademoiselle Vilette."

He became increasingly pale and stared at them with watery blue eyes. "She's dead?" he stammered.

"Apparently you're one of the few locals who doesn't know about this."

"I don't own a television. The mindless garbage it spews upon society is unbearable. I haven't read today's newspaper either."

"She died Saturday evening," Adel informed him.

"My God. That's ... but why are you coming to me with this?" He looked over at the neighbour who was no longer pretending to clean her window but had pricked her ears, and was listening to the conversation.

"Mademoiselle Vilette was murdered and you were one of the last people to have seen her alive." Adel spoke loudly enough to be heard by the nosy old woman.

"Come in," he urged them. "Not everyone needs to know why you're here. I have an impeccable reputation and don't want to let two overzealous and insensitive civil servants ruin it." He let them both go ahead of him and seemed to struggle with not pushing them out of sight and earshot of the old lady next door. It was a tiny house, hardly bigger than Sandrine's cottage but crammed with shelves overflowing with books. Monsieur Salazar steered them to a sofa covered with magazines, which he quickly collected and stacked on the floor. They slowly toppled and slid to one side, but he left them there.

"I had nothing to do with Mademoiselle Vilette's death, absolutely nothing," he began as soon as they were seated. "There's not much more to say."

"Is Pierre Salazar your real name or a pseudonym which you use to write crime novels?"

"Of course it's my real name, I fully stand behind what I publish. Incidentally mine are not crime novels in the classic sense, but rather socio-critical considerations that develop in the context of an illegitimate plot."

"Do you make a living from this?" Adel asked.

"A living? Of course not. You can get rich with shallow and carelessly written tear-jerkers but not with art, at least not in this country of cultural philistines. These days Victor Hugo and Émile Zola would have starved to death."

"And how do you make a living?" Adel asked, although they already knew.

"High school teacher of French and Philosophy," he replied

with little enthusiasm, adding, "in Saint-Malo. I also direct a theatre company."

"What did you want with Mademoiselle Vilette the day she died?"

"Like I said, I had nothing to do with her death. I didn't even know she'd died."

"But you visited the woman shortly before she did. For what purpose?"

"Who's said such a thing?" He straightened up. His gaze darted wildly back and forth between Sandrine and Adel. *Like a cockfight*, she thought and bit back a grin.

"Monsieur Pascale, the neighbour. He saw you in the stair-well several times, including the day in question."

"The steroid-fuelled guy who followed and molested her? You'd better investigate him. I believe he's capable of anything," the man said vehemently.

"What did you want with Mademoiselle Vilette?" She skipped confirmation that he'd actually been there. It seemed obvious to her, why else would he be so upset?

"She regularly reviewed my books."

"Not especially benevolently, from what I hear."

"She didn't understand them."

"So, also a cultural philistine," she couldn't resist.

"That would come pretty close to the truth."

"Why did she want to talk to you?"

Monsieur Salazar rubbed his hands together. The cracking of his joints broke the incipient silence.

"All right," he said suddenly. "She wanted to speak to me about my most recent book. For once, she seemed to have enjoyed it and she had some questions about several passages, the implications of which she could not fully understand at her tender age."

"And you were kind enough to explain these passages to her."

"I did not go into her apartment. She seemed to be expecting another visitor and was cleaning up, at least she had one of those feather dusters in her hand. We made an appointment for next week. I gave her a signed copy then left."

"Where were you between ten p.m. and midnight?"

"You're asking for an alibi? You can't seriously think that ... I am a man of art." He looked at Sandrine with an open mouth.

"Routine, Monsieur Salazar."

"I was here. Over there at my desk, working on my new book."

"Any witnesses?"

"Definitely not. Absolute silence is essential when writing."

Judging by the slightly neglected condition of his living space, the man hardly received any visitors, even when he wasn't working on his book.

"What time were you at the Rue de la Cloche?"

"Around five-thirty or six. I wasn't in the building for more than five minutes. The guy that identified me can certainly attest to that. Strange that he recognized me, he doesn't look like he can even read."

The unflattering description that Aubert Pascale had given of him, she kept to herself.

"Did you notice anything about Mademoiselle Vilette? Did she say who else she was expecting?"

"She struck me as quite ordinary. One of these shallow bloggers who skim books then mistakenly think they can criticise them. And no, I didn't ask her who she was dusting her apartment for because it was just a chat in the stairwell. She didn't think it was appropriate to ask me in."

"Some people are rude," murmured Adel. Sandrine

assumed he was thinking about the irony that the author had also refused to invite them into his house.

"We found your book in the woman's studio," said Sandrine.

"That would be the signed copy I mentioned. I wanted to make sure she had one. Some of these self-proclaimed literary critics just grab a free copy off the internet if the blurb isn't enough for them to form an opinion."

"So, I assume Mademoiselle Vilette liked the book."

"Of course."

"She didn't review a lot of crime novels, why did she make an exception for you?"

"You can say what you want about the young woman, but she made definitely made it a point to mention local artists."

"But she also discussed English-language works."

"Not ... that ... I ... know of," he said protractedly. "What makes you think that?" The intensity with which he studied Sandrine increased noticeably.

"There was a novel by a certain Sarah Mason in her studio. *Deadly Sins Will Hunt You.* Ever heard of it?"

"No." It came like a pistol shot. "I don't read foreign books. Especially those which haven't been translated into our language."

"Too bad, that could have helped us."

"I don't know how. The book would hardly have killed her. I suppose she owned a lot of such banal novels."

"I assumed that this would lead to a dead end," Sandrine admitted.

"If there's nothing else, I would like to prepare for my lessons. There are still exams to be graded."

"We're done for now. If we have any further questions, we'll contact you."

"Hopefully not. I want to have as little as possible to do with a murder." He jumped to his feet. "I'll take you to the door."

· · ·

"He threw us out," said Adel and slammed the car door shut.

"Obviously he wanted us out of his house," Sandrine agreed. "But that's not unusual. Think about Madame Drouet, she was reluctant to let us into her apartment. I'm sure she counted her porcelain figurines after we left, not that we would have stolen one. We're not exactly popular guests."

"Not when we're on duty anyway." He started the motor and drove off. The curtain moved. Pierre Salazar was watching them. As was the neighbour who was still cleaning the same window. Sandrine gave her a friendly wave and the woman instantly disappeared inside the house.

"I thought the book was one of our best leads." Adel seemed irritated.

"It is, but I didn't have to let him know that. If he did kill Aimée Vilette, he's now wondering how much we know or can find out."

"I looked around and didn't see a television. If our writer made the video, all he can do is view it on his ancient PC. Not exactly a pleasure."

"I noticed that, too. At the moment it's hard for me to imagine how he draped the victim on the table, lit the scene and operated the equipment. The man didn't seem to be one of the most cunning."

"Definitely not. Especially after seeing the condition of his home."

"Aimée Vilette had regularly slammed his crime novels, which can really upset an author. But why should he go nuts now? They say his last book isn't that bad."

"You haven't read it, have you?"

"Since when do I have time to read? I trust Rosalie's opinion."

"So it must be true. The woman knows her stuff." He looked at her. "Do you think she could autograph one of her novels for me? For my older sisters, they're into Hugo Delacroix. For whatever reason. How the man solves his cases is completely unrealistic."

"True." She suspected that the amorous adventures that Commissaire Hugo Delacroix engaged in during investigations had a big part in the series' success.

"You're right though, it doesn't make much sense. Salazar should have killed her long ago but not now, when she was going to give him her first decent review. Unless something else happened that we don't know about."

"One of us should definitely read the novel," Sandrine decided. "Unfortunately, I don't have any time this evening."

"A date?"

"No. I'm letting myself get beaten up."

"I'd better not ask any more questions, everybody has their own personal preferences." Adel grinned.

"Don't be silly. I have a date at the gym and I'm afraid that I'm going to take a beating."

"My sympathies. The guy who spent the night at your house?"

"No. A woman I'm not particularly fond of."

"Ah. The girlfriend of the guy who spent the night at your house?"

"Definitely not. Now let's concentrate on the case."

"Then off to our goose breeder."

Mark Bergier's farm was on the outskirts of Saint-Coulomb, a big village between Saint-Malo and Cancale.

Several buildings whose best times were behind them were

clustered around an unpaved courtyard that had been sodden by the night's rain. Sandrine was pleased that she had put on her sturdy shoes. She watched Adel who got out of the car carefully. The yard certainly wasn't the right environment for the brigadier's stylish black leather shoes. He sniffed loudly and made a disgusted face. Country life wasn't his thing.

"What are you looking for here?" a grey-haired woman shouted from an upstairs window.

"We would like to speak with Monsieur Bergier," Sandrine called up to her.

"He's over in the meadow feeding the geese." She gestured in the direction of the barn. Sandrine waved thanks at the woman and crossed the yard.

"Don't slip, otherwise your chic outfit will be ruined."

"I should get a transfer to Paris or another big city," grumbled Adel.

"We followed a gang of cigarette smugglers through the sewage canals. In contrast, here it smells like a flower meadow in spring. I've also discovered dismembered corpses in landfills or human remains floating in chemical waste, stuff eating through the thickest leather shoes."

"All right. I see what you're getting at. It's not too bad here."

"Well, I don't want to lose my best brigadier."

Behind the barn stretched an expansive meadow surrounding a pond. A huge flock of white geese crowded around a tall man distributing feed from a bucket. Sandrine assumed him to be Marc Bergier. She stayed behind the fence and waited until he noticed her. The man froze in his tracks and for a moment they made eye contact.

"Don't run away," she murmured to herself. "Don't run away, we'll get you anyway."

As if the farmer had heard her, he shooed a few geese aside and walked towards her. He dropped the buckets and stuffed both hands deep into the pockets of his work trousers, which were held up by a pair of wide suspenders.

What the author had lacked in height, this giant could have easily given him.

"Police?"

"You were expecting us?"

"Yup. You took your time. I was expecting a patrol car yesterday."

"Sorry, we're not that fast," Sandrine apologised. "Why did you think we were going to pay you a visit?"

"It's obvious. The girl on the radio is dead and I yelled at her pretty savagely. A few thousand people must have heard it."

"Do you have something to do with her death?"

He pulled his trousers up, took his hands out of his pockets and crossed his arms defensively in front of his chest. "Nah."

"Then can you answer a couple of questions for us?"

"And if I don't? Will you two drag me to the police station?"

"My colleagues would take care of that."

"They wouldn't dare."

"Oh, yes they would, no problem. However, afterwards you would need someone to take care of your farm for a minimum of twenty-four hours. That's how long you would be stuck in a cell whether you answer my questions or not. Maybe you have money to spare for a lawyer but he wouldn't be able to get you out any faster."

They looked each other in the eye for several beats. Then the giant nodded. "All right, what do you want?"

"You had a fight with Mademoiselle Vilette, we know that, but about what exactly?"

The man gritted his teeth and balled his hands into fists. Adel stepped aside and Sandrine noticed out of the corner of her eye his hand moving closer to his gun.

"Did the woman anger you that much?"

"A spoiled city slicker, railing against honest peasants. Let her eat her veggie burgers."

Sandrine looked around. "I see neither pigs nor cattle here. Are you upset about burger patties?"

"No, that junk from fast food places is only good for the garbage can." He pointed to the stalls. "Foie gras. My family has been making goose liver paste for generations, but suddenly it's not okay?"

"Well, the geese do get pretty tormented when they're stuffed, I understand."

He took his cap off and scratched the back of his head. "Organic farming and petting zoos won't feed seven, or who knows how many, billions of people, who only want to spend a couple of cents for their Sunday roast. Factory farming is the only option as people are not willing to pay an acceptable price. That's how I see it. The animals are definitely on the wrong side. But what's left for farmers who are unwilling to sell their farms?"

"So Mademoiselle Vilette was bad for business?"

"Oh, farming is getting worse and worse. We used to export a lot but people like that girl ruined the business. These so-called animal rights activists have managed to get foie gras banned in most countries."

"But not here in France," Adel interjected.

"No, fortunately not. Our politicians have recognized that foie gras is part of French tradition."

"I didn't know foie gras was made in Brittany."

"Most of it comes from the south-west. From Perigord, the Ecke and surrounding areas. But there's also a long tradition here."

"So you argued about that?"

"Exactly." He exhaled loudly. "Actually, I really didn't care about the girl but that night I simply freaked out. At some point the dam just bursts. I should have refrained from the email thing. Honestly, I even wanted to apologise but then I put it off for too long. But now, it's no longer possible."

"Are you familiar with this?" Sandrine pulled out a photo and held it up to the man.

"Yes."

"And?"

"It's a stuffing tube for geese but nobody has used them for a long time. The metal pipe slits the throat too easily and the animal bleeds to death. Today we use the flexible plastic kind."

"Do you own this kind of pipe?"

"I'm sure there are a few of my father's lying around some-where in the barn."

"This one says M.B. Could that stand for Mark Bergier?"

"Definitely not."

"So it's not a darning pipe from this farm? We could prove it." That was a lie, but Sandrine took the chance that the man would believe she was capable of it.

"I didn't say that, only that those initials definitely didn't stand for Marc Bergier."

"Get to the point," she urged him.

"It could stand for Michel Bergier. My father. If it's one of ours."

"Who can get a hold of these things?"

"The barn is not locked and anyone can enter. I wouldn't be able to hear them. Except if someone came in through the back." The man grinned and Sandrine shot him a puzzled look.

"Have you ever heard what a racket two hundred geese can make? They're better than a watchdog. Even the ancient Romans kept geese to protect themselves against burglars." He straightened up and nodded in confirmation. He seemed proud of his animals.

"Where were you Saturday between ten p.m. and midnight?"

"First in front of the television, then in bed."

"Can anyone confirm that?"

"My mother usually falls asleep before I do. After that not even the worst thunderstorm can wake her up."

"Can you check to see if one of your stuffing tubes is missing?" Sandrine asked.

"I don't have to. The one in the photo is mine. But I have no idea how it got to where you found it. Did it have something to do with the murder?"

"It's what knocked out the woman."

"Then someone is trying to frame me. I was here on the farm. Anyway, I didn't kill anyone just because of goose liver paste and a couple of stupid comments on the radio."

"Present yourself at the police station sometime today and give your statement to Brigadier Dubois for the record." The man started to say something but Sandrine wouldn't let him. "Otherwise I'll send someone to fetch you."

"Okay, but it will be later on in the afternoon, I have my hands full till then."

"That works. We'll be waiting for you."

"There's a garden hose in the courtyard. I'm sure your colleague will want to wash the dirt of honest work off his fine leather shoes."

"Thank you," Sandrine replied. "Then we'll get on with our honest police work."

She turned around and left the man standing there. She felt his hostile gaze on the back of her neck.

"What do you think?" asked Adel, as he took off his wet shoes and put them in the back of the car.

"The man has no alibi, the murder weapon belongs to him, he appears short-tempered and has a motive."

"I see no solid motive," he replied. "Just because they screamed at each on the radio, does that mean he killed her? I don't think so."

"Times change. His livelihood gets slowly destroyed. He can't access the people who make the laws and regulations. Aimée Vilette is a well-known figure around here who represents all those he sees as enemies. Why shouldn't he try and make an example of her? If the woman had been killed in a crime of passion, this is the first man I would think of. But I don't trust him with the entire planning. Can you imagine Marc Bergier organising and videoing the scene? I can't."

"The woman was laid on a kind of altar, on which she was sacrificed. He knows all about butchering. How many geese choke to death while being stuffed?"

"A lot, I'm afraid," she said, thinking out loud. "But you're right, he probably wouldn't be able to operate the equipment. And he doesn't seem like someone who would know Japanese calligraphy either."

"Let him off the hook?"

"Not for now. My gut tells me the man knows more than he's telling us. We'll keep the pressure on, maybe he'll come up with something interesting at some point."

"Then let's look at the next person on the list: this Chardon," said Adel. "The psychiatrist."

"Did Inès inform him of our visit?"

He took a look at his cell phone. "The man is out this morning. His secretary is expecting him around one o'clock and has reserved time for us."

"We should be back in Saint-Malo shortly before twelve. That should be enough time for lunch."

"Good idea. Which restaurant?"

"Well, the crêperie recommended by Inès was excellent and the service was very friendly and informative."

"Do you know what she's been up to?" asked Azarou.

"No idea."

"You've been telling everyone that you've been thinking about quitting the police force. I like working with you, as do most of the others."

"Thanks for the compliment."

"Compliments can be well-meaning white lies, but I mean this in all seriousness. You're the most capable leader that we've had in our department and luckily, Matisse agrees."

"What are you getting at?"

"Inès is trying to welcome you into our big family. She wants you to feel at home so that you can sign the damned application which is on your desk."

"You know about that?"

"It's an open secret."

"It's hard," she said thoughtfully.

"Nonsense. You were made for this job."

Matisse had said the same thing, too, as had the last murderess they'd arrested. Did these people see things more clearly than she herself could?

"No matter what, I'll definitely stay until we catch Aimée Vilette's murderer. After that I'll have more time to think about the proposal."

Her cell phone rang, interrupting their conversation. It was Rosalie. She had never called during her working hours before.

"One moment, it won't take long," she excused herself and took the call.

She listened in silence. "Then we'll see each other there."

"Did something happen?"

"It was Rosalie. She found out something about Pierre Salzar and wants us to meet for lunch."

"Did she say what it is?"

"She's a writer, so naturally, no. The woman enjoys being part of a real murder case and tries to keep the suspense up as long as possible."

"Does she know what happens to witnesses who call the police with a ground-breaking discovery and don't immediately come up with it right away?"

"They're usually killed before investigators arrive," she said. "Commissaire Delacroix definitely had some experience with that."

"Should I come with you?"

"It's not necessary. Just drop me off at Plage du Sillon. On Mondays Rosalie meets with her agent and some writer friends for tea. I'll meet you later at the police station."

* * *

Sandrine got out in front of the small café on the Chausee du Sillon.

"*La Boîte de Chocolats,*" she whispered. A fitting name. Rosalie had a weakness for chocolates, plus this was the name of a crime novel with Hercule Poirot, one of her favourite investigators.

Through the window she saw her friend who was sitting alone at a table set for seven or eight people.

As soon as Rosalie saw Sandrine, she waved her in.

"What is so urgent that you had to interrupt my investigation to meet with you?"

"Who said anything about interrupting? I'm bringing you a good step forward."

"I'm very curious."

Rosalie ordered two coffees. "The chocolate cake here is excellent, would you like to try it?"

"It's still too early in the day. A drink is enough."

"It's probably too much sugar for me, too." She looked at the waiter. "We'll stick with coffee, Richard."

Sandrine watched the man until he was out of earshot. "Spit it out, what have you found? I hope that I don't end up regretting giving away too much yesterday."

"Not at all. Actually you didn't tell me much, which seemed interesting at first glance."

"I've since met with Pierre Salazar."

"Pompous guy, isn't he?" She wrinkled her nose slightly. "An artist who looks down on all other writers that actually sell their books."

"That's about right."

"I read his new crime novel."

"Yesterday evening?"

"Yes," she said. "It's still full of Salazar's typical metaphors and idioms but the plot isn't bad. Much better than his other books. With some interesting twists. Just before the end does it become clear who the murderer is. And that's saying something for this man."

"Good for him. Hence the benevolent review that the victim prepared." Sandrine took the cup from the waiter and put it on the table in front of her. "After all the panning, that must have been balm for his battered soul."

"That's his personal dilemma. On one hand, he considers himself a man of letters who writes unfazed by the taste of the masses, on the other hand, the man thirsts for praise and attention from the very people he pretends to despise. It's a tricky situation." Rosalie picked up one of the chocolates that lay on the plate with the tips of her fingers and popped it into her mouth with relish.

"If he wanted to kill Mademoiselle Vilette, why would he do it now? He was finally getting the recognition that she had denied him for so long. Now her death is a bitter setback for the man."

"Commissaire Delacroix wouldn't let him off the hook that easily," Rosalie replied. Judging by her grin she was very pleased with herself.

"And what might the famous investigator have discovered that I'm missing?" She played Rosalie's little game, in order to get the information quicker.

"He would have wondered what an English-language crime novel was doing in Aimée Vilette's apartment since she had never reviewed foreign-language books before. So why this one?"

"Did you read it?"

"I finished it at three this morning," she said proudly. "This is why I need a good dose of caffeine to get through the writers' meeting without falling asleep at the table."

"Plagiarism?" Sandrine took a shot in the dark.

"Almost." Rosalie sipped her coffee and picked up another chocolate.

Sandrine drummed her fingertips on the tabletop while waiting for her friend to continue.

"He didn't copy it, at least in the strictest sense," she finally went on. "Our friend stole the exact same plot but then moved the story from Cornwall to Brittany and swapped the characters' names."

"That's not plagiarism?"

"No. As long as he doesn't take entire passages, it's not. Ideas and actions are not protected by copyright."

"But as I see it, that's hardly a motive for murder."

"You met him. The man hates his job. Standing in front of a gang of uninterested students and trying to introduce them to Voltaire and Camus drives him into the depths of despair. Writing is the most important thing in his life. His lifeline. If

Aimée Vilettte had made it public, it would have ruined him as a writer. Not even his old friend Grégoire would have published anything by him again. People have killed for a lot less."

"The mouth is the root of misfortune," murmured Sandrine. "Was this the bombshell that Aimée had spoken about?"

"Exactly. Whoever killed the woman wanted to shut her up. And who knows the power of the word better than a writer?"

The victim was knocked down in her studio. Even a slight man like Salazar could have put her on the table and tied her up. It was entirely possible.

"She revealed his secret."

"Bull's eye! Exactly. The woman had it in her power to destroy his reputation as an artist. That would have killed him," Rosalie said. "Only figuratively, of course."

"When you take away the thing a man loves the most, it is not uncommon for him to attack to the extreme."

"I agree, though it's hard for me to imagine Pierre Salazar as a murderer."

"Thank you very much. You've really helped me a lot."

"My pleasure."

"So now we have to talk to Pierre Salazar again," Sandrine decided. She'd almost removed him from the list of suspects.

"Here come the first people." Rosalie turned to the front window, with a view of the sea. The woman whom Sandrine had met with Rosalie at the house and a man in an elegant grey suit waved to her.

"Who is the man with Madame Marchal?"

"Madame? Don't let her catch you calling her that because it makes her feel as old as she actually is. And I feel the same way. Just stay with Odette. Her companion is Grégoire Argent, her publisher and also Pierre Salazar's."

"I'd better get going."

"No way. You should definitely talk to both of them. Odette

wasn't only in contact with Aimée but she also knows Pierre Salazar and Dominique Petitjean, who the newspaper says discovered the body."

"I find it hard to imagine her and the photographer being friendly."

"In her wilder times, she posed for him now and then as a model. When she was short of money."

No one in the café escaped the boisterous woman's arrival. She loudly greeted the waiter and kissed Rosalie's cheeks. The writer clearly loved making a diva-like entrance. Her publisher radiated an inner calm or maybe resignation, like someone who recognized the weakness of his companion but nevertheless appreciated her.

"Grégoire Argent," he said, introducing himself. "And you must be the famous investigator that Rosalie likes to talk about and that one reads about in the newspaper."

"Investigator, yes, but famous remains to be seen and what's in the newspaper is mostly bogus."

"She's investigating the case of poor Aimée Vilette," Odette Marchal told him.

"Tragic, really tragic. I really appreciated the woman," said Grégoire Argent. "She was a real treasure for our region."

"She wasn't always friendly to her authors."

He made a face. "I guess that's right. Poor Pierre, in particular, has suffered some harsh criticism from her. But on the whole, I can't complain. She was mostly benevolent to local artists."

"Bad publicity is better than no publicity at all," Odette said. "Writers need to have thick skin."

"That's easy for you to say. Your reviews are just wonderful," Grégoire said, flattering her. He sat next to Sandrine. "In fact, I just recently talked to Pierre Salazar, he is an old school friend of mine. The man lives for art. Last week he thought about to cancel the publication of his new book." He looked at Rosalie. "He suddenly found the style too lurid and ordinary. It was his first work that did well in advance sales."

"But Grégoire was able to talk him out of it. Probably nervousness again." Odette ordered a double espresso and Sandrine wondered whether the woman really needed something to get her blood pumping any further. She already seemed to be pretty wound up. Probably just the excitement before the launch of her book, Sandrine guessed.

"I would imagine a cancellation so close to publication would have financial consequences."

"Grave consequences. The edition is printed, the advertisements are running, all costs that cannot be recouped if the book fails or even worse, doesn't appear at all."

"Have you been in contact with Mademoiselle Vilette in the last few weeks?"

"Oh, am I under suspicion?" The man appeared to be amused.

"We all are, until Sandrine catches the murderer," Odette remarked. "If I may say that, Sandrine?"

"But of course."

"I telephoned Mademoiselle Vilette several times in recent days. She had a review copy of Pierre's book and one from Odette. She seemed to like both of them and offered to introduce them on her social media channel. For a medium-sized publisher like mine it was a totally wonderful advertisement, and free of charge. But personally I haven't met with her in weeks. I can't remember ever seeing her at a reading or any other event that we hold regularly at our house."

"We definitely have a copy of my book with us, right?" Odette asked the man.

"Of course. However, I think that Madame Perrot is not exactly a fan of our young adult books."

"She can give it away as a gift."

The publisher pulled out a paperback from his briefcase and gave it to Odette Marchal who signed it and then gave it to Sandrine. "Thank you. I appreciate it." She leafed through the book superficially. "I hope I'll have more time soon, then I will definitely read it."

"But only after you've read *Oyster Murderer*," Rosalie admonished her.

"Of course." She looked at her watch. "I have to leave now. My colleague is already waiting for me."

"Then we won't keep you any longer," Grégoire Argent said. "Catch the murderer of that poor woman." He held two thumbs up.

Sandrine said good-bye and left the café. Outside she took a deep breath. The short walk to the police station would do her good.

Except for the two brigadiers, the large open office was deserted.

"All the others are in the canteen," Renard Dubois said as he held up a Tupperware container. "My wife put me on a diet. I'd rather stay here and nibble on the carrots than watch them eat. And Luc is keeping me company."

"Understandable." She sat on the opposite side of the desk. "Is there any news that can help us move forward?" she asked Brigadier Poutin.

"I called through the list of people who sent insults and threats to the radio station. There were a couple of unpleasant guys but everyone had an alibi for Saturday night."

"Verified?"

"So far all are water-tight but I'm not done yet. Renard is helping me with the rest," said Poutin.

"Pity. At least it narrows the circle of suspects further."

"The film provided zero clues," said Dubois. "A rather harmless little film. Nothing borderline or illegal. It wouldn't upset a soul these days." He handed her the cassette. "I checked the actors who played the parts. No one was underage at that time and nobody came from Brittany. I would assume that these people are not in this business any more considering the age of the film."

"Thanks for taking the trouble to watch this."

"No problem. During my time in vice, I had to watch a lot of different things."

* * *

Sandrine went into the conference room. The victim's photo was pinned on the board. She wrote Salazar's name on an index card and pinned it next to Aimée Vilette's photo. The author had lied to her, that much was certain. Aimée had caught him copying another book's plot line and as an influencer she could have destroyed his reputation. According to neighbours, there had been loud arguments several times in the past few days. It wasn't hard to guess what about. She must have confronted him with the knowledge. Otherwise why would he have spoken to his publisher about stopping publication? In the end, it did not happen. Whether he had come to some kind of agreement with the victim or he knew that she could no longer speak out, put him at the top of the suspect list. She would pay the author another visit. But she doubted whether Aimée Villette took his fraud seriously enough to announce a special broadcast about it on local radio. Arianne Briand, the program director for the local radio station was exactly right: literature did not cause tempers to flare up in this region. She stepped up to the bulletin board and looked at the young woman's photo. It had to be something else, a more personal topic.

She wrote the names Odette Marchal and Grégoire Argent on one card each. The publisher was one of the suspects. He also had a lot to lose if Aimée Vilette accused one of his authors of stealing a large part of a foreign novel. It would tarnish his reputation, plus withdrawing the book from publication would represent a significant financial loss. If Pierre had complained to him, Grégoire Argent also had a valid motive to remove Aimée Vilette from his path. She made a note to put someone onto the publisher's finances. They wouldn't be able to access bank documents given the slim allegations but Inès should be able to pick something up in the rumour mill.

"The cassette does not seem to get us anywhere," said Adel when he entered the conference room and sat next to her. "I talked to Dubois about it. He agrees with me."

"My gut tells me there's more to this thing than we realise," replied Sandrine.

"What could it be?" asked Adel.

"None of the participants, neither the actors nor the producers have any connection to Saint-Malo or to Aimée Vilette. Dubois said the plot was of a very poor standard. Even the locations where it was filmed was somewhere in the southwest. Nowhere do I see a connection to our case, but it will not let me go," said Sandrine.

She held the VHS cassette in her hand and gazed at it intently, but in vain, for any kind of sudden enlightenment.

"The only person that I can think of who owns these things is Dominique Petitjean. We saw them in his apartment. Do you believe he sells them at the flea markets?"

"Surely there are people who collect things like this. Everything seems to have its fans these days." Sandrine flinched. "Wait a minute." She took off the paper cover and examined the inside. "It looks like the remains of a label here."

"Could be, but maybe it's just a smudge."

"We'll send this to Mazet in the lab. I want to know what this is."

"Be careful not to get too distracted by this idea," Adel said, sounding worried.

"Don't worry. I won't let the other evidence get left aside," she reassured him though she couldn't estimate how successful she'd be. She knew her history and how she could fixate on what she thought was promising.

"Who is Odette Marchal?" He pointed at the index card that she'd pinned on the board.

"An author who had something to do with the victim and Salazar. She also knows Petitjean."

"And how did you find that out?"

"Rosalie claims that in the nineties, she modelled for him."

"That was a long time ago."

"She must still have some contact with the man." She gave him the book she received from her at the café.

"Authors are vain. She couldn't help but give me a copy."

He flipped through it. "What should I be looking for?"

"On the last page. Petitjean appears in the photo credits. The portrait next to the biography came from him and it's certainly not twenty-five years old. He must have taken it recently. We'll be paying the man a visit. I want to know what kind of relationship he still has with Odette Marchal. An even more of a burning question is how he explains his fingerprints on the victim's laptop and desk."

"We have a meeting with Phillipe Chardon. After that we can go to Petitjeans's place."

"Agreed. Let's get out of here."

"Ah, the police." The tanned and casually dressed man stood up behind his desk and came toward them. Sandrine's first impression was that he spent significantly more time on a sailboat than in his practice. She suspected that his clientele were not members of Saint-Malo's lower class.

"Thank you for taking time for us, Monsieur Chardon." The image that dominated one of his white painted walls immediately caught her eye. A huge breaking wave threatened to tear several small fishing boats down into the deep. Centred in the background loomed a cone-shaped snow-covered mountain. Her father had a print with a similar motif.

"You like it?" The man stood by her.

"'The Great Wave off Kanagawa' by Hokusai," she said. "Always impressive."

"You're familiar with Japanese wood prints? Astonishing."

Sandrine did not respond to the slightly concealed insult. After Salazar and Odette Marchal, she'd met her quota for narcissists today.

"Not particularly, but Katsushika Hokusai's work is quite unique." She stepped up to a dresser which spanned the entire width of the room under the picture. "I see you have a penchant for calligraphy."

"An innocent hobby of mine. A friend of mine made me try it for the first time decades ago." He opened the lacquered boxes which contained an inkwell and several brushes of different sizes.

"Maybe you recognize this?" Adel held up a photo of the Japanese characters the perpetrator had written on Aimée's stomach.

"*Kuchi wa wazawai no moto*. An old saying."

"The mouth is the root of all misfortune," said the brigadier.

"I confess, I'm impressed. Little did I know that our police would promote a broad general education of its members."

"We are investigating the case of the death of Mademoiselle Vilette," Sandrine said.

"As you of course know, I cannot give you any information about my patients. You understand."

What she understood was that he used the word patient instead of client, unlike his colleague, Leriche. Everything in the office was designed to impress and instantly convey who the authority in the room was. There would be no dialogue between equals here.

"Your patient is dead. She would hardly be able to raise an objection."

"There are rules we have to follow. Bring me a court order, then we can continue this conversation."

"If you insist, we will," she replied.

"Then it will be a pleasure to give you any information you want. But until then ..." He raised his open hands which was probably meant to express regret, but Sandrine did not believe it.

"From what I understand you are obliged to stay silent about the therapeutic sessions, but it is possible for you to give us information about Mademoiselle Vilette that does not concern therapy. Isn't that correct?"

"Of course. However I never had a relationship with her that went beyond the professional."

"You stopped treating her," Sandrine said. "You don't need to confirm it, that's a fact."

"Since you already know, I won't deny it."

"Did the reason for her stopping her treatments have anything to do with your work?"

"Absolutely not." He shot her an angry look.

"Someone must have done something terrible to her which turned her normal behaviour completely upside down."

"It had nothing to do with the therapy."

"Good, then you're free to talk about it."

The man pressed his lips together until they were only visible as a thin line. Sandrine had tricked him and he didn't try to hide his anger. He went back to his desk and sat down without offering her or Adel a seat.

"I have no knowledge of what might have happened to her outside of my therapy that had traumatised her so much. The girl had withdrawn from everyone, including me." He picked up a pen and rolled it between his fingers.

"Do you have a theory?"

"No, I don't appreciate conjecture and I ignore people's chatter as best as I can. You know people say many stupid things in these small towns."

She pulled up a chair and sat down close to his desk. She wouldn't let this guy intimidate her.

"So, what did people say?"

"As I said, complete nonsense."

"I'd like to hear it."

Phillipe Chardon tossed the pen on the table. "You'll find out about it anyway. It was rumoured that there was sexual abuse in her family. Her mother remarried soon after her husband's suicide."

"The stepfather?"

"I don't want to accuse anyone."

"But?"

"That was the gossip. He never commented on it and there was never a police investigation. Therefore, there's nothing more to say." She wondered if this was the necessary clue to the bombshell the woman was going to announce. What could be more personal and dramatic than abuse in the family? She had to see the stepfather.

"Thank you. I find that quite informative."

"Then we're finished? I have patients that are waiting because of you two."

"One last question: have you ever had a meeting with Aimée Vilette in Saint-Malo?"

"No, I have not. As far as I know, she visited my colleague, Dr. Leriche. There was no reason for her to visit me." The word *colleague* came out hesitantly over his lips. He didn't seem to have much appreciation for the psychologist.

"Oddly enough, she had your name in her appointment book. Double underlined."

"Maybe she'd planned to get in touch with me. But she didn't do it. You are welcome to inquire with my secretary." He looked very conspicuously at his watch. "That would answer your last question. I wish you every success in your search for the one responsible for her death."

"If we have any more questions, we'll contact you."

"Of course. It would be best to bring the court order with you next time."

"We'll do that," she replied and stood up. He didn't bother to walk them to the door.

* * *

She held her finger firmly on the doorbell.

"I'm busy," cried Dominique Petitjean through the closed door. "Come back later."

Adel hit the metal door with the flat of his hand. "Police. Open up or we'll kick the door down."

The sound of steps got closer. They heard a key turning the lock. Petitjean opened the door just enough to look out.

"I'm busy making a living. I'll have time for you in an hour." The stench of cigarette smoke and a strong alcohol odour hit them. She tried to imagine how Aimée Vilette must have felt around him. Sandrine grabbed the doorknob and pushed it with a quick jerk.

"Hey!" the man yelled in shock. She put her right hand on his chest, shoved him aside and went by him towards the living room studio.

"You can't go in there," he shouted.

"It looks as though she might very well do so anyway." Adel followed Sandrine. They could hear the sound of bare feet running away and a door slammed shut. She assumed someone had fled to a bathroom or an adjoining room. It wasn't her job to find out who was with this sleazy guy, so she decided to ignore his visitor.

"Do you have a warrant?" He had overcome his surprise and stormed into the room behind them. "Otherwise, get out of my apartment."

"Do we have a warrant?" she asked the brigadier.

"I'm afraid not. Should I go get one?"

"Too much trouble." She turned to the photographer. "I must have misunderstood you. Sorry, I thought you invited us in. Now I don't have any other choice but to take you to the police department."

"You're going to arrest me?" he stared at Sandrine in amazement.

"Not yet but you are this close to it." She held her index finger and her thumb close together. "I will book you for misleading the police."

"You can't do that," he stammered.

"I'm tired of being lied to. And especially by the likes of lousy liars like you. One night in a cell will definitely bring your memory back again."

"I didn't lie." He looked at Adel, who sat on the sofa. "Am I a suspect? Why? Because I found the body? The woman had been dead for half a day."

"Let's start with the false statements," Sandrine said. "Then we'll work our way up to property damage or theft and see if we end up in murder."

The man dropped into his chair and stared at her with wide-open eyes. "What do you want to know?"

"Everything, from the beginning. What time did you enter the apartment?"

"At nine. I've already put it on record."

"What did you want there?" She stated the question quickly like a gunshot and with a hard edge to her voice.

"To submit photos."

"Mademoiselle Vilette had already kicked you out of her life. So again: what did you want there?"

"That is a lie. We were business partners."

"Nonsense. The woman only hired you for commission work. Nothing more. She would never have involved someone like you in her business."

"Why are you insulting me?"

"I'm not. These are the facts. Take a look at the mirror over there and ponder for a second what Aimée Vilette must have thought of you."

"What?" He made eye contact with Adel, as if the man could help him.

"Again. What did you want in the apartment?" pressed Sandrine.

"I already told you."

"Show me the photos!"

"What?"

"Show me the photos you wanted to deliver," she continued.

"I don't have them anymore. They're lying around some-where in the apartment."

"We didn't find anything and forensics is pretty damned thorough."

"Then I probably took them home with me and threw them away. I was in shock."

"What did you do when you discovered the victim?"

"Called the police, what else?"

"Immediately?"

"Of course. After I emptied my stomach."

"Your call came in exactly five minutes after nine."

"Yes."

"What were you looking for on the deceased's desk and laptop?"

"I wasn't at the desk," he said defensively. He wiped his sleeve over his forehead. The interrogation seemed to have sobered him up. She leaned towards him and put her hands on the arms of the chair. Petitjean backed away from her.

"I've had a terrible day. Because of liars like you I had to skip lunch and my blood sugar levels are dropping rapidly. Now I'm becoming extremely unpleasant and really bitchy." Out of the corner of her eye she saw Adel nodding in agreement. "Your fingerprints were all over the desk and the laptop, the photos don't exist and a witness testified that you arrived well before nine o'clock. Lies, lies and more lies." She drew herself up. "Adel, call a patrol car and tell them to take this guy to the police station. I'm sick and tired of this."

"What should we do with the visitor who fled to the bathroom?" the brigadier asked. She turned to Petitjean again.

"Should we check it out?"

"Maybe our help is needed," said Sandrine.

"Don't do that!"

Adel took his cell phone out of his pocket. "Shall I call forensics so they can look around? They'll have some fun in this dump."

"Stop!" yelled Petitjean. "All right." His shoulders sagged and his face turned white.

"Spit it out," she urged him.

If she lessened the pressure, he would try to slip through their fingers again.

"All right. Yes, the tramp sent me a fucking letter saying that she didn't want to work with me anymore. No more orders. Someone told her some nonsense."

"What did you want with her?"

"I wanted to make it clear that she couldn't get rid of me so easily. In the last few years I was good enough for her, gave her special prices and suddenly she got pictures from some other guy. Probably somebody fucked her and worked for her for free. But not me. Without me she would still be some unknown hobby blogger."

"You demanded your share of the business?"

"I was going to but ..." He shook his head. "There she was, dead on the table. What a fucking sight. I still feel sick thinking about it."

"And you took the opportunity to help yourself to her desk? What did you steal: money, documents?"

"I panicked, thinking that they would blame me for the whole mess and I was looking for the damned letter. She was really conscientious and kept a copy for her file."

"And what did you do with it?"

"I stuck it in the shredder, what else?"

"And the laptop?"

"I couldn't get in. Password protected."

"And after that?"

"I called the police." He looked at Adel again as if he was looking for an ally. "Honest." Petitjean sank deeper into his shabby armchair. All resistance had vanished. "You can arrest me right now, if you want to."

"I'll think about it." She believed him but she let him sweat it out for a while. "What did the woman see in you that she put up with you for so long?"

"She wasn't any better than me. She just pretended to be nice."

"What makes you think that?" Adel asked.

"On the last visit, the so-called respectable lady stole one of the pornos." He pointed at the closet where Sandrine had noticed VHS cassettes. "It was one of my favourites."

"Home-made video or acted in?" Adel gave him a warm smile.

"Both. That's something a person can get attached to. I'm just sentimental."

"I can understand that, most everyone would feel the same way," said the brigadier, playing the compassionate cop.

Sandrine took her cell phone out of her trouser pocket and looked for the picture of the cover of the VHS that she'd found in the apartment. She held it in front of the man's face.

"This one here?"

He glanced at the picture on the cell phone and shook his head. "Nah, I've never seen that one before. Who knows, maybe the girl collected videos like that?"

"Could be," said Sandrine thoughtfully. An unpleasant feeling arose in her. Someone had tried to trick her.

You think you're so damned smart, don't you? she thought. *But don't celebrate too soon.*

"What was the name of the film?" asked Adel.

Petitjean thought for a moment. "*Hot Desire Beyond Walls*," he said finally.

Sandrine shrugged.

"It was shot here in Saint-Malo. You know: the wall around the old town. These days that type of stuff wouldn't lure anybody out from behind a kitchen stove, but back then, it was a bestseller. At least in the area."

"Do you have another copy? Out of pure sentimentality."

"No, that's why I got so upset."

"Too bad. I would have liked to have seen it."

Petitjean gave her a sceptical look. "You're kidding, right?"

"No. Honest." But not for the reason the man probably had in mind. There was something on that tape that was really important to somebody. Maybe even important enough to kill for. "When was the last time you saw Mademoiselle Vilette?"

"When she was here to hand me the letter personally and insult me. Beginning of last week."

"And after that?"

"First thing Sunday morning. But that hardly counts."

"Someone said they saw you on the Grand Rue on Thursday. You got into a shouting match."

"Impossible. I wasn't even in Saint-Malo on that day."

"Where were you?"

He tapped on the camera which lay on the table next to the armchair. "Working. At a friend's wedding. In Morlaix. There are nearly two hundred witnesses and I also have pictures. There must be selfies of me and the groom in it."

"Then our eyewitness must be wrong." The alibi was too easily verifiable for him to be lying again.

The shot in the dark had done nothing. "Did Mademoiselle Vilette mention to you which story she wanted to talk about on Sunday?"

"No. No idea."

"Did you notice if she was fighting with or afraid of someone?"

"The woman only talked about work. She was constantly preoccupied with her research and articles and they were always so incredibly important. Blah, blah, blah. Just stuff that nobody really cared about."

Sandrine stood up. "Go to the police station and put your testimony on the record. Today. Understand?"

"Yup. I don't want you kicking down my door on your next visit."

"Give your guest our best regards." She nodded to him and left the apartment.

"Thank you for playing along," she said to Adel who walked next to her.

"Playing along?"

"Well, that I was spiteful and bitchy because lunch was cancelled."

"Well, that wasn't really a lie."

"I'm never bitchy."

"The man is a disgusting character, but a murderer? I have my doubts," he said, ignoring her objection to being bitchy.

"But I am really hungry. I really didn't feel like eating at Boîte de Chocolats. I wanted to be gone before Rosalie's writer friends got there."

"Let's get some take-out."

She looked at her watch. "I have to meet with the victim's parents this evening. Inès signed me up for six p.m."

"Shouldn't I come along?"

"Conversations with relatives are always difficult. This won't be any different."

"Worse than usual, I'm afraid."

"Could be. Are you considering the abuse rumours mentioned by the psychiatrist?"

"It would explain the sudden change in her behaviour. So you have to address it."

"I can't run up there and ask the man if he had abused his stepdaughter."

"I trust you to have more sensitivity," Adel assured her.

"Let's eat first." She headed for the Papillon Rouge. The brigadier sighed deeply and followed her.

"Madame Commissaire. Back with us so soon," greeted Jamila.

"The quiche was so delicious."

"Hello, Jamila," said her brother, whom she'd ignored so far.

"Hello, Adel. I see you have to get a new boss before you can bring yourself here to eat?"

"That's not true. I would have liked to come sooner, but I have a full time job."

"And I don't? First school, then I work here three days a week then do homework in the evening."

"All right. But I'm here now."

The girl leaned towards her. "I made friends with the chef and Adel can't stand him though he hardly knows him."

"Let's not fight. Lieutenant Perrot is surely not interested in our private lives."

"I have no intention to. I behave professionally at work. What will it be?" Jamila asked.

"I'll take a galette complète and a Badoit."

"Excellent choice."

"And you?"

"Just water," said Adel.

She maintained eye contact with him as she tapped her right foot on the wooden floor.

"All right, I'll also try the galette. A vegetarian one."

"Good." She stuck her pad in her pocket and went into the restaurant.

"Forgive me. Jamila can be quite exhausting. It's the age," he said to Sandrine.

"I find her extremely pleasant ... and refreshing."

"That's what one would call it, when one wasn't responsible for her."

"Pass some of the responsibility on. After all, you have three other sisters and your parents."

"They have no idea what could happen to a girl," he said and looked at the door that she'd disappeared behind.

"Slowly that list of suspects is filling up," said Sandrine. "Even though I don't have a real favourite yet."

"I would push Petitjean further back on the list. I doubt whether he's said all he knows. We will definitely have to interview him more than once."

"I agree with that. If he wanted her to keep employing him, why would he want to kill her?"

"Who do you think would be capable of this crime?" Adel asked.

"Someone much cleverer than Petitjean. Someone who left a bunch of clues to confuse us. One of the entries in her calendar and the Japanese characters lead to Phillippe Chardon, the crime novel to Salazar and the threatening letters and the stuffing tube to Marc Bergier. We know the reasons that the author and the goose farmer would want to silence the woman," summed Sandrine up.

"Sounds logical. Now we have to uncover the psychiatrist's motive."

"That will become evident as soon as we find out more about him. Chardon is opaque. I have no idea what kind of game he's playing with us. If the abuse did indeed take place, the person responsible for it would have panicked that that was the bombshell she was about to drop. My gut feeling is the man knows more than he's sharing with us."

"Is the stepfather on the list?"

"Maybe. This evening I'll scrutinize him closely to get a good first impression."

"Who else?" asked Adel.

"Salazar. The staging of the death would appeal to a crime novelist. Also his publisher, Grégoire Argent. We have to take a closer look at him; he would have had a lot to lose if she had made the theft of ideas public."

"What about the psychologist? Maybe something went off the rails during a therapy session. The victim visited her on the day of her death and Suzanne Leriche knew a lot of the details of her private life."

"It would be a possibility but I don't see a real motive there."

"You have it again," he said suddenly.

"What?"

"This look. Like a hunting dog who's picked up the scent and won't let anything throw him off the track."

"Nonsense. I'm just thinking about what our next steps should be."

"This is different. You were made for this job."

"Says who?"

"Actually, everybody who's ever worked with you."

Jamila came out of the restaurant into the narrow veranda and put the food on the table in front of them.

"I'm done with my shift in half an hour and then I'll come to the police station and make a report."

"You can go with Adel. He can take the report."

She nodded at her brother.

"Great. Enjoy your meal."

Sandrine stabbed the fried egg with the tip of her knife and looked at the yolk which slowly spread out over the ham and crème fraiche.

"No appetite?" asked Adel.

"Yes, very much." She shoved her thoughts aside and devoted herself to eating. Her cell phone rang. It was Inès. She picked up and listened to the office manager. "That's unusual but I can arrange it," she said. "We won't be seeing each other again today. Send me the address."

"Did she discover something?"

"No. The mother of the victim has asked Inès whether I could bring Madame Leriche with me during the family visit later. The two know each other through the victim's therapy. I'll pick her up and take her with me to Saint-Brieuc. Maybe I'll get something interesting about the family from her during the ride."

"Do you intend to let her participate in the interrogation?"

"We're not that far along yet, it's simply an interview, not an interrogation. Nobody in the family is under suspicion right now."

"Will Suzanne Leriche be there?"

"It might be advantageous, Madame Vilette might open up more with her there. If the family insists, there's nothing I can do about it." She lay money on the table and stood up. "I'm scheduled to show up at six p.m. at the parents' home. It's getting pretty tight if I have to pick up Suzanne Leriche. See you tomorrow."

"Have a nice evening."

"You, too." She smiled at Jamila then said good-bye.

Her idea of a nice evening was very different to what was planned. Talking with the parents of the victim, who were desperately looking for answers and then going into the studio to train with Lilou Lanvers were not exactly plans she looked forward to.

* * *

The wind picked up again and shook her old Citroën's spongy suspension as Sandrine made her way to Saint-Brieuc. A few miles beyond the Saint-Malo city limits, she turned onto a side street that should lead to Suzanne Leriche's house. The path meandered past fields and small groves until she arrived at a high gate that was framed by two massive towers with pointed slate roofs. She pulled the note with the address that Inès Boni had given her from her pocket and compared it to the destination in the navigation systems. This had to be it, even though it looked like the entrance to a mediaeval castle. She pushed the revolver shift into first gear and drove slowly through the open gate. Lined with old oak trees, the driveway led to a larger square in front of a long multi-storied castle made of the typical natural stone found in Brittany. The builder of the complex must have had a weakness for towers because the main building was adjoined by another.

Above a large arched front door, a lamp illuminated the way. Suzanne Leriche stepped out and waved at her. The wind made her hair flutter like a blond flag and she drew her scarf tighter around her neck. Sandrine drove to the front door and the woman ran down the stairs. She opened the door and sat in the passenger side. She was holding an overnight bag and a sturdy raincoat rolled up in her hand and threw them in the back seat.

"Thank you for taking me with you. I hate to drive by myself."

"My pleasure, Madame Leriche."

"When I'm over sixty, I might accept the title of Madame. Like I said yesterday, I prefer to be called Suzanne."

"As you wish."

Sandrine drove around the plaza in front of the mediaeval building. "At first I assumed I was wrong about this place. But this is a real castle."

"You could say that. When my parents took it over, it was a dilapidated ruin. It took a while for it to look like this. But the work was worth it for all of us."

"You live here with friends?"

"The remnants of an old hippie commune." She looked over at the house. "Today, most of them are respected citizens. We have a lawyer, two tech people, a professor of political science, and luckily a few talented craftsmen, whom we require to do some repair work, but also some artists and philosophers. And even a farmer who manages the land that belongs to the estate."

"And a psychologist who takes care of the harmony?"

"Harmony is over-rated. Conflicts must be confronted otherwise they grow like cancer," she answered. "We have our quarrels like in any home where a lot of different people live together. But all in all, we live pretty well here. I would never move to a city, even to tranquil Saint-Malo which is already too crowded for me." She looked at Sandrine. "I heard you're from Paris. An interesting city."

"That depends. My job didn't always lead me to the prettiest places."

"Of course. And what brought you to Brittany? Excuse me, it's an old psychologist disorder. We believe that everybody has an inner urge to share their life's story with us."

"No problem." She turned onto the two-lane road leading to Saint-Brieuc. "I had some problems with my superiors. Undoubtedly self-inflicted problems."

"Any conflict always involves two."

"Well, ninety percent of the responsibility was mine. My Uncle Thomas would say 'the child caused a front end crash'."

"Was the crash avoidable?"

She thought a while before she answered. "The direction was right but I was going too fast and overlooked a red light. In a figurative sense, of course." In fact, she hadn't overlooked the red light but ignored it. She had broken into a suspect's house to look for evidence and was almost caught.

"And then you moved here to heal your wounds?"

"You could say that. I inherited a house in Cancale and moved in to sort out my life. Technically, I've been suspended by the police prefect in Paris and temporarily loaned out to the local police station." She wondered whether she said too much about herself to a woman she barely knew, but she trusted Suzanne Leriche. One could probably characterise her as an outstanding therapist.

"Until I push myself to take another path or the police prefect throws me out, I'm making myself useful in Saint-Malo."

"Very successfully, from what I hear."

"Thanks for the compliment."

"That was no compliment. Like I said, we have a lawyer in our little community."

"And you asked him about me?"

"Of course. I wanted to make sure the investigation was in good hands. Aimée was a special person and she deserves the best investigator."

"A compliment after all." Sandrine clicked on the turn signal and changed lanes. Her foot was firmly on the gas pedal and at a snail's pace, the car pushed past a truck.

"I wasn't expecting this car. Impractical but really nice. One of the last French classics. A family heirloom," said Suzanne. "My parents also had a Citroën, 'ugly duckling'. It was practically mandatory back then. I did my first driving lessons in it."

"I spent most of my summers learning how to drive my duck up and down the Emerald Coast but you certainly had enough room to practise driving at your castle."

"True. Actually too much. Garden, pond and lawn maintenance is a lot of work."

"Gardening is rather meditative, a female friend once said to me. But I have no first-hand experience with it." She was glad she had a tenant like Rosalie who kept the garden in good shape.

"She's absolutely right." Suzanne leaned towards Sandrine.

"Unless you own one of those riding lawn mowers and use it to hunt down foxes who sneak in to catch ducks."

Sandrine laughed. "Sounds like fun."

"Enormously. And luckily I never caught one, just scared them to death with the noise the mower makes."

* * *

They crossed over the Rance, the river that separated Saint-Malo from Dinard. The forest stretched down the slopes to the riverbanks. The light of the setting sun reflected on the smooth water; sailboats were anchored on both sides. From here it was only a short distance past the tidal power station to the English Channel.

"I'm guessing you weren't being entirely unselfish to take me with you," Suzanne Leriche said suddenly.

"You caught me. I was hoping in the interim you might come up with something that could help me."

"I thought about it for a long time," she replied. "I wish I could give you a clue but I don't have the slightest idea about who could have done this to Aimée."

"I met her boyfriend."

"An interesting person. He was good for her. In my opinion, he wouldn't be one of the suspects but I assume that you can't tell me the details of the investigation anyway."

"At least nothing internal. We can talk about things that make it in the newspaper."

"You and one of your colleagues met with Philippe Chardon."

"That wasn't a question, was it?"

"No, I ran into him on one of my daily walks along the wall. Although it may not have been entirely coincidental. Anyway, I've never seen him there before. He doesn't seem like the type of person that likes to walk in very windy weather."

"May I ask what he wanted?"

"He wanted to talk about Aimée. Her death hit him pretty hard. After all, she was once one of his clients. Back in Saint-Brieuc."

"With us he clammed up and invoked medical confidentiality. He didn't strike me as someone who was seriously affected by her fate."

"In your job you have to deal with victims of severe violence," said Suzanne, "but a lot of them are already dead. My clients go through similar things but survive. Highly traumatised people come into my practice on a daily basis and we dive down deep into their life stories. Every psychotherapist has their own way of protecting themselves from the monstrosities that human beings do to each other so they don't roll you over and drown you like a wave. I have my way and Philippe has his."

"He keeps his distance from others?" Sandrine asked.

"That's how it seems to me sometimes."

"What happened in Saint-Brieuc that caused Aimée to quit therapy and withdraw completely from the outside world could be the key to solving this case. I have to find out."

"We didn't talk about that. It could have been anything. Perhaps Philippe was too direct or too quick in his approach which caused her to crawl into her shell but it probably had nothing to do with the therapy."

"He talked about rumours of possible sexual abuse."

"Did he?"

Sandrine noted the astonished tone of her voice. "It seemed to me that he wanted to point me in a certain direction without revealing any details of their sessions."

"Aimée never mentioned anything about it but it would certainly explain a lot about her behaviour."

"Your colleague vaguely pointed in the direction of the stepfather."

"François?"

"You know the man?"

"Superficially. Marie, Aimée's mother, met with me every now and then. He accompanied her and waited for her. We hardly exchanged two sentences but he seemed like a pleasant person."

"Do you believe he could do something like that?"

"I believe anyone can commit murder when overwhelmed by fear but for this man to molest his kid? I would find that hard to believe."

"His stepchild."

"I don't know," she said. "You'll meet him this evening then you can come to your own conclusions. You are much more the expert than I am when it comes to evaluating the criminal aspect of a person's character."

If her information was correct, François Deloir was a doctor at the city hospital. Marie, his wife, had kept her old married name and worked as a nurse in the village. They didn't live directly in Saint-Brieuc, but in Les Rosaires, a little village a few miles away.

Sandrine found a parking place diagonally opposite the house which was directly by the sea. Huge stone block breakwaters and waist-high concrete barricades protected the road on stormy days from waves that could tower over the flat beach. *A perfect place for surfing*, she thought as she got out of the car.

She rang the doorbell and a man opened the door shortly thereafter. Judging by the deep circles under his eyes and rumpled clothes, he had hardly slept, if at all, in the last few days.

"Monsieur Deloir?"

"Yes. I guess you're from the police." He nodded at Suzanne

Leriche. "Marie has been waiting. Come in." He stepped aside before Sandrine could show him her police ID.

"Lieutenant Perrot ..." she began but he turned without a word and led them into the living room.

"Madame Leriche is here, so are the police," he said.

Marie sat on a wide sofa, looking forlorn. To Sandrine, she appeared to be an older version of her daughter, only her hair was shoulder-length and her eyes were red, as if she had been crying recently. The woman looked up at her, clearly exhausted.

"Please sit down. Can I offer you something, coffee or tea?" her husband said.

"We don't want you to go to any trouble," Sandrine declined.

"It's no trouble and I'm glad to be able to do something." He put his hand on the back of his wife's shoulder who clutched it.

"In that case, we'll take two cups of tea," Suzanne Leriche decided and sat down on the sofa next to Marie Vilette, and took her free hand. "I'm so very sorry," she said compassionately.

"Thank you for coming." Her voice was low and raspy.

"It goes without saying."

"No, it does not," she replied.

The man disappeared in the kitchen and Sandrine observed both women. With Suzanne's arrival a little more life had returned to the mother's eyes.

"The police were here on Sunday, but they couldn't tell us much. How did my daughter die? Who did this to her?"

"I wish I could answer your last question but unfortunately I'm not able to do so right now. I promise we'll do our best to find out."

"Lieutenant Perrot is a competent investigator. If anyone can find the perpetrator, she can," the psychologist assured her.

"It won't bring my daughter back."

"Nobody can. Unfortunately. But it helps to ease the pain of not knowing."

"Tell me what happened without glossing over anything," she said. Her husband came in with two cups. He heard his wife's last sentence. He looked at Sandrine and nodded in agreement. A young man in his late twenties entered the room behind her. Probably the victim's stepbrother.

"Your daughter was found in her apartment on Sunday morning," she began and reported what they had found. However, she left out some details and spoke in broad strokes. When she came to the end, the room was completely silent. Tears ran down the mother's face and Suzanne put an arm around her shoulders.

"Why? Do you have any idea why someone would do something so terrible?" Marie asked, her voice trembling.

"We won't know until we catch the culprit," she said.

"You are the police and you know your way around. What do you think? You must have some sort of guess," the woman insisted.

Sandrine briefly made eye contact with the psychologist, who nodded back at her.

"I could be wrong," she began, "but I think the male or female perpetrator acted out of fear."

"Fear? Fear of Aimée?" Her eyes widened and she stared at Sandrine. "She wouldn't hurt anybody."

"Your daughter hosted a show on local radio, as you know."

"She seldom visited us," François Deloir said. "So we never missed her Friday show, it was almost as if she was sitting here with us."

"Then you must know that Aimée announced a special broadcast on Sunday evening."

"Of course. I changed my on-call duty to be there."

"She wanted to make something public, something personal

but she didn't tell anyone what it was. Maybe she suggested something to you?" Sandrine asked.

"No. She called on Thursday. I told her that we were looking forward to hearing her on the radio on Sunday. She backed off from telling me what she was up to. It was supposed to be a surprise." Marie turned her head and looked at the young man.

"Did she mention anything to you, Christophe?"

"No. We didn't talk with each other that week. The new restaurant had just opened and I had a lot of work to do. She sent me a couple of text messages, that's all. Nothing unusual. The only surprise that I know of was that she intended to introduce Sébastien to the family. But that's hardly a thing that she would talk about on the radio."

"Her boyfriend?" Marie Vilette sounded surprised. "She has never brought a boyfriend home."

"Because she had never met anyone whom she was really serious about," her son replied.

"It could be an event in her youth here in Les Rosaires that is connected to the crime."

"What do you mean?" The woman made eye contact with the psychologist.

"She was in psychological treatment back then, as far as we know?" asked Sandrine.

"Yes, with Dr. Chardon."

"Can you tell me why?"

"I'm partly to blame for that," answered Aimée's mother in a low voice.

"Don't say that," François interrupted. "You are not to blame for what happened."

"I left my husband," she continued. "Our marriage was long gone. Charles had psychological problems."

"He would get drunk and beat you," the man said, summing it up succinctly.

"At some point, I just couldn't stand it any more and escaped from my marriage. Aimée came with me."

"You met Monsieur Deloir after that?"

"No, our relationship started before that." She gave him a gentle smile. "Charles hanged himself a year later. Of all people, Aimée found him in the attic. She was always quite sensitive and the sight of her dead father took a toll on her. Beyond our ability to help her, she needed professional help, so she went to see Dr. Chardon once a week."

"But Aimée abruptly stopped the treatment," said Monsieur Deloir.

"That's right," Marie said. The father stood up. Obviously he did not have the inner peace to stay sitting on the sofa.

"We cannot rule out that something happened at that time. An event that traumatised your daughter."

"We thought so, too, but she vehemently denied it. We couldn't force her to talk about it," explained Madame Vilette.

"Did she speak to you?" Sandrine asked the son. "It's often easier for siblings to talk about things between them than to the parents."

"Unfortunately not, for a few months she totally sealed herself off. We were step-siblings but we had a close relation-ship. She even pushed me out of her life for a while. I had no idea what might have happened."

"Do you also believe something happened to her?" Sandrine asked.

"Of course," said the mother. "A person does not change like that overnight. I don't know what happened but it broke Aimée. It took her a long time to bounce back enough to make arrangements to see Madame Leriche. Thanks to her, she came back to life."

During the conversation, it became increasingly clear to Sandrine that she would not make any progress until she found out what happened here ten years ago. But she had no idea where to start.

"I'm exhausted," Madame Vilette said and leaned back into the sofa. "I would like to end the conversation now."

"Of course. If you can think of anything else, please give me a call." She laid her business card on the table and stood up.

"I'll accompany you outside," Monsieur Deloir offered.

"Sure." She got the impression that the man had something he wanted to get off his chest.

"I need one," said François Deloir and pulled a pack of cigarettes out of his trouser pocket. "I haven't smoked in five years but now ..."

"I can understand that. What you're going through can break you."

He walked across the street, past the concrete barricade protecting the parking bays and leaned back against it.

The lighter clicked and a flame lit up his face, drawn by grief. The end of the cigarette glowed red. The man inhaled deeply and emitted a cloud of smoke, which a fresh breeze blew away. François Deloir looked over the dark sea that lay behind the breakwaters. The tide drove masses of water toward land. Some windsurfers used the last light of day to race at breakneck speed over the white crests of the waves. Living here in the summer had to be paradise. Had Aimée found her love for the sea in this place? Maritime Lifestyle. That's what Aimée called her social media presence.

"Thank you," he said suddenly.

"For what?"

"That you didn't mention it to Marie."

"What do you mean?" Sandrine asked though she knew

exactly what he meant. She wanted to hear it come out of his mouth.

"This rumour. Les Rosaires is a small town and Saint-Brieuc is no different. People couldn't help but notice how poorly Aimée had been doing. Someone started the rumour that she was being sexually abused. It didn't take long for them to open their mouths and point in my direction."

"Allow me to ask the question ..."

"You can save your breath," he interrupted. "I had nothing at all to do with that. Aimée was like my own child, even though I never pushed her to see me as her father or to restrict contact with her biological father. I never wanted to take his place." He drew on the cigarette. "I loved her and I believe she loved me, too."

"How did Aimée react to the rumours?"

"She was trapped in her own world for a long time. She didn't notice what was going on around here at all. It was only after she met Suzanne that she slowly opened up to life again. She saved my daughter from the darkness."

"And later on? She could have made it clear that it wasn't your fault. Why didn't she do that?"

"Because we never told her about it."

"You kept it a secret from Aimée?" she asked in astonishment.

"Of course. She had suffered enough and had just gotten back on her feet with great difficulty." He stubbed out the cigarette on the concrete barricade. "It was hard to bear the looks and people talking about me behind my back but I could stand it. Aimée would have blamed herself for it. It was better that she never found out."

"She knew about it. But only recently." The son had come up behind them. The wind had drowned out his footsteps.

"None of us told her."

"Believe me, she knew about it." He joined them and took a cigarette from his father's pack. "I didn't want to say anything in front of Mother but I guess that's the bombshell she was talking about. I had to promise her to keep my mouth shut."

"That's why you came here from Paris? Despite the opening of the new restaurant?"

"She asked me to. So you wouldn't be alone when you heard it on the radio."

"Did she say who did this to her?" asked Sandrine.

"No. She was so sorry that people here thought that her stepfather had anything to do with it. She was determined to set the record straight."

"So she died because someone believed they had to prevent her from making the sexual abuse public?" François Delois carelessly dropped the cigarette pack. "She was murdered because she wanted to help me."

"No. This was her own decision. She had been carrying that weight around for a long time. It was clear to her that she had to get that weight off her back in order to start a new chapter. In any case, she wanted it to happen before she introduced you to Sébastien."

Sandrine pulled up the zipper on her rain jacket and wrapped her arms around her upper torso. It was time to say good-bye. Both men needed some time to themselves.

* * *

"I didn't think Léon would be able to persuade you." Lilou, who was a hand's breadth taller than Sandrine, seemed like a fixture in the studio. She couldn't remember not seeing the woman with the wiry figure and bright-red close-cut hair work out on any given evening. One probably had to do that to get to her level. Sandrine really did not expect her to thank her for her support.

The woman seemed to have a tough exterior and she seriously doubted whether there was a soft core underneath. So far she hadn't seen anything soft about her.

"I'll try not to hurt you," Sandrine joked, while tying her shoes.

"That worked great last time," replied Lilou with a smirk. "I can't remember you even touching me. I'm sure you felt the same way. You have to improve your aim if you want to hit. But it must be really hard with such terribly long arms." In fact, Sandrine had taken several hard hits and only repaid a few. "Must be nice to be able to tie your shoes without bending over," joked Lilou and dug out two red-black punching mitts out of her bag and handed them to Sandrine. "Let's take it easy. Just gentle punching to warm up."

"Fair enough." She doubted that the term *gentle* meant the same to Lilou as for other people.

The punching mitts were rectangular and slightly curved. A solid leather glove was sewn on the back. The front side was made of thick artificial leather with a white hitting circle that made aiming much easier. Sandrine relied on the woman hitting precisely otherwise sparring could become quite painful very quickly. They both climbed into the ring. Sandrine had already warmed up with a light workout and she pushed her hands into the gloves of the punch mitts. They were tight and she could barely move her fingers, but they were better protected that way. The men working with the dumbbells looked over at them. They were obviously curious about how Sandrine had become a sparring partner. She had only registered with the fitness studio at the beginning of the year and she hardly knew anybody by name. In Paris, she'd started training when she was very young, actually as soon as she'd learned to walk. Her mother was of the opinion that a woman shouldn't run away but be able to defend herself.

"He's coming later," said Lilou.

"What do you mean?"

"Um, Léon. You were looking around for him."

"Nonsense."

"Whatever, but during training, I need you to be able to fully concentrate. Don't let the guys distract you. Understand?"

"*Oui, mon général.*"

"Good attitude. On those terms, we'll get along just fine." Lilou turned to face the onlookers. "Don't you people have anything better to do?" she shouted at them.

Sandrine lifted her mitts to shoulder height. Immediately the first punch landed exactly on the white striking point and her hand bounced back a bit from the blow. Now she knew what the woman meant by gentle.

"Keep the tension and move faster. You're moving so slowly even my grandfather could land a punch."

Sandrine danced a little to the side, her hands moved quickly but Lilou landed a punch every second. The clapping of leather meeting leather echoed throughout the studio. She was amazed at how hard and precise the woman hit. She would put money on her at the championships.

After a half hour, Sandrine's muscles and shirt were soaked in sweat, as if she had run a marathon. The woman still punched tirelessly in rapid succession with the same precision as she had at the beginning of the training session. Out of the corner of her eye she saw Léon, who came to the ring and leaned onto the ropes.

A sharp pain shot through her left calf when Lilou kicked her. "Ow!" Sandrine cried and raised her arms up to keep her balance, but it was too late. She crashed backwards onto the mat. The air shot out of her lungs.

"Breathe easy." Lilou knelt beside her as Sandrine attempted to catch her breath.

"Never turn your focus away from what you're doing. As soon as we let men distract us, we're screwed."

"Thanks for the lesson." The intended sarcasm was lost while she was gasping for air.

"That's enough for today. I'm going to take a shower. I need to catch the last bus," Lilou said and took the training mitts which Sandrine held out to her.

Léon came through the ropes. "Was that really necessary?" he hissed at Lilou.

"Stop. She was right. I didn't pay attention and got my punishment. Just like in real life." She held out her arm and he pulled her onto her feet.

"How's it going?" he asked her.

"Up until the last minute? Actually, really well. That woman is a beast. I'm sure she could have pounded me for quite a while longer."

"Yup." He watched until Lilou disappeared into the locker room. "I wouldn't want to mess with her either."

He held one of the ropes and she climbed out of the ring.

"How's the hunt going?"

"Read the newspaper. I'm not allowed to divulge anything."

"So bad?"

"You can take it whichever way you want to take it."

"I'm sorry."

She looked at him with astonishment.

"Did you know the victim?"

"No, but as long as you haven't caught the perpetrator, we're not going to see you at the barbecue and I would like to put something on the grill for you. Because I'm an excellent cook."

"That sounds so nice. And I'm an excellent guest. As soon as I catch the guy, I'm in."

"Friday. We'll start at five p.m.," he said. "Unfortunately I have to go to work afterwards."

"I'll do my very best to hurry up the investigation." A barbecue with friends sounded so pleasant. So far, she hardly knew anyone in the area. Just a few who weren't involved in police work.

"That would make me really happy." He sounded sincere.

"Me, too."

"Have you decided yet whether to stay here, or move on like a nomad?"

"This falls in the same category as the barbecue. The murder case has priority. I've got to take a shower now. We'll see each other Friday," she said as a good-bye.

She had two and a half days to catch the perpetrator if she wanted to attend the barbeque as a pleasant reward. That was cutting it pretty close. Exhausted, Sandrine dropped onto the bench in front of her locker and stretched her legs. Her eyes burned as she wiped the sweat from her face with a towel. A round Bluetooth speaker hung upon a hook and the music of Alan Stivell's celtic harp filled the shower room It probably belonged to Lilou who was already taking a shower. She took off her wet gym clothes and threw them in the open locker. Her stuff needed to be washed as urgently as she herself did. With a bottle of shampoo and a towel, she went into the shower room which was separated from the dressing room by a frosted glass pane.

"That good-bye was pretty fast," Lilou said, as she greeted Sandrine. Dense shampoo foam sat on her head and Sandrine couldn't resist a smile.

"Why not? He's here to train, not to chat."

"I'm not so sure of that."

Sandrine didn't answer and squirted a dab of shampoo into her palm.

"I've known Léon for some years now. He's a nice guy," said Lilou.

"So it seems," Sandrine replied evasively.

"Certainly, especially when compared to the murderers and man-slaughterers that you usually have to deal with."

"Or to corpses."

"I forgot about that," she agreed. "Anyway, Léon seems pretty interested in you." Lilou grinned and put her head underneath the shower jet. Foam ran down her body and the bright red hair reappeared.

"Perhaps," she said curtly.

"Try not to hurt him."

Sandrine stopped lathering her hair and looked at Lilou in amazement.

"I have no intention of getting between you two."

"Don't be ridiculous. He's only a good friend. Besides, I'm in a committed relationship."

Strangely enough at that moment, she thought about Arianne Briand, the program director of the local radio station. They expressed themselves in the exact same way.

"You have to take the bus?" Sandrine changed the subject. She didn't know the woman well enough to discuss her private life in the shower. She also suspected Lilou didn't like her very much.

"Yup. My junk car is in the shop again."

"Where do you live?"

"A small village on the Rance, south of here."

"I can take you."

"That's not necessary. I can still catch the last bus."

"Don't be silly, I'll drive you. It's kind of on my way," she lied.

"All right. Thank you."

Lilou took a towel off the hook, rubbed her hair dry and left the shower room.

"What is this: a chariot from the Middle Ages?" Lilou stood in front of Sandrine's 2CV and studied it extensively.

"An heirloom from my aunt. The last thing I have left of her," Sandrine teased the woman.

"I'm sorry. It's really a beautiful car. And it has a convertible top. It must be so pleasant in summer."

Sandrine unlocked the door. The "ugly duckling" did not boast a central locking system.

"Hold on," said Lilou, pressing the old military bag into Sandrine's hands then climbing into the passenger seat.

"What's in this, millstones? What should I do with it?"

Sandrine handed the heavy bag back to her then also got in.

"Curious?"

"An occupational infirmity."

The woman opened the buckles of the bag and pulled out a dark lump that looked like stone and was about double the size of her fists. She handed it to Sandrine who weighed it in her hand.

"Iron ore?"

"Lucky guess." Lilou took it back and packed it up again.

"Why are you carrying this around? Are you going to slam the bag over someone's head?"

"Not with this," she replied. "A week of work went into that." She blew her breath out powerfully between her lips. "We built a kiln to recover the iron ore."

Sandrine pulled the choke then started the car. "Like in the Middle Ages? What do people call that? Live Action Role Play?"

Lilou's eyes widened and for a moment she stared at

Sandrine in amazement. "It's called experimental archaeology. I don't wear pointy elf ears or dress up like a female orca then frolic around."

"Excuse me, I just thought ..."

"You don't have any idea what I do outside the studio, do you?"

"No. I don't know where you work either." She shoved it into first gear and the duck chugged along.

"The ancient Celts built kilns and filled them with iron ore and charcoal. They forged swords, knives and other vital tools from the iron they obtained. I made it with my class. Yesterday evening we made a fire, used the bellows to keep the temperature up overnight and pierced it this morning. The chunk is a product of a lot of work."

"Your class?"

"I teach history at the high school."

"Oh, sorry."

She waved her hand. "It's all right. Hardly anyone knows what I actually do for a living."

"It certainly sounds very interesting."

"It is. But the next step is going to be really exciting."

"And what would that be?"

"We take the ore to the forge and work on it further."

"May I see how it comes out?"

"I'll have to ask my students." Lilou grinned. "Cops are not necessarily on the top of their friends list."

"I can understand that."

"You have one of my colleagues on your radar," she said unexpectedly.

"Who are you talking about?"

"Salazar. French literature and philosophy. He's convinced that you want to make him look bad because you're stuck on the Vilette case and need someone to blame."

"That's what he said? Well, the man is an author so dreaming up wild fantasies is probably a basic requirement."

"Well, he doesn't have the goods. Most of his students would perform a dance of joy if you locked him up."

"Doesn't surprise me. But we only questioned him as a witness who knew the victim, nothing more." She looked at Lilou. "Do you believe he's capable of murder?"

"The man is a weakling. He identifies with the self-created heroes in his books and portrays them in such an exaggerated way. Pierre doesn't have anything else in his life. He hates his job as a teacher which is why the students despise him. If someone came and took his writing away, I don't know how he would react. He'd probably kill himself rather than another person."

"I hope he had nothing to do with the woman's murder, even if that means his students have to continue to put up with him," said Sandrine thoughtfully. The man had a motive that Lilou had just confirmed. Aimée could have taken away his life's purpose with her knowledge of his deceit. And Pierre knew that. Perhaps he felt so cornered that he saw no other way out. *I'm going to find out.*

She left the woman in a remote hamlet in front of an old farmhouse.

"Thank you."

"Wasn't a big detour and I'm not tired."

"Not just for driving but otherwise. I didn't think you'd agree to help me. Not after what happened."

"I'd been drinking and I had a big mouth. I got what I deserved."

"True," she said as a good-bye and walked away.

A Mysterious Video

Sandrine ran through the light rain and held her jacket over the fresh baguette and the bag of croissants. She knocked on Rosalie's front door with her elbow.

"It's open," her friend called out, who never locked her door from the inside. It was a miracle that no one had ever broken in. Burglars were probably deterred by the motion sensor light on the facade facing the street and the alarm system, which was never turned on.

Rosalie was waiting in the kitchen for her. On the massive oak table were plates, large café au lait cups and two glasses of orange juice, but also a vase filled with peonies, still wet from the rain. The smell of freshly brewed coffee filled the room. Sandrine set the baguette on the wooden cutting board and tipped the croissants into a bowl placed in the middle of the table.

"That should be enough."

Rosalie looked at the vast assortment of croissants. "For today and the rest of the week."

"I'll take what's left over to the police station. My colleagues always seem to be hungry." *Mainly Poutin. The man spends half his work hours eating and smoking.*

She sat down in her favourite place where she could look out the lattice windows through the pine trees to the sea. Dark clouds piled up over the horizon. It would be an unpleasant day. Definitely not a good day to ride to work on the motorcycle.

"The weather is unlikely to change today," Rosalie said as she pushed a bowl of steaming coffee towards Sandrine. "Lots of wind, clouds and rain. A perfect day for writing."

"Good for you."

"It sounds as though your case is as dark as the weather." She picked up a croissant, spread some salted butter on top and bit into it with relish.

"I have a bunch of people who could have profited from Aimée's death but no tangible evidence to pin down the perpetrator."

"It will come," she said consolingly. "If I know you, you're on the verge of finding something you've missed thus far."

"I hope so. In any case, thanks for the tip about the book."

Rosalie looked over the edge of the coffee cup which she held with both hands. She ran the tip of her tongue over her upper lip and licked up some croissant crumbs. "I was afraid you wouldn't appreciate me interfering."

"Don't worry. It was a valuable tip. We'll probably have to talk to this writer again." *And with his publisher. Preferably at the police station.*

"A complicated case if one can believe what's written here." Rosalie slid an open newspaper across the table. The title page featured a picture of the building at Rue de la Cloche. A red arrow pointed at the victim's apartment. Madam Drouet, the elderly owner of the building, would most definitely disapprove as she probably did of most things. Sandrine pulled the news-paper closer towards her. The little information the Commissaire had released was mentioned and exaggerated with wild speculations. Deborah Binet's by-line was just below the article.

"I know this journalist. This woman wants to climb the career ladder, therefore for her the end justifies the means."

"She managed to get a hold of this story, which suggests that her methods were successful. There aren't many murder cases here; some colleagues will be quite upset that she snatched the story away from them."

"So it seems," said Sandrine. She suspected the journalist was boasting to her newspaper colleagues about her excellent relationship with the team of investigators with the hope of receiving inside information. Well, if the woman could deliver something tangible she would return the favour.

"Anyway, some of my old acquaintances have appeared in the investigation," said Rosalie.

"Do you mean Salazar?" Sandrine ripped a finger-length piece off the baguette and cut it lengthwise.

"Yes. But also Grégoire Argent, Dominique Petitjean, Odette Marchal, Suzanne Leriche's parents and a few others."

"Do they all know each other?" She put the knife with which she was going to spread a dab of strawberry jam back on the plate. "This is really interesting."

"Of course. Saint-Malo is a tiny town."

"Tell me!"

"In the nineties, they were a pretty wild group. Not Suzanne Leriche, but her parents."

"Were you there also?" wondered Sandrine.

"I knew some of them but not especially well. At that time I was still too young, in high school, to party all night at the clubs. Around here they were all pretty famous or rather, notorious. They managed to sink a boat at the Saint-Brieuc yacht marina. Odette was probably stoned and crashed into the quay wall at full speed. But the exact course of events has never really come out."

"How did you know I spoke with Suzanne Leriche? She doesn't appear in the article," asked Sandrine, astonished.

"It's an open secret. You questioned her while she took her daily walk along the wall. Half the city saw it."

"That's probably true," said Sandrine. "So Suzanne Leriche's parents were part of this group then?" She bit into her baguette and crumbs from the crispy crust fell on the table.

"Old hippies. Sex, drugs and rock 'n' roll as they say. But actually very nice people. After Odette's crash, the clique disbanded. She ended up in an addiction clinic, Suzanne's parents went to India for some years, Petitjean continued to work as a photographer, and Grégoire founded a successful publishing company."

"Was Chardon a part of this scene?"

"The pretty Phillippe. Sure. From what I heard he donated the happy pills for the parties. But I've lost track of him for a long time now."

"He worked as a psychiatrist in Saint-Brieuc and now here in Saint-Malo," Sandrine said.

Rosalie thoughtfully stirred her café au lait "Hard to imagine that man does anything voluntarily for others. He was a kindred spirit of Odette's: excessive self-love."

"I had the same impression. The guy is a prime example of arrogance."

"But basically a coward. As soon as the police showed up to ensure the peace, he would immediately disappear."

"If they're all involved, I might find a motive there."

"Unlikely. That was twenty-five years ago. Most of the crimes would be null and void under the statute of limitations and Aimée Vilette would have been a baby then. Commissaire

Hugo Delacroix would rather snoop around in the last couple of weeks before the crime."

"But he doesn't have a boss or the press breathing down his neck who want to see results, preferably yesterday."

"No, but my investigator is driven by an enterprising publisher who wants the new manuscript on his desk soon."

"Why aren't your books published by Grégoire Argent's company?"

"My agent thought my future would be better served at one of the major publishing houses. She was undoubtedly right. Crime novels were never Grégoire's passion."

"Until Pierre Salazar."

"Old male friendship, perhaps. No idea what binds those two."

"What kind of publisher publishes a book by an unsuccessful author year after year? The company must take a huge loss."

"I don't know the numbers, you need to ask him about that yourself."

"Then I'm off to find out." She finished her coffee, stuck the rest of the baguette in her mouth and left the house.

* * *

It was pouring with rain and Sandrine ran a few yards from her police department parking place to the rear entrance. Her hair was soaking wet and she wiped her cheek off with her hand. She hung her rain jacket on the wardrobe at the entrance of the large open office.

"It should clear up by this afternoon," said Inès, who threw her a dry towel. "An umbrella might be uncool, but it sure is practical. Especially here in Brittany."

"I'll remember that for future reference."

The brigadier was sitting at his desk and looked over at her.

"How was last night with the Vilettes?"

"The parents were on edge which is not surprising. Suzanne Leriche stayed there overnight."

"Did you confront the stepfather with the rumours?"

"He raised the issue on his own initiative. The man knew about the sex abuse gossip and how he was accused of it at the time. He assured me that Aimée would not have heard about the accusations."

"Daughters can find out a lot of things without their father's knowledge." Inès sat down with them. She probably spoke from her own experience.

"The stepbrother confirmed it. According to him, she only heard about the gossip last week. So that was the bombshell she had planned to make public. Another piece of the puzzle we can work with."

"I'd like to know who gave birth to those rumours," said Adel. "And who abused her. I assume that this will be the murderer. There are a lot of suspects. Do you believe the father had nothing to do with this? After all, most cases of abuse come from people who are close to the victim."

"I can't say with certainty but my gut tells me he really loved her. And his son confirmed his version of the story."

"Maybe it was the other way around. Maybe he abused his stepsister and the father is protecting him."

"Anything is possible." Sandrine stretched her legs and leaned back in her chair.

"I would exclude both of them," said Inès unexpectedly.

"You know these people?" Adel seemed surprised.

"No. But it doesn't make sense."

"What do you mean?" Sandrine asked her.

"I grew up here and have an excellent network. If I don't know them, then they're completely blank slates around Saint-

Malo." The brigadier nodded in agreement. "A daughter accuses her entirely unknown family of abuse." She looked at Adel first then Sandrine. "In my opinion that wouldn't be explosive news that required a special broadcast. Especially one that would need the backing of other influencers. I suspect it's someone better known in the area who has significant influence."

"That seems quite logical," Sandrine agreed.

"Chardon," Adel said. "He could be behind both the rumours and the abuse. His family is wealthy and influential."

"He was her psychiatrist back then. The possibility exists but we have no evidence," said Sandrine. "Aimée Vilette didn't accuse him or file a complaint. Without her as a witness, it would be very difficult to prove abuse."

"There is something," he replied. "I showed Jamila photos of the suspects. Also some from the website of the group practice. She's willing to testify under oath that Philippe Chardon was the man that Aimée Vilette was fiercely arguing with on the Grand Rue a few days before her death. When we asked him, he denied it."

"Then we'll pay him another visit. This time without warning, so we can take advantage of the element of surprise."

"A search warrant wouldn't be a bad idea," murmured Adel.

"That would be difficult since our psychiatrist is in the same golf club as prosecutor Lagarde," said Inès, shooting down his pipe dream. "The evidence we have against him isn't really strong enough to pin one's hopes on."

"I heard some of our suspects were in a clique in the nineties. Can you do some research on this?" asked Sandrine. "Odette Marchal was supposed to have caused a boat wreck in Saint-Brieuc, a report of which should be found in the newspaper archives or perhaps with colleagues in the Coast Guard. I would also like to find out everything we can about Grégoire

Argent's publishing company. First and foremost, how it stands financially. How hard would it hit him if he had to cancel the publication of Salazar's crime novel?"

"If the victim had exposed the author as an idea thief, the book would no longer be saleable, not least from being a public relations fiasco. He might even be sued for damages. That's a solid motive," said Adel.

"I'll see what I can find." Inès wrote some notes on her pad, which she always carried with her. "What else?"

"According to Petitjean, the title of the cassette which Aimée allegedly stole from him was *Hot Desire Beyond Walls*. Can you find out where we can get a copy? I would like to take a look at it."

"Searching for porn is really something new and exciting," said Inès.

"Then you certainly won't get bored." Adel smiled mischievously.

The brigadier turned to Sandrine. "Does any of this makes any sense at all? We're assuming that the motive for the murder is sexual abuse, that happened over ten years ago in Saint-Brieuc. That's fifteen years after the film was shot."

"Just a gut feeling, nothing more," Sandrine answered. "We're probably just wasting our time but I don't want to be accused later of not following up on every possible clue."

"All right. It's your decision."

"Anything new from forensics?"

"Nothing jaw-dropping," said Adel as he leafed through his notebook. "To date, Marie has had a hard time decrypting the hard drive. She won't give up, I should say but her chances of success are pretty abysmal. Stade Rennais is more likely to win the championship. The stain on the inside cover was more than likely a label. The ink has smeared so it will be hard to make it readable again, but they're trying. Marc Bergier's fingerprints on the pipe are old." He looked up from his notepad. "There was a layer of dust over it. The man hasn't touched that thing anytime recently, at least not without wearing gloves."

"If he had been careful enough to think about wearing gloves, our goose breeder would have thought about wiping off the old fingerprints and not using a weapon that could immediately be traced to him. That should take the man out of the game." After the interrogation, Sandrine had crossed him off the list of suspects. The idea that this rather dull guy was familiar with Japanese calligraphy was practically negligible.

"What do we start with today?"

"With Salazar."

"That will be difficult," said Adel. "The man didn't answer his phone and he called in sick at his school. Perhaps we already came in too close to him and he's fled."

"Then we'll need to drive to his house. If he's disappeared then we'll put an all points alert on him."

Sandrine looked outside. It was still pouring buckets. "We'll take your car," she said to Adel.

"Of course, since my car's roof isn't leaking."

* * *

The car's rubber wipers squeaked over the windshield. For fractions of a second the house was visible before the driving rain obscured it again.

"It looks abandoned," said Adel. They sat in the warm car and put off the inevitable.

Sandrine looked up from the passenger-side window into the cloud-covered sky and sighed. It didn't look like the rain was going to stop any time soon.

"This weather doesn't help much," she said. "I'm going over, you stay here. No reason for both of us to get soaking wet."

Before he could answer, she pulled up her rain jacket's zipper, put her hood over her head, got out and shut the car door behind her. She marched quickly to the front door and pressed the doorbell with her pointer finger. A cheesy melody rang out. She rang several times but nobody opened the door. She ran back.

"What crappy weather." She shook out her rain jacket through the half-open car door.

"What should we do? Put him on the wanted list?"

"He called in sick at the school but he's not here either. What else can we do? We need to talk to him."

"Perhaps he's at the doctor's and had to turn off his cell phone."

"Could be but I don't want to take the risk of him packing his things and then disappearing, never to be seen again. At the moment he has the most compelling motive for the crime."

Adel picked up his phone and called the police station. He spoke briefly with Dubois and vertical creases appeared on his forehead.

"Bad news?" In this case, it was hardly unusual.

"Petitjean lied to us. There's no video with that title. Dubois and Inès have checked all relevant directories and websites. They found nothing."

"What reason would he have to lie to us about such an apparently trivial thing?"

"We have to ask him in person."

"Get Inès on a search warrant for Salazar's house."

"I didn't expect he'd be here, so I already prepared the paperwork. It should go pretty quickly unless the prosecutor backs down. I don't believe that Salazar's playing golf with Lagarde right now."

"Good. Let's drive over to Chardon's now. I'm curious to see what lies he conjures up for us this time."

Adel typed a text to Inès before he drove off.

* * *

"Dr. Chardon is very busy right now unfortunately." The lady at reception was trying to stall them. "I'd be happy to make an appointment for you."

Sandrine winked at Adel.

"That would be incredibly kind of you." He leaned forward slightly. "Mademoiselle Pradel," he read on her name tag. "Not everybody is as helpful as you are." Resistant to irony, the woman pulled the keyboard of her PC towards her and opened the appointment calendar.

"What day would be ... Stop! You can't do that," she yelled behind Sandrine who had marched to Philippe Chardon's office door. The woman jumped up.

"Does next Thursday work for you?" asked Adel.

"Excuse me?" she stammered, stopping in irritation.

Sandrine opened the doctor's door without knocking. The psychiatrist sat behind his expansive desk and gazed at her in amazement. "What are you doing?"

"You just went ahead when I was about to make an appointment," said Adel innocently, following her.

"Monsieur Chardon, forgive me." The receptionist tried to move in front of them but Adel blocked her way. "I couldn't stop them," she cried.

"We're in luck," said Sandrine to Adel. "He's here and surely has time to answer a few questions. We can save ourselves an appointment."

"All right, Fleur, you can go, and take these uninvited guests with you on your way out."

"We don't want to disturb you, Monsieur Chardon. If this is inconvenient for you, then we'll of course go," said Sandrine and walked towards Fleur. "Please cancel all appointments for this afternoon." She looked at her watch ostentatiously. "Afterwards a patrol car will pick up your boss for an interrogation at the police station."

"Unlike you, I'm busy. My time is short and expensive," the man told her.

"I totally understand that. My uniformed colleagues will sit quietly in your waiting room and drive you to the police station as soon as you have time. Madame Pradel doesn't have to worry. The men will bring their own coffee in thermoses."

"You want to do what?" He stared at her with an open mouth. "You want two policemen to squat in my office? That's not possible. How would that look?"

"It would look like you lied to the police and know more about the sexual abuse of Mademoiselle Vilette than you've told us. Perhaps out of self-interest."

"Self-interest? Are you suggesting ... His cheeks turned blood red and he leaned both hands on the desk and stared at her aggressively. "I will file a complaint against you."

"You're welcome to do that. After the interview I will send a colleague to the interrogation room who will take up the complaint, okay?"

"Fleur, get out of here!"

She wordlessly fled the office.

"You've toyed with us long enough," she snarled at the man. "Why did you lie to us yesterday?"

"I'm not allowed to give any information about my patients without a court order."

"You claimed not to have seen Mademoiselle Vilette for a long time."

"That's true."

"We have witnesses that say you had a very loud fight with her. On Thursday, on the Grand Rue in front of the Papillon Rouge to be exact."

"Who says that?"

"People who are ready to identify you in a line up."

The man took a deep breath. "All right. I happened to run into her on the street."

"Why did you lie to us?"

"Somebody had just killed the woman, do you think I wanted to end up on the list of suspects?"

"Lying to the police doesn't exactly make you look innocent."

He leaned back in his chair and looked up at her. "Of course, hindsight is always 20/20."

"What were you arguing about?"

"Insignificant stuff. I don't remember why she got so upset."

"You're lying," she said.

"How dare you!"

"It was about the abuse she suffered."

The man abruptly fell silent and bit his lower lip.

"Out with it," she told him. "Otherwise I have no choice than to take you with me down to the station. I can only guess how much this would damage your reputation."

"Yes," he confessed. "She insinuated that I had spread rumours about her and her father. That was an allegation that I couldn't let stand."

"And did you threaten her?"

"Threaten? No. All right, maybe with my lawyer if she continued to spread these lies."

"Did you go to your lawyer?"

"No. I didn't hear from Aimée again until you two showed up here and told me about her death."

"Where were you on Saturday evening?"

"At home. But I can't come up with an alibi. I am a confirmed bachelor and ended the day with a glass of red wine and a good book."

"Well, that's quite inconvenient," Adel said.

"Since I never touched the woman, I'm not afraid of your investigation." His anger had vanished and his voice sounded scratchy. He picked up the glass of water in front of him and took a sip. "Is that all?"

"For starters," she said. "Come down to the police station, we need to officially record your statement."

"I'll be there."

At the door, Sandrine turned to face him. "Did you sexually abuse Aimée?"

Phillipe froze then slowly replied, "No, I did not."

"If you're lying, we'll find out." She left the man alone and followed Adel who had already left the office.

They said good-bye to the receptionist, who gave them a dirty look, then stepped out into the rain.

"They found Pierre Salazar's car," Adel informed her. "It's in Dinard, in front of Grégoire Argent's publishing house."

"They're both up to their necks in this. I'm exactly in the right mood for these two men. Did Inès find anything about the publisher's finances?"

"We can't access his bank accounts without a court order and right now, the evidence against him is far too slim. Rumour has it that the man has his back against the wall. Madame Marchal's new book has to be a success, otherwise the future looks pretty dim for his publishing company."

"Please ask some colleagues to keep an eye on Salazar's car. If Salazar tries to leave, they need to stop him. How long will it take us to get there?"

"Fifteen minutes, depending on traffic, maybe more."

"Let's go."

"And what about Petitjean?"

"He lied to us, too. We will talk to him later."

They sprinted through the rain to the car and quickly got in.

* * *

The villas still bore witness to Dinard's glorious past, the oldest seaside resort in France. The publishing house was located in the city centre. Adel stopped in front of a whimsical three-storey building. A metal sign with ornate lettering hung on the blue lattice of the courtyard entrance: Maison d'Édition Grégoire Argent.

A police officer got out of a patrol car and walked toward them.

"Brigadier Azarou?"

"Yes. And my colleague, Lieutenant Perrot. Good job finding the car."

"Thank you. The owner hasn't shown up. Do you still need me?"

"We may have to take a suspect to Saint-Malo for questioning. Could you do that?"

"No problem. I'll let the office know." The man went back to his patrol car parked on a side street.

Sandrine rang the bell and pushed against the courtyard gate as soon as the buzzer sounded. A young man opened the front door and let her in. "Monsieur Argent and his visitors are waiting for you," he said, leading Sandrine and the brigadier to a conference room.

At an oval dark-red mahogany table, sat Grégoire Argent, Pierre Salazar and to Sandrine's surprise, Odette Marchal. The publisher stood up and moved two chairs to the table. "Please sit."

"Good morning, Madame le Commissaire," Odette Marchal said in greeting with a slight smile on her lips. "It seems we are constantly running into each other these days."

"Lieutenant, to be exact," Sandrine said, correcting the writer.

Pierre Salazar sat on his chair with slumped shoulders, avoiding eye contact with Sandrine and Adel as they sat across from the three.

Odette Marchal stood up and straightened the gold chains around her neck. "I suppose I'm no longer needed here. I really have nothing to do with this painful matter."

"Do you know what brings us here?"

"Of course. Pierre confessed to everything. A mistake but not illegal."

Sandrine raised her eyebrows. "So you don't believe that he had anything to do with the woman's death?"

"That is ridiculous. He wouldn't hurt a fly."

"Stay here, Odette," said Salazar in a low voice. "There's nothing more to confess that you haven't already heard."

The woman looked at her and Sandrine nodded. If the man felt more comfortable in her company, Odette could stay.

"You lied to us, Monsieur Salazar. You had a solid motive to get Mademoiselle Vilette out of the way. You can't give us an alibi either."

"Yes, I lied to you, I admit that. But at that moment, I panicked, thinking you would try to frame me for murder."

"So there was never a benevolent review?"

He hesitated, then nodded. "She'd found out that I got an idea or two from another novel. But I didn't copy one word. My book is an independent work, not plagiarism and I abide by this point." The man looked at her directly for the first time. "This is not a crime."

"The entire story line was stolen by you, just like the majority of characters and their development throughout the story," replied Sandrine. "And you are correct, but even though this not illegal, wouldn't your reputation be in tatters after Mademoiselle Vilette's disclosure?"

"It would have been his death," Grégoire Argent said. "Well, only his literary death, of course."

"For someone for whom writing is so important as it is for Monsieur Salazar, it certainly seems a credible motive for murder."

"No!" he shouted, looking for help from his friends. "Not at all." He slumped even more and gazed at the tabletop in front of him. "I write about murders but I don't commit them. I would never be able to do that."

"What were you doing on Saturday at the victim's apartment?"

"That brat lambasted my books mercilessly as if she could even recognize the value of true literature." He glanced up at Sandrine with a tormented look on his face. "For years my books were ignored. I was desperate. Something had to happen and I decided: if readers insist on junk, then they should get it. So I took a trashy novel as a template and ..."

"Copied it," Adel ended his sentence.

"You don't understand."

"I don't have to. But answer my colleague's question: what were you doing in the victim's apartment?"

"Surrendering. She had won and wanted to savour her victory."

"What does that mean?" asked Sandrine.

"The girl had threatened me. If I didn't withdraw the book from publication, she would make my misstep public. I couldn't let that happen under any circumstances."

"So you silenced her? 'The mouth is the root of all misfortune'."

"No. I caved in and agreed to not publish the book. In return, she promised never to review any of my books again."

Adel held his notepad out and tapped on it with his index finger.

"You came around six o'clock. There is a witness for this."

"That's true."

"How long were you in the apartment?"

"Not very long. She kept me at the door. She pretended to be waiting for visitors and wouldn't let me in. I was there for about ten minutes. There wasn't much to discuss."

"Do you at least know who she was expecting? That might help you."

Odette laid a hand on his shoulder. "Don't worry. We believe in you and won't abandon you."

"Certainly not," Monsieur Argent agreed, though he hesitated briefly.

"Thank you," replied Salazar quietly.

"Do you know who she was waiting for?" asked Adel again.

"I never asked and the girl hardly told me anything. We were both happy to bring this unpleasant discussion to an end."

"When did you inform your publisher of your plagiarism?" Sandrine kept an eye on Grégoire Argent. The man wasn't a good actor. His reaction would reveal whether he was lying or not.

"This morning."

"Four days after the meeting. You took your time," said Adel. "Did you want to reconsider your decision?"

"It takes courage to admit your mistakes and even more in front of your friends. I'm certainly not a brave person. But I stand by my word and will withdraw my book from publication."

Sandrine looked at her watch. Jean-Claude Mazet and his team should have arrived by now. "Monsieur Salazar, as we speak your house is being searched by the police. If we find any further incriminating evidence, I will arrest you. My colleagues will take you now to the police station, where your statement can be recorded. In the meantime, maybe you can think of something else you'd like to share with us."

The brigadier stood up, opened the door of the conference room and waved to the waiting policeman. Salazar rose and went out, dragging his feet.

"You're being pretty tough on poor Pierre," said Grégoire Argent. "That guy could never hurt anyone. At least physically."

"Some of his books bordered a little on mayhem," Odette interjected. "But it's true that Pierre would make an absolutely incompetent murderer. Not even our friend Rosalie could make him into a credible criminal."

"If I've learned anything in my profession, it's that under the right circumstances anyone can become a murderer."

"That might be true," said the publisher thoughtfully.

"You used to be a tight-knit clique, so I hear."

"One could say that," answered Odette. "Both of us and Pierre. You've already met Philippe. Then there is Petitjean. He has a photo credit in my current book. A blast from the past," she laughed quietly.

"Don't forget our two hippies." Argent smiled as if remembering some unforgettable moments.

"The Leriches?"

"Exactly. Every now and then they brought some of their perpetually stoned friends with them."

"Strange that so many of you appear in connection with this investigation."

"A coincidence, I can only assume," the publisher said defensively. "Our wild times are long behind us. Today we are the establishment we deeply despised a quarter century ago."

"You founded a successful company."

"You flatter me," he replied with a smile. "A small publishing company in a tough industry. As less and less people read from year to each year, we feel it. On top of that, more and more books come on the market each year. But we have to get through it as best as we can."

Sandrine placed her forearms on the table and scrutinised the man closely. "From what I heard, Pierre Salazar's crime novels didn't fare very well."

"You must have heard that from Rosalie," said Odette. "It's hard for the rest of us to keep up with her success." She looked at Grégoire. "I'm afraid I must be going now. What publisher wants to disclose his company's finances when one of his authors is present?" She rose and smiled at Sandrine. "Give my regards to Rosalie, we absolutely must meet again soon." Then she picked up her Louis Vuitton bag and said good-bye.

Grégoire Argent watched her until the door closed behind her. "What a woman," he muttered.

"But also exhausting, I would guess," Adel said.

"Oh, yes. For days, we've been running from one appointment to another. She has energy that those in her age group can only dream about."

"When will the new book be published?" Sandrine asked.

"On Thursday. That evening she has a radio interview. We're going to Paris this weekend for a book signing. In a few more days, the hype should settle down a bit."

"Shouldn't Salazar's crime novel have also been published on the same day?"

"Oh yes, of course, but on a much smaller scale."

"If times are so hard, why would you publish a commercially unsuccessful book by Pierre Salazar every year?"

"A good question which I've been asking myself more often lately." He leaned back in his chair, which creaked softly. "Pierre and I have been friends for decades. We've all made careers to a certain extent. For me, it's the publishing house, for him, literature. I couldn't help but support him."

"You were willing to take a loss for friendship's sake?"

"Oh, I didn't lose a lot of money. We kept editions small, maybe a hundred copies. He sold most of them at readings. Some of them are on the shelves of booksellers and he drives by frequently to see if they're still there. Being a published author means a lot to him."

"And yet, he ultimately jeopardizes it?"

"Strange, isn't it? At some point even the most ardent writer will grow weary if he doesn't achieve a certain level of commercial success. Anyway, that's my experience."

"What will you do with him now?" said Sandrine. "Instigate court proceedings to recover your losses?"

"Oh God, no!" replied Argent.

"But you're sitting on a stack of books you can't sell right now," said Sandrine.

"Pierre will bear the costs, I'm not worried," he stately calmly.

"But?"

He reached onto the shelf behind him and pulled out a paperback. *Deadly Sins Will Hunt You.* "This novel was really worth reading. I wish he actually had written it himself."

"This Sarah Mason will not be pleased."

"On the contrary," the publisher replied. "I submitted an offer for publishing rights to the author shortly after his confession. This book will sell very well. Maybe I should share a percentage of the profits with Pierre, after all, he's the one that discovered it." Grégoire Argent seemed to be very satisfied with himself.

"Would the situation be similar if you had to recall Odette Marchal's books back?" asked Sandrine.

"Do you have any idea of the number of books she has in circulation? We are talking about a completely different scale here. Please don't tell me her stories were somehow stolen, too."

"Don't worry, I'm just trying to get a picture here."

He took off his glasses and cleaned them with a small cloth. "Understand this. The publishing house is solid enough to absorb the small loss from Pierre Salazar's books but not the demise of Odette's. That would be my ruin. However, in that situation I would rather kill the author than the woman who uncovered the scandal, if your curiosity goes in that direction."

"Was Aimée Vilette one of the many appointments that you've had in the last few weeks?"

"Not that I can remember. She rarely discussed children's or young adult books, which did not stop me from sending her a copy. But we also checked out a number of other book bloggers." He put his glasses back on. "Some of them were so annoying that I could have easily killed them myself. But Mademoiselle Vilette wasn't like that. She was a very intelligent and quick-witted conversationalist."

"Well then, we won't keep you any longer." Sandrine stood up and said good-bye.

Monsieur Argent accompanied her and Adel to the door. The rain had diminished and the sun shone brightly through the clouds. Maybe it would be a pleasant day after all.

From the restaurant's covered terrace on Dinard's seafront, Sandrine enjoyed the view of the beach and the sea. She hadn't missed the opportunity to see some of the city. She ate her salad, which for a tourist restaurant, was surprisingly tasty. The morning rain had driven the bathers away and she guessed that the cook had a lot less stress on him today. In front of them stretched the fine sand of the Plage de L'Écluse, which would otherwise be very busy. On the rocky outcrops which framed it, the old villas with their pointed roofs and turrets left their mark on Dinard's panorama.

"We haven't found out very much," said Adel who had just finished the last bite of his vegetable quiche.

"More than I expected, to be honest," said Sandrine.

"Chardon admitted that he'd had a fight with the victim, that's all. Maybe it's true that she wrongly accused him of giving birth to the rumours, who knows? Our author admitted to having visited Aimée Vilette but claims he never entered her apartment. We can't prove that either man is lying. The financial loss that Grégoire Argent suffered from Salazar's book is too insignificant for murder." With a frustrated look, he sipped his coffee. "We haven't made any progress at all."

"I wouldn't say that. Salazar confessed to stealing ideas either out of honest regret or to make him look better in front of us. I can't say which of those is true, but I also find it difficult to see him as the murderer. The man has neither the imagination for the staging nor the courage to commit such an act," said Sandrine.

"He had motive and opportunity."

"And he happened to steal a stuffing tube from Bergier before-hand? Do you believe that he's able to memorise Japanese characters quickly? Unlikely. We also have a witness who testifies to having seen him at six o'clock. The murder didn't happen until ten p.m. at the earliest. He would have had to stay in the apartment for at least four hours without leaving fingerprints or DNA. As messy as his house looked, I think that would be quite impossible."

Sandrine ordered two additional café creams. "Rosalie claims the man doesn't have a trace of creativity or imagination. Something our killer has in extraordinary abundance. The longer I think about it, the less Salazar comes into question for me as the perpetrator. More like Chardon, the psychiatrist. He lied to us on our first visit and only ever admits it when we can clearly prove it to him. I'm sure he lied to us again today."

"But we can't prove it."

"Not yet."

"Okay, so we ruled out a suspect but we're no closer to identifying the real culprit."

"My gut tells me that the solution is right in front of us, but we just can't see it. Not yet."

"I hope you're right."

"We're going after Petitjean," Sandrine decided. "If both Inès and Dubois doubt the existence of the film, therefore I assume he lied. But why? It was a trivial thing."

"Aren't you getting a little too obsessed with this tape?" wondered Adel. "There could have been anything on it. We'll probably never find out."

"She connected a video-grabber to her laptop and copied the film. There's a copy somewhere in her directory. I bet that this is the key to finding the murderer."

"If Marie is already in despair over the encryption, we'll never be able to see it."

"Then we'll have to solve the case without the cassette."

The waiter put the two café creams on the table, then she asked for the bill. It was time to return to Saint-Malo.

* * *

Sandrine hit the door with the flat of her hand. Petitjean had not responded to the bell. Since music was blasting out of his apartment, he should be there. He was probably entertaining a woman or he was too drunk to hear them.

"Let me try." The brigadier came out of a neighbour's apartment, rattling a bunch of keys. "The man often leaves his keys inside or loses them. That's why he left a spare with his neighbour." She stepped aside and he opened the door. "Et voilà." Adele let her go in first.

"Monsieur Petitjean, it's the police," she called out in the hall. No response. The apartment seemed to be deserted. Sandrine carefully pushed open the door and entered the studio. Petitjean wasn't there and Adel turned off the music.

"Horrible stuff, like what Inès listens to," he grumbled.

"He certainly had visitors." On the table were two glasses, one half-full, the other empty, and the ashtray was overflowing, mostly with yellowish and pungent remains of Gitanes cigarettes. The entire apartment stank of cold smoke. But an unpleasant sour smell also hung in the air.

Adel picked up the bottle and looked at the label. "With that kind of booze, it's no wonder he threw up. From the way it reeks in here, it seems as though he didn't make it to the bathroom."

She opened the door to the next room and stepped inside. It was the bedroom. A large metal frame bed took up half the room. In front of it were two lamps and a camera tripod. Dominique lay lifeless on the bed, naked and with a gag in his mouth.

"Adel!" she called out. "Come here."

"Allah!" she heard him exclaim behind her as she stepped closer to the bed.

"Stay where you are," she warned him and pulled out a pair of blue plastic over-shoes which she always carried inside her jacket. She slipped them on easily, and a pair of disposable gloves. She crouched beside the head of the bed and felt his throat for a pulse. His skin had cooled and she searched in vain for a heartbeat. Dominique Petitjean was dead and probably had been for quite a while. Rigor mortis seemed to have set in. His hands and feet were tied to the bed posts with cable ties. Clotted blood was on the man's wrists and ankles. What caught her eye was the gag. It looked like the perpetrator had used Petitjean's sex toys. A black plastic ball attached to a narrow leather strap was stuck in his mouth. None of his neighbours would have heard him scream even without the loud music. His eyes were bloodshot and wide open. Vomit oozed from the corners of his mouth and nostrils.

"He suffocated," said Adel, who was scrutinising the scene from the door. He cleared his throat. The sight of the deceased man was clearly turning his stomach.

"With his blood alcohol level, the shackles and the gag in his mouth, he had no chance of surviving when he threw up."

"A sex accident? His sex partner panicked and took off?"

"I don't think so." She pointed at the lamps and the camera. "This is how Aimée Vilette's murder was staged."

"I bet the memory card is missing."

"The man is wiry but certainly not a weakling. That's why the empty bottles. The murderer filled him up before he dragged him here."

"Let's see what Dr. Hervé says. I bet he finds drugs in his stomach as well as the alcohol. After that, any child could have tied the guy to his bed. Our perpetrator always plays it safe."

"Why kill the man?"

"He was a bastard, but not stupid. He was definitely keeping something from us. I assume he found out why Aimée Vilette had to die and who was responsible."

"And told the wrong person?"

"It could have happened that way. But that is pure speculation. Let's see what forensics and pathology bring to light."

Adel phoned Jean-Claude Mazet. "You can stop what you're doing there. We have a body here ... Yes, another one. This has priority."

Sandrine stood up. She'd seen enough. Forensics would do the rest.

"They'll be here in about a half an hour. A patrol car will come, too, to block off the crime scene. I'll get the team together," Adel said.

"Let's go to the police station. Matisse will be expecting a report."

"We don't have much to report. And Petitjean won't be talking anymore."

"Our boss will have to live with that for now." She realised that after this second murder, the press would pounce on Commissaire Matisse, and the prosecutor and the examining magistrate would put additional pressure on them. She was glad not to be in his shoes.

* * *

They ran into Inès who was about to roll another bulletin board into the conference room. "Poutin and Dubois are already here, Commissaire Matisse and Monsieur Lagarde are on their way."

"The prosecutor?"

"Two deaths in one week is unheard of in Saint-Malo. The press, his superiors and the politicians are breathing down their necks."

"I can imagine." And she had nothing tangible to show them. Matisse would stand by her but in the long run, he wouldn't survive. The longer the investigation dragged on, the louder the calls for a responsible person's head to roll. As much as she appreciated her boss, it wouldn't be his.

"Here come the two of them," said Adel.

"Good morning, if under these circumstances one could even speak of a good morning," the commissaire greeted them. The prosecutor contented himself with a nod, ignoring Adel.

"Give me a report." Matisse looked at his watch. "The president of the general council and the prefect are waiting for me to call back, I can't put it off any longer."

"Come in. The rest of the team is already waiting." She went ahead into the conference room and greeted the brigadiers Dubois and Poutin. "Inès, stay here, it will go fast so we can do without coffee and cookies."

"I would take one," Poutin remarked.

"Let's get started while you are in the kitchen getting some," said Sandrine succinctly. The fact that Inès took care of the coffee was due to her friendliness and efficiency. Serving her colleagues was by no means part of her duties. The man twisted his mouth and remained seated. In the presence of the chief of staff, he decided he didn't want to be the one to take care of his culinary needs rather than be present at the meeting.

"At one o'clock, Brigadier Chief Azarou and I found the body of Dominique Petitjean." She took a picture that Inès had printed from the table and pinned it on the new bulletin board. "At this point we barely know anything else. Forensics and pathology have only just begun their work."

"Give us your first assessment," Commissaire Matisse demanded.

"Without wanting to anticipate what Dr. Hervé will say, I suspect the time of death to be late last night. Rigor mortis had already fully set it before our arrival, which suggests a period of between six and twelve hours."

"The neighbour from whom I got the key complained about the loud music. It started around ten p.m. At midnight she heard the front door slam and saw a figure walking away," said Adel. "However, she wasn't able to identify them. The woman is over seventy and very near-sighted. Anyway, the loud music continued unabated and she went over to complain. Petitjean didn't hear the doorbell. I would assume that he was already dead at this point."

"How did he die?" the prosecutor said, breaking his silence.

"Forensics and pathology have to sort that out," Sandrine answered.

"Your assessment," Commissaire Matisse urged again.

"The man reeked of alcohol, empty bottles cluttered the living room and one was under the bed. We'll get his blood alcohol level over the course of the day, but I would assume he was dead drunk. The large gag in his mouth made breathing extremely difficult. He was unable to breathe when he vomited." Sandrine sent the photo she had taken with her cell phone onto the projector.

"Choked on his own vomit," Dubois murmured, "like a seventies rock star."

"The man was into the BDSM-scene?" Poutin's mouth twisted in disgust.

"We don't know if the gag was put on voluntarily or if it was forced. Perhaps at that time he was unconscious," replied Sandrine. "The zip ties that were used," she moved to the next photo, "are also unusual in the scene. This variety cuts into the skin easily and creates bloody injuries."

"So you think this isn't an accident but a murder?" Matisse looked at her and waited.

"My first assessment is that someone killed the man."

"It doesn't seem to me that the two cases are related. Except for the fact that he's worked for Mademoiselle Vilette from time to time, as well as other people in the area, there's no other connection thus far. The man has a terrible reputation and not many friends in Saint-Malo, so I've heard," Lagarde said.

"A serial killer would be bad for the city's image," muttered Dubois, just loud enough to be heard. He had understood why Lagarde was reluctant to attribute the two murders to the same perpetrator, although it seemed obvious to everyone involved.

"I don't want to hear that kind of talk, understand?" the

prosecutor told him. "That word will not be used in this investigation. Imagine if the press becomes aware that some police officers are even considering something like this."

"I'd be surprised if we don't see any such speculation in the news tomorrow," said Commissaire Matisse. "The more sensational the article, the better the newspaper sells."

Lagarde turned to Sandrine. "Please don't tell me that you think it's a serial killer, too."

"If you're talking about a psychopath wandering around Saint-Malo indiscriminately killing people, then surely not.'

The prosecutor sighed in relief. "Thank you."

"But I do assume it's the same perpetrator."

"What makes you think that? Both victims live in different social circles, had little contact with each other and Mademoiselle Vilette's murder had no sexual implications similar to this one."

She took a deep breath. The man wasn't stupid but in this case for some reason he refused to acknowledge the obvious.

"The crime scenes were staged in detail. The lighting was professional and both crimes were recorded. In both cases the killer took the memory card. Both victims died of suffocation. I bet forensics will prove that it's the same cable ties, too."

"I agree," said Matisse. "We have to look for a single perpetrator and a connection between the two victims."

"Philippe Chardon," said Sandrine. "The man knew both of them. Petitjean from his youth here in Saint-Malo and Aimée Vilette through his treatment of her in his practice."

"That doesn't mean much. He probably had hundreds of clients," Lagarde said.

"We suspect the first motive is in connection with events that took place when she was in therapy with Dr. Chardon."

"You suspect. That's not a lot to go on."

"Perhaps Petitjean knew more about the murder and

needed to be silenced. In both cases, it was about brutally snuffing out the victims' lives to save their own skin. The woman with the pages of a novel, the man with a gag. The message is hard to miss. To solve this case, we need a search warrant for Chardon's apartment and practice. If possible also for Aimée Vilette's client file."

"Again, only your hunch?" The prosecutor waved her off. "I will not ruin the reputation of a respected psychiatrist without your bringing me tangible evidence. Out of the question."

She had expected this decision and yet she felt abandoned by him.

Lagarde stood up. "I have to go back to the prosecutor's office. See you at the press conference this afternoon." He said good-bye to Commissaire Matisse but ignored the rest of the team.

"What's next?" asked Dubois after the prosecutor disappeared.

"You and Poutin go to the crime scene and question the neighbours. Maybe for once we'll get lucky and somebody will have noticed something. Inès, would you gather background information on Chardon?"

"It's as good as done," she answered.

"Adel and I will go through the existing clues again in peace."

Dubois stood up. "Come on, Luc," he told his partner who rose clumsily.

"What concerns you?" Matisse asked, when they were alone.

"The perpetrator is playing with us. He always seems to be one step ahead."

"What do you mean exactly?"

"He leaves clues that lead us in a certain direction, some of which prove to be wrong quite quickly, like Marc Bergier, the goose farmer. Others I'm not so certain about." She sat down on a chair and scrutinised the bulletin boards on which hung photos, index cards with descriptions and connecting arrows. Only a few clues merged onto one picture.

"My gut told me that the VHS tape played a role. But it's also possible it's something that led us on a wild goose chase, which cost us a lot of time and attention."

"It led to Petitjean."

"Now he's dead which excludes him as Aimée Vilette's murderer."

"Maybe Lagarde isn't totally wrong and the clues incriminating Chardon are also fabricated to mislead us."

"The killer throws clues in our path so we can't clearly see what's ahead."

"Shovel the dung out of the way and you'll see it," Matisse advised her.

"Thank you for your trust."

"If anybody can do it, you can. But first we have to get this press conference over with this afternoon. The press is expecting the head of the investigation. The hyenas are no longer satisfied with just me and Lagarde."

"I'll do my best to be there on time."

"I'm counting on you."

After the commissaire left, Sandrine stayed alone in the conference room and continued staring at the bulletin board. Something was hiding in plain sight, but what?

Her cell phone rang and she picked up the call. It was Suzanne Leriche and she sounded upset.

"What's happened? The press? In front of the house? Do you have any idea where the information came from? All right, I'm on my way."

She jumped up and ran out of the room. "I have to go to Les

Rosaires, to the Vilette's," she called out to Adel. "Someone sent the press to the family house."

"Should I come with you?"

"I can do this alone. There are enough important things for you to do here. As a last resort, you might have to represent me at the press conference."

"Don't do this to me!" she heard him call out before the door closed behind her.

* * *

Sandrine steered her ugly duckling into the parking bay along the street then stepped firmly on the brake. The car shook then stopped. The reporters who besieged the house turned. Cameras clicked and a horde marched toward her.

"Lieutenant Perrot!" cried Deborah Binet, who was among some of her colleagues. "Are you here to make an arrest? Is Monsieur Deloir the murderer of his stepdaughter?"

"I'm here for only one reason: to ensure peace, law and order."

"Are the rumours true that Aimée Vilette was sexually abused?" one reporter shouted over the heads of others. "Was it the father or the brother?"

She marched to the entrance of the house and stood on the stairs leading to the front door. "Calm down," she cried. The reporters fell silent slowly; only the clicking of the cameras could still be heard. "How did you come up with such nonsense? There is no reason to harass the family this way."

"Are you going to make an arrest or not?" Deborah Binet reiterated.

"I'm not arresting anybody here," she replied. "There's no reason to do so whatsoever."

"Her stepfather is said to have abused her for years," cried an angry woman from the second row.

"Tell me who started these fabrications." She pointed at the female journalist who took a step to the side and hid behind one of her colleagues. "It's silly, baseless stuff. Somebody pulled a nasty joke on you. Everybody needs to go home."

"Can you assure us that the allegations are baseless?"

"Does the abuse that has taken place here have anything to do with the murder of Dominique Petitjean?" The journalists fired question after question at her.

"You're behaving like a horde of immature children. Just because someone whose identity is currently unknown is spreading wild speculations, you're terrorising an innocent family who are in the midst of grieving for the death of their daughter. Shame on you." She demonstratively looked at her watch. "In an hour I will personally attend a press conference at the police station in Saint-Malo. You should all hurry because we close the doors punctually. Whoever shows up too late must wait outside. That is a promise and people who know me know I am serious."

The reporters hesitated until Deborah Binet lowered her cell phone which she'd used to take photos of Sandrine.

"Will you comment on the rumours?"

"We'll share any information which we're allowed to disclose for investigative purposes."

"So far the police haven't been especially cooperative or successful," grumbled a bearded colleague of Deborah's.

"We're working on this case as fast as we can. Because of your childish behaviour I'm standing here unnecessarily instead of investigating the crimes."

Some journalists packed their cameras into their bags and made their way to their cars.

"Do you have a suspect?" Deborah Binet tried her luck again.

"Why are you here?" she asked the woman and went to her. "Who told you about these rumours?"

The journalist pulled a note from her jacket pocket and gave it to Sandrine.

"Someone sent an email to the editorial offices of the local newspapers."

She read the few lines attentively: "'Aimée Vilette was sexually abused by her stepfather for years. When she decided to go public with her story, he silenced her. Within a day, police will arrest him.' Anonymous bullshit. And you fell for it?"

"If you kept the press informed about the investigation, we wouldn't have to pursue every little lead that comes our way."

"That's what the press conference is for."

"You owe me something. So, do you have a suspect?"

Sandrine glanced at her watch again. "Time is running out."

"You still owe me." Deborah Binet turned around and went to her small sports car. Shortly after, she raced away.

Sandrine had no doubt that she would see the woman at the police station where she couldn't so easily evade her questions. Someone opened the door behind her and she turned around. It was Suzanne Leriche.

"Thank you for coming. We wouldn't have gotten rid of that mob without your help. None of us dared leave the house."

The parents were sitting on the sofa and looked up when she entered the living room. Christophe, the son, wasn't there. He'd probably gone back to Paris.

Sandrine sat on the armchair. "Do you have any idea who started this rumour?"

"It's been buzzing through the city for years. This is nothing new. We've almost gotten used to it, as much as possible anyway," said Marie Vilette.

"Someone deliberately stirred up the journalists. An anonymous source claimed that today we would arrest Monsieur Deloir for the murder of his stepdaughter. Of course everyone wants to be on location to report on it."

The man stood up and stared at her. "This is absolute nonsense."

"Of course. Nobody's accusing you of anything. You can rest assured."

"Now the whole city thinks we're paedophiles," Marie blurted out. "We can't go anywhere anymore."

"Take a holiday for a couple of days. I'm pretty sure that we're on the culprit's heels." Anyway, that's how the killer seemed to see it. Sandrine couldn't imagine any other reason for these hysterical falsehoods. He must feel the walls closing in on him. That's why he caused this disruption. Mainly to distract them from their investigation. Maybe the murderer wanted her to get out of town for a while, knowing the Vilettes would call her for help. If so, she had fallen for this manoeuvrer. What could he be up to?

"I have to go back to Saint-Malo. The journalists won't bother you any more today. To be on the safe side, I'll ask my colleagues to patrol here more often."

"Thank you, that would be nice." Marie Vilette seemed relieved. Judging by the dark circles under her eyes, it looked like she had hardly slept in the last few days.

"I have to go to town, too. May I come with you?" the psychologist asked.

"Of course."

Suzanne Leriche said good-bye to the family and brought her small overnight bag with her. The two women left the house together.

About thirty journalists filled the room, firing questions at police and prosecutors' office representatives. Lagarde had taken over the leadership role but as soon as the criticism and allegations of incompetence became louder, he turned it over to Sandrine.

"Is this a familial crime and do you suspect Mademoiselle Vilette's father?" Deborah Binet seemed to be fixated on the abuse story and would not let up.

"Monsieur Deloir is not under suspicion. There are no signs of abuse in the family. However, someone seems to be spreading this rumour, thereby making police work more difficult," she said. "If anyone knows who is behind this campaign, we ask you to share this knowledge with us."

"Do the police have any suspects at all?"

"Of course," she replied concisely. There was no way she could mention names at this press conference.

"Are the two cases connected?" called a reporter, who sat in the first row.

"We're not assuming that's the case at this point," Prosecutor Lagarde cut in before Sandrine could answer.

"Is that also your opinion, Lieutenant Perrot?" the reporter turned directly to her.

"We value the experience of the prosecutor's office representative. Monsieur Petitjean's body was found ..." she looked at her watch, "only three hours ago. We have to wait for the results of the forensics team's investigation before we can verify a connection."

"Do we have a serial killer in Saint-Malo?" Deborah Binet called out loudly.

Lagarde winced as he stood beside her. The man had expected and feared this question.

"Nothing about these tragic events supports such a suspicion," Sandrine answered.

"There is no reason to frighten the inhabitants of Saint-

Malo with theories that have been plucked out of thin air," the prosecutor said, trying to drown out the journalists.

Adel stepped into the room and waved at her.

"I have to go. Something's happened," she whispered to Commissaire Matisse.

"We'll be ending soon anyway. I can handle the rest without you. But hurry and catch the bastard before the serial killer idea gets any more traction."

She stood up and marched through the room toward Adel.

"Why are you leaving?" shouted a journalist behind her.

"Has another murder occurred?" All heads jerked round and thirty pairs of eyes stared at her.

"I have answered all your questions, and at present I cannot contribute more to the current state of the investigation. Unfortunately, I must apologise, but Prosecutor Lagarde and Commissaire Matisse remain at your disposal." She ignored the questions that were hurled at her and went through the door that Adel held open.

"What's going on?" she asked him as soon as they were safe from eavesdroppers.

"They've arrested Mademoiselle Vilette's boyfriend."

"Sébastien Duvall? On what grounds?"

"The man stormed into Philippe Chardon's office, verbally abused and assaulted him. Our psychiatrist got in a few good shots before his colleagues were able to separate them."

"That's hard for me to imagine." The photographer hadn't given her the impression that he was capable of violence. "Where is Duval now?"

"He didn't try to flee and our colleagues picked him up. He's sitting in one of the interrogation rooms. I assumed that you would want to speak with him right away."

"Definitely. If something threw him for a loop enough to

attack Philippe Chardon, he might have found out information that could help us."

They walked together to the interrogation room where the photographer was waiting for them. Sandrine stepped in first and Sébastien Duval jumped up instantly.

"You must arrest that pig," Duval shouted angrily.

"At the moment, only you are under arrest," Adel replied. "And that's for assault. If Monsieur Chardon presses charges, it's not going to look very good for you since there were half a dozen witnesses to the attack. Now sit down, please."

Apparently intimated by the brigadier's harsh tone, the man obeyed but never took his eyes off Sandrine. He seemed to expect some degree of compassion from her. "The guy had it coming and then some. If they hadn't stopped me then ..."

"You would have done nothing at all," she said, cutting him off. Further threats would only hurt the man at trial. He slid restlessly back and forth on his chair, seemingly fighting the urge to jump up again.

"Please remain seated," Adel advised him.

"You can't let him get away."

She scrutinised the man. He himself had not been left unscathed. His left eye was red and beginning to swell. Tomorrow at the latest, it would turn into a real black and blue shiner.

"Did Chardon do this?" she asked.

"Him? No. The bastard was hiding under his designer desk. I owe this to one of the policemen who refused to lock the man up."

"Let's start at the beginning. Why did you enter his practice, threaten and then attack Philippe Chardon?"

"It was him," he blurted out. "He molested Aimée."

"Calm down, Monsieur Duval. Someone's playing dirty games with Mademoiselle Vilette's family." She took the note that the journalist had given her out of her pocket and laid it on the table in front of the man.

"Monsieur Deloir, the stepfather, was also accused of the same thing. The press got a hold of this email and I was forced to go to the family's house to ensure the peace."

"Was that all?" he asked.

"That was enough to rile up the press. Did you receive a similar message?"

"Similar? No." He shook his head adamantly. "I have no idea what this nonsense is." He tapped his index finger on the paper. "Aimée sincerely loved her stepfather, like a real father. He can't have had anything to do with the abuse. Utterly out of the question. It was Chardon. Somebody sent me photos that were unambiguous."

"What kind of photos?" asked Sandrine immediately.

"Terrible ones." His voice gave out and Adel handed him a plastic bottle of water. Duval took a big gulp. "Photos of Aimée. He abused her." His hands clenched the edge of the tabletop and he breathed slowly to calm himself down. "He must have murdered her to silence her." His face lost all colour. Sandrine wondered whether that thought had come to him at that moment.

"We don't know that."

"Who else could it have been?"

"Where are the pictures?"

"At home. In Saint-Lunaire."

"Did they come as an email or by post?"

"A motorcycle courier brought an ordinary envelope. I didn't think anything of it, lots of agents send their documents that way, so I opened it and found the photos."

"Was there a written message?"

"Yes. The sender of the pictures wrote that Philippe

Chardon had abused Aimée. That I should better confront him before he escaped justice."

"Is he clearly recognizable in the photos?"

"Who else could it have been?"

"We need those photos."

"Can you promise that the guy will be punished? More than ten years have passed."

"The statute of limitations has not yet expired. For minor victims it's thirty years. The man will not escape punishment. If you hand over the photos, I can get Chardon's house searched." His cooperation was unnecessary. Sandrine could have immediately obtained a search warrant and confiscated the photos, but she wanted his help.

"He must not get away," he said, his voice raw.

"Can you promise you're not going to pull any more dumb moves?" she asked the man urgently. From the corner of her eye she noticed the puzzled look Adel sent her.

"I'm not going to touch this guy again, if that's what you mean. I wasn't thinking clearly after I saw those photos. All that matters now is that he is held responsible."

"I'll drive you home now so you can hand over the pictures. Okay?" He nodded with resignation. "If Monsieur Chardon does not file a complaint, we'll drop the case."

"Thank you."

"Wait for me here." Sandrine stood up and left the room.

Adel followed her into the office. "What are you doing with this man?"

"I'll put him in my car and we'll get the photos. That's the most important thing right now."

"You really want to release this man then drive him to Saint-Lunaire?" The brigadier tugged nervously on his left earlobe. "That's taking a huge risk."

"Are you worried about me?" Sandrine grinned at him. "He

doesn't seem like a habitual thug and I'm quite capable of keeping him off my back."

"I'm not worried about you," he replied. "I know where and how you spend your evenings. It would be pretty stupid for him to mess with you."

"Then where's the risk?"

"You like the man and think he's harmless, that's obvious. If these photos actually exist, I trust that he'll want to finish what he started today."

"I'll take full responsibility for that," she said. "If Sébastien Duval had really wanted to kill the psychiatrist, he wouldn't have shown up without a weapon. The man saw the photos and he blew a fuse, which I can fully understand. He stormed into the office in a blind rage and went for the throat. Surely this is his first fight since kindergarten."

"He can easily do it again."

"He's had time to calm down by now. I don't believe that he'll freak out again, now that he knows we're taking over."

"I would sleep better if we could keep him overnight in a cell."

"He's a victim, not a criminal who belongs in a cell."

"Your decision."

"We're a team. If you insist, I'll leave him at the police station and drive alone to Saint-Lunaire."

Adel thought about it then nodded. "You're right, he's gone through enough."

"Good. I'll get on the road right away."

"Wouldn't it be better if I joined you?"

"I can do this alone. As soon as I get these pictures, we'll be able to see if we can use them or not. In the meantime, I need someone at the police station who can go over the results of forensics from Dr. Hervé. With a bit of luck, Mazet found something interesting in Dominique Petitjean's apartment. Otherwise prepare the paperwork for a search warrant for Chardon's house. With these photos in his hand, the prosecutor should give in. He'll be happy with any activity that makes him look good to politicians."

"I'll keep you posted and give you an update on the Chardon search warrant request. Call me as soon as you know whether we can use the photos."

"I will. The warrant should apply to both his home and practice. If he molested Aimée Vilette, she probably wouldn't have been his only victim. I bet he's keeping the pictures around to look at them again. We need to act quickly before he destroys the evidence."

"I'll do my utmost. Commissaire Matisse and Prosecutor Lagarde are in the building. I'll catch both of them as soon as the press conference ends."

She stuck her service revolver into her shoulder holster and got underway.

* * *

"Take this," said Sébastien Duval and handed Sandrine the key to the front door. "My hands are shaking." She opened the door and he went upstairs. "My landlady lives below but she went to her aunt's in Chinon for two weeks."

The curtains were drawn but substantial light came in through the skylights into the living room. It was limited to essential furnishing, like Aimée Vilette's apartment, but the décor revealed a lot about the man who lived here. A few, probably carefully selected, travel souvenirs were discreetly displayed and framed photos hung on the walls, mostly portraits.

"From your project?" she asked Duval to pull him out of his dark thoughts.

"Yes."

"A blacksmith?" She pointed at a broad-shouldered man with a leather apron who smiled happily for the camera.

"One of the last blade-smiths in Brittany. Another portrait of him hangs in the Paris exhibition."

"When I'm in the capital again, I'll surely go in and look at it."

"Are you interested in photography?"

"Just a little hobby. Mostly landscapes."

He went into the kitchen and came out with a manila envelope. "They're in here." He lay it on the living room table and she took a pair of disposable gloves out of her jacket pocket.

"Sorry, I touched everything. My fingerprints must be all over it."

"You couldn't possibly have imagined what you were going to find." Instead of stamps, the postmark of the courier company was printed on the envelope. The probability that the sender left any DNA traces behind was low but forensics would still look for some. Sébastien sat on the sofa and watched her intensely. It felt like he didn't want to miss her reaction to the photos. She hesitated.

"I would understand if you didn't want to see the photos again. It's no problem if you want to go into the kitchen again."

"No. That's not necessary. I'll never get those images out of my mind anyway."

Sandrine opened the envelope and pulled out a handful of photos. Even though it had been more than ten years ago, it was unmistakably Aimée Vilette. Wide-eyed and frightened, the naked girl stared at a man who stood in front of her. Sandrine could clearly see how tortured and humiliated she was, and she cursed silently that the guy had his back to the camera. Size and stature could be determined, but it was impossible from this perspective to positively identify him. She'd seen enough and put the photos back. She only kept the letter that was sent with the package.

These pictures were taken by Philippe Chardon. He abused your fiancée in his office. It was signed, *A Friend.*

"Someone is calling for revenge against your girlfriend's former therapist but the man is not visible in the pictures. What makes you believe what the sender is saying is true?" She herself was convinced that it was Chardon. The Japanese wood-print he had taken to his new practice hung on a wall, and on a dresser stood a reddish-brown wooden box, where he stored his calligraphy set.

"It's the man's office. I was there once to drop off a photograph he had bought," replied Duval. "I remember the copy of a sculpture by Rodin on his desk."

"You are an excellent observer."

"That's what my job entails." He pressed both hands upon his knees as if he was trying to stop them from shaking. "What will you do now?" He looked at her tensely.

"We'll ask him about the photos."

"For what purpose? You have to arrest that man. He ruined Aimée's life."

"First I need more evidence."

"What other evidence could you possibly need?"

"The photos aren't enough. Your observations are only evidence that they were taken in his former office in Saint-Brieuc but they are not incontrovertible proof. The man himself is not recognizable. The photos could have come from anyone."

"You can see from her eyes that she didn't do this voluntarily." He couldn't keep himself on the sofa. The man jumped up and paced back and forth in front of the window. Suddenly he stopped and looked at her. The pain of the loss was written all over his face.

"How can I help you take this man down? Aimée was definitely not the only one he molested."

"First of all, you absolutely must stay away from Chardon. He hasn't pressed assault charges yet but that could change quickly if you try it again or even come close to him."

"It's hard, but I'll do it. What else?"

"Consider carefully whether you can find out Aimée's password. Your girlfriend was a professional. Perhaps she'd already recorded a video naming Philippe Chardon as the perpetrator. That would help a lot."

"She is ..." He couldn't bear to say the word *dead*. "In that case, there would be two statements. Who would you believe?"

"Aimée," she said decisively. "Your statement plus these photos would be hard to refute."

"I'll think about it," he promised.

"Can I leave you alone now? Perhaps we can find someone to keep you company?"

"I'd rather be on my own."

"As you wish. I need to get back to the police station."

"These pictures," he added. "You promise that they won't be published, right?"

"We'll keep them under lock and key. However, I cannot prevent some of my colleagues from examining the photos and the envelope. Maybe we'll get lucky and find a useful clue."

"I have to live with that."

"I promise you we'll bring the man to justice."

Sébastien Duval remained silent, opened the curtains and looked out of the window to the sea, where the tide had gone out. Sandrine left him alone and went to her car.

"I have the pictures," she said to Adel on the phone. "Everything indicates that they were taken in his former office. Unfortunately the man himself is not identifiable in the photos. Is he still in the hospital? Okay … then we'll meet in front of Chardon's house in Saint-Malo. I'm curious what explanation he's going to offer us." She ended the conversation and started the duckling's engine. She wouldn't need more than a half hour, even with the slow car.

* * *

Adel was waiting in front of the property. He leaned his hip against his car's fender as he looked at her. "You actually left Duvall in Saint-Lunaire?"

"He won't do anything stupid and definitely won't attack Chardon again. I gave him a thought-provoking task that will keep him distracted and busy at the same time."

"The psychiatrist has refrained from filing a complaint so far."

"The pictures are in the car. He can't be identified, but there's much to suggest that they were taken by him. He's likely more concerned about his freedom and wants to keep the police away as much as possible."

"After the fight, he cancelled all his appointments and did not return to his office. His car is not in his driveway and there's no movement inside the house. Looks like he's not here."

"Is he answering his phone?" Sandrine asked.

"It's turned off. If I were in his shoes I would have already thrown it into the sea."

"You think he's gone into hiding?"

"Hard to say. Since he's not recognizable in the photos, a good lawyer could get him out of this. But his reputation as a psychiatrist would be ruined."

"As long as we can't prove anything right now, we should consider the possibility that he's innocent. Just because he's an arrogant snob doesn't mean he's a criminal. First François Deloir was accused, then shortly afterward Philippe Chardon. Someone is playing a game with us, and I don't know who and to what end," she said. *Maybe he hoped that Duval would kill Chardon.* Sandrine's phone rang. It was Commissaire Matisse. "Yes ... in front of Chardon's house. What about the search warrant? ... No, the man is not indisputably recognizable in the photos, but now he seems to have gone into hiding. I assume that he's evading questioning and perhaps even on the run." She walked up and down in front of Adel's car, while she listened to her boss. "Then we'll wait," she said and ended the call.

"Anything new?"

"Matisse is going out on a limb with Lagarde. The fact that Chardon disappeared makes him look guilty. This should be enough for a search warrant, he hopes."

"What do we do now?"

"We make sure that man is not in the house." She stepped up to the property's gate. Behind it was a white block of concrete and glass, an eyesore in this neighbourhood of old Brittany villas. Twilight was upon them, but apart from a light over the door, the whole house was dark. Sandrine pressed a button on one of the angular concrete columns that framed the gate. Nothing happened. She grabbed the top of the gate and jumped over.

"We can't just ..." Adel started to protest.

"The search warrant is on its way and there's danger in delay," she insisted. "We have to at least look inside."

"What kind of danger? There's nobody home."

"Chardon's crimes have been discovered. He is ruined professionally and he's terrified of doing a long bout in prison. I think it's likely that this man is toying with the idea of killing himself. We definitely have to prevent his suicide."

"That guy? He might do anything but surely not ..." Adel

hesitated. "When I think about it, it seems somewhat understandable." He climbed over the courtyard gate and followed her.

"I'll ring the doorbell, you look around the back yard."

"No monkey business!" he couldn't resist saying, before he turned and disappeared behind the house.

Sandrine pressed the doorbell with her index finger. The sound of a Japanese bamboo flute surrounded her. *Nice ringtone,* she thought while waiting in vain for a sign of life. Chardon must have made the decision to immediately vanish after Duval confronted him with the photos. Did he use the intervening time to pick up a few things and make possible evidence disappear? That's what she would have done in his place. Sandrine took a step back and examined the house. Upstairs, a window seemed to be slightly ajar. She looked around. No one was in sight.

With the lock-picks she always carried with her, she could open the front door with no problem but in the short time she had, she probably wouldn't be able to switch off the alarm system before it activated. There was a sign on the door with the name of the security company which would show up if the alarm went off. Philippe Chardon probably hoped that this would deter possible burglars. The open window was tempting but she decided to wait. Her illegal intrusion into a suspect's Paris home had earned her a demotion and pending disciplinary proceedings. She wouldn't make that mistake again. Her phone vibrated: a text message from Inès. The examining magistrate had approved the search warrant for his home but not for his office.

"That's good enough for right now," she muttered. Sandrine pulled herself up to the roof of the garage attached to the house. The down pipe of the rain gutter seemed stable. Nevertheless she shook it to be sure. *It'll take my weight.* With both hands on the pipe and her feet pressed up against the wall, she climbed to the upper floor. The window was slightly ajar. That meant that on this floor there was either no alarm or it was not armed. With one hand, she continued to cling to the pipe and with the other she pushed open the window. No sound. She exhaled with relief. With a little momentum, she made it onto the windowsill and climbed into the house. An unused bed stood at the shorter wall opposite the bedroom door. A guest room, she guessed, and at any rate, she didn't recognize any personal belongings that would indicate that this was Philippe Chardon's bedroom. The hallway ended with a free-standing staircase without a railing that led to the ground floor. She went down, turned the light on and opened the porch door to the garden.

"How did you get in?" asked Adel. "Oh, never mind, I don't think I want to know." She stepped aside and let him in.

"Mazet and his people are on the way. They're bringing the search warrant with them. We're perfectly legal here."

"Good to know," he answered her succinctly. The brigadier hated it when she freely pushed the boundaries of legality.

He walked a few steps further and looked around. Heavy wooden partitions hung on the perimeter walls of grey exposed concrete, allowing areas of the home to be partitioned off as needed, but for now they were all folded together and the lower floor formed a single coherent living space. Through the floor-to-ceiling glass fronts, the last light of day fell onto the reddish-brown parquet floor.

"I'll look down here," she said. The kitchen area was meticulously tidy. She pulled on some gloves and opened the dishwasher. A plate and a cup were inside, along with croissant crumbs and blobs of jam.

Therefore, Chardon had had breakfast alone.

She heard Adel's footsteps on the stairs on his way to look around. She decided to take a look at the man's desk. The chair was comfortable and rocked under her weight. The desktop was scrupulously clean and bare except for a writing pad, a pen holder and an external DVD drive. The corresponding laptop was nowhere to be seen. Either Chardon had taken it to work or had picked it up when he decided to flee. She opened up the drawers. Just writing stuff and paper. In the lowest drawer were more beige envelopes, like the one that the courier had delivered to Duval. She picked up the top one and poured its contents onto the desk: documents, application and invoices. Nothing that interested her. Certainly no incriminating photos.

"Found anything?" Adel asked, coming back downstairs.

"Not so far. The guy took his laptop. I would've liked to have that," she sighed. "Chardon was in the house after the fight. Everything is neat and tidy except for socks and a T-shirt on the bedroom floor. The man was here, rushed to collect some things then fled. Something must have really frightened him."

"Probably Duval, confronting him with the existence of the photos."

"The question remains: who gave the pictures to Aimée's boyfriend? Our psychiatrist certainly didn't."

'I can't offer more than a vague theory.'

"Let's hear it."

"Chardon and Petitjean were friends for decades. Aimée Vilette's photos look as though they were taken in secret. Maybe Chardon needed help installing the camera and who could do it better than a photographer like Petitjean? He may have copied some of the pictures either for his own perverse pleasure or to secure the possibility of a later source of income."

"Are you talking about blackmail?"

"It might be hard to prove but I found something that could help us." The brigadier placed a black leather mask and a whip with a short handle on the desk. "This stuff was in the back corner of his wardrobe, the first place every half-way experienced police officer looks."

"Well, weird but not illegal."

"In addition, they're the same brand as the gag that was shoved into Dominique Petitjean's mouth. There was also a pack of cable ties among his socks."

Sandrine whistled softly. "I'm sure Mazet's crew can find out if these things belong to the same person. This could link him to Petitjean's murder."

"Perhaps the theory of blackmail between old friends is not so absurd after all."

"Chardon assumed he had gotten rid of his accomplice with the murder. No wonder he panicked when Duval showed up at his practice, knowing about the photos. Slowly, the puzzle pieces are coming together. But we're still missing the laptop. I'm sure that the footage of the murders is on it."

"It's nine o'clock. We can forget about having an evening off."

"Sorry, did you have plans?"

Adel smiled with embarrassment. "I had arranged a witness testimony meeting which doesn't have to take place at the police station."

"How officious of you. Even in your spare time." Sandrine shot him a wide grin. "I suppose this is about the testimony of the neighbour, Geneviève Drouet. Yes, she had some holes in her story. I'm glad you're willing to do this, it saves me a trip."

"I thought you'd see it that way. After all, you took it upon yourself to interview the owner of Club Équinoxe after hours."

Sandrine's smile disappeared. "Have we really come so far that we can't separate our work from our private life?"

"Occupational hazard for police officers, I'm afraid."

"I'll stay here until Mazet and his people show up. You can

make a quick getaway, we'd both just be standing in their way anyway. And remember, women love romance."

"Romance is my middle name. But what are you planning on doing?"

"Our colleagues are scouring the city for Chardon. I'll pay a visit to the man's friends and see if he's shown up there."

"You could just call. That would be easier. Besides, nobody has to let you in without a search warrant."

"I want to look them in the eye when they answer, that's enough for me right now. The guy's somewhere and he's probably with one of them. I want Chardon to know we're looking for him. The more pressure, the more likely he'll make a mistake."

"Good luck."

The doorbell rang. Through the glass pane she recognized Jean-Claude Mazet. She told him to come through the back garden because she hadn't found the house key or the code for the alarm system yet.

* * *

Grégoire Argent opened the door. He was dressed casually and elegantly, as if he intended to go out. Although honestly, she had never seen the man dressed any other way.

"Lieutenant Perrot, what an unexpected surprise," he greeted her.

"Really?"

"Of course. I thought I already told you everything I know about this terrible incident."

"Incidents," she said, correcting him, emphasising the "s" at the end of the word. "May I come in?"

"Of course, how inattentive of me." He stepped aside and let her walk past.

"Let's go up the stairs. This villa is both my home and workplace."

"I imagine there's still a lot of work to be done on the eve of a major publication."

"Oh, yes, work rarely lets up, especially for us smaller publishers." He went up the stairs in front of her and led her to a living room on the top floor. Two opposite windows were open and the gentle breeze made the leaves of a book on a table flutter. He smelled slightly of sweet tobacco smoke. The man offered her a seat on a dark brown Chesterfield sofa.

"Something to drink or are you on duty?"

"I'm driving, so I must refuse."

"Then at least an espresso so you don't fall asleep while driving. I can't let anything happen to Rosalie's dear friend. She would never forgive me." Without waiting for an answer, he went into the kitchen. A short time afterwards, he came back holding a dainty little cup. He poured himself a cognac in a bulbous glass and took a seat in the armchair opposite of her.

"Thank you." She put a sugar cube in the thick foam that covered the espresso and watched it sink in, slowly disintegrate and disappear.

"I assume this is a business visit. How can a simple publisher help you at such a late hour?"

"You are friends with Monsieur Chardon."

"Philippe." He swirled his glass and gazed at the amber liquid running down the sides. "Since ancient times, but you know that."

"Just like Odette Marchal."

"I assume you are a conscientious investigator and know her biography."

"Just in broad strokes."

"She was the most alive of all of us. Any room she entered, she lit up like a star." His voice seemed to come from afar, as if he were remembering better times. He sighed and took a long, deep sip. "It happened the way it had to. She was greedy. Too much of everything. Alcohol, drugs, parties. On top of that, an almost self-destructive tendency to date the wrong men. Odette disappeared at some point. I didn't know what had happened to her. After ten years she suddenly appeared at my door. Like a new person. With a manuscript that inspired me."

"Not just you, so I've heard."

"That's right. She crawled out of the darkness and found her way into the sunshine."

"Did you or Chardon ever have a relationship with her?"

"No." He shook his head. "I certainly didn't. Odette probably found me to be too boring."

"Did she think Philippe Chardon was also boring?"

"I would guess not. He was her saviour when she went wild again. His family is extremely wealthy and has a lot of influence in this area."

"She sank his boat, so I've heard."

He laughed quietly. "Yes, she did. High on his pills, she hit the sea wall with full sails." He shot her an amused look. "But that's all long gone now. I don't want to get anybody in trouble."

"Chardon must have been angry."

"He just laughed. A wonderful story to share at parties is more important to him than the cost of repairing the boat. His insurance company probably paid for the damage anyway."

"Did he have a relationship with Odette Marchal?" she said, coming back to her question.

"Not that I know of. Rumour has it that he has a preference for younger girls. It would be best to ask Rosalie. As far as I know, he arranged to go sailing with some of her friends."

"Younger girls? How young?"

"No idea. Dominique teased him about it sometimes. That was one of the few things that could really annoy him."

"The way you describe Philippe Chardon, I have a hard time imagining the man taking up a profession to help other people."

"We felt the same way back then. We were thoroughly amazed. Why are you asking about him? Did something happen to him?"

"We're looking for him, but unfortunately he's disappeared. He's suspected of having been involved in the murders of Aimée Vilette and Dominique Petitjean."

"Philippe?" He stood up and looked at her in amazement. "I can't imagine that. Dominique was his friend."

"Why not? Wasn't he capable of violence?"

The publisher sipped his cognac, held it in his mouth for a moment.

"Philippe is capable of many things," he finally said. "But he would never kill anyone."

"He didn't strike me as a pacifist."

"Don't get me wrong. He would stop at nothing when it came to saving his own skin, but he wouldn't do it himself. Philippe has the means to leave that type of thing to others."

"Are you talking about a hit man?"

"I don't know much about your work, but yes, that's what I would call it."

"Has he contacted you during the course of the day?"

"I haven't heard from him in a while, let alone seen him. In fact, I was hoping we could use Odette's book launch celebration to meet up and chat about old times."

"Then he didn't come here to hide from the police?"

"Not at all," he said without hesitation. "But I understand if you're suspicious. It's part of your job. If you want to, you are welcome to look around. This house isn't especially big."

"That won't be necessary. I take you at your word." She stood up. "I won't disturb you any further."

"Have you already been to Odette's or is a visit to her the next thing on your list?"

"What makes you think of Madame Marchal?"

"Isn't it obvious? You're searching for Philippe. What better way than to canvas his old friends?"

"I seem to be easy to read."

"You are logical, and that is quite understandable. In addition, I occasionally publish crime novels. As an old-fashioned publisher I read my authors' books, and don't leave that job solely to the editors."

"Does Madame Marchal live nearby here?"

"Everything in Dinard is close by. She lives in a villa just above the Plage de l'Ecluse."

"A posh neighbourhood."

"She can afford it."

"Then I hope her new book will be as successful as the last one."

"Thank you. We are very confident." He looked at his watch. "I'll take you to the door."

* * *

The buzzer sounded and Sandrine entered the building. On the second floor someone opened the door and waited for her.

"Good evening, Sandrine. Nice to see you again." Wearing a gold-coloured kimono, it was evident Odette Marchal had no intention of leaving the house. She stepped aside and let Sandrine in.

"I'm assuming that Monsieur Argent has told you to expect me."

"That wasn't a question, was it? So no need to deny it."

"You opened the front door without asking my name. So you knew who was ringing your doorbell."

"How careless of me. Rosalie warned me about how clever you are."

"A warning would only be appropriate only if you had done something wrong," replied Sandrine.

"My God, who hasn't?" She pointed at a sofa with a chaise lounge that covered the length of the living room. "Take a seat." Odette sat down, sinking deep into the soft cushions. "I am a more mature woman now, but not everything that I did in the past would have pleased the police."

"Are we talking about parking violations or something more serious?" Sandrine sank on the other end of the sofa, realising it would be hard to fight your way off it and still look halfway elegant.

"Why would you think that Philippe would try to hide here with me?" she asked, changing the subject.

"Because you're friends."

"That was a long time ago. Now, I would rather describe our relationship as a sentimental acquaintance. We've hardly seen each other in the last few years."

"When was the last time you had contact with him?"

"We met earlier this week in Saint-Malo for coffee and to chat about old times. I realized then how old we've become and that we don't have much in common anymore. Philippe and I live in two different worlds."

"Did he talk about the incidents of the last few days?"

"Do you mean Aimée Vilette's death? Only marginally. He mentioned that he knew her briefly. When he lived in Saint-Brieuc. But that was more than ten years ago."

"If I can be indiscreet: have you ever had a relationship with Monsieur Argent or Monsieur Chardon?"

"Very direct and exceptionally indiscreet," Odette replied, smiling. "To satisfy your curiosity: no. I love Grégoire for other reasons and as far as Philippe goes, I'm not sure whether he is interested in women. At least, I've never seen him with a girlfriend."

"You are close to Monsieur Argent, otherwise he would never have picked up the phone immediately after I left his house."

"That's always been the case. He believes that he must protect me from this evil world and won't forgive himself for having failed to do so in the past."

"Has he?"

"Like any good friend, he glorifies my character flaws. Nothing and no one could have protected me from myself at that time. Especially not him. He was entirely too nice but also a weak person." With a dismissive gesture, she seemed to want to banish the thought. "That was a long time ago. Today, we're best friends and business partners."

"Does he feel the same way?"

"Ask him yourself. Only he can give you an honest answer. But you're not here because of my relationship with Grégoire, but to see whether I've hidden Philippe from the police under my bed?"

"That is correct."

"Take a look around. But you won't find Philippe here."

"That won't be necessary, I don't think you're lying to me," said Sandrine. If the woman was trying to hide this man, she certainly wouldn't do it in this apartment.

"Why are you looking for him? Did he have something to do with these terrible murders? Grégoire implied something along those lines."

"We want to talk to him about that."

"I just can't imagine that he would kill Dominique. The two – as unequal as they are – used to be quite inseparable. I can't remember them doing anything individually."

"There are things that make him look suspicious presently.

221

We're looking for him to give him a chance to speak up," said Sandrine carefully. She had no intention of revealing her knowledge of the photos of the abuse.

"I'm sorry that I'm unable to help, but I will call the police if Philippe contacts me. I promise."

"Thank you. I can't expect any more than that." With both hands, she braced herself on the edge of the sofa and struggled out from the cushions. "I heard that Arianne Briand asked you to participate in her radio show."

"The program director of the local radio station? Yes, she did. She has an engaging nature. I said yes to her. Thursday evening, I'll answer her questions. You should do the same. Us women are often too muzzled in this society."

"I'll think about it." Sandrine said good-bye. Odette Marchal walked her to the door and stayed there until she left the house.

Thus far, her search for Philippe Chardon had been in vain but she had learned a lot about the relationships within the clique. *I don't know whether this will get me any further*, she thought as she got into her car.

A Night Meeting

"How did the interview with Mademoiselle Drouet go?" Sandrine asked her assistant when she saw him in the office the next morning.

"Very pleasant, but unfortunately no new information for the case."

"How unfortunate but also quite predictable. Perhaps our colleagues will have been more successful."

"Matisse called, he's on his way. The boss expects results."

"Then we won't disappoint him." She waved at Brigadiers Dubois and Poutin to follow her into the conference room.

"Did you call Mazet?"

"Already done. He should be here soon. And the doctor sent a preliminary report that Inès put on your desk."

"I'll take a peek while we wait for the rest of the team."

At that moment, Matisse and Mazet came into the open office together.

"Well, I guess I'll have to postpone that."

"How does it look? From what I've heard, we've found the perpetrator," her boss said in greeting.

"We can connect him to the abuse but whether we can

connect him to the murders remains to be seen. I hope the forensic department has evaluated the most important evidence."

"I hope so too. I put some pressure on Lagarde to apply for the search warrant. If Chardon isn't our perpetrator, then I'll owe the man a big favour and that's not something I would relish."

"We're getting closer to the answer. The prosecutor will soon be able to hold his press conference and name a perpetrator. Then you're even."

"I hope so," Commissaire Matisse grumbled and sat down.

After sharing last night's event with the rest of the team, she pinned a photo of Chardon on the bulletin board. "At the moment, this man is not the only suspect but our prime suspect. He and the first victim know each other from her time in therapy at his former practice in Saint-Brieuc. We know he lied about his relationship with her several times. On Thursday, before the crime, a credible witness observed a dispute on the street between him and the victim which he ultimately admitted to. We assume that he sexually abused the then-underage Aimée Vilette. This is supported by the photos that an anonymous sender sent to Sébastien Duval, Aimée's boyfriend. Although he cannot be identified for certain, Chardon's escape speaks for the authenticity of the photos. After the conversation with her stepbrother, we are currently assuming that the bombshell which she was referring to is the disclosure of the abuse at the hands of Chardon who wanted to prevent this at all costs and may have used violence to silence her. It seems to us that Dominique Petitjean was privy to and perhaps even involved in the abuse. The anonymous sender could have easily been him which was reason enough for Chardon to get rid of him. That's our theory so far."

"Unfortunately, we can't go any further with just a theory.

The man's family is very influential in this area and his lawyers will tear us apart if the charges are not watertight," Matisse declared. "As of yet, we can't conclusively prove either the abuse or the murder."

"Then why would he have run away?" Poutin asked.

"To visit his rich aunt somewhere in the country and recover from the fight. Completely irrelevant. The man isn't guilty of a crime just because he isn't sleeping at his home. We can't even prove that he knows we want to speak to him," Matisse growled at him.

"Let's look at the results of the forensic medicine and the clues that were found at the crime scene and at the house," Sandrine decided and nodded to Inès, who had a copy of the report from Dr. Hervé in her hands. "I haven't been able to read it yet, but could you give us a brief summary?"

"Of course. Dominique Petitjean's blood alcohol count was two and half per thousand. The results of his toxicological study will take up to two weeks more."

"Good job. The guy was probably barely standing even when he was conscious," Dubois interrupted. "Wouldn't have been difficult to drag him onto the bed and tie him up."

"Due to the special shape of the gag, a large part of the oral cavity was filled. When he vomited, as we had already suspected, he died of asphyxiation," Inès continued.

"External interference triggering vomiting?" asked Matisse.

"Dr. Hervé believes that one or more blows to the abdomen may have triggered the vomiting response. But he won't be able to give more details until after the full autopsy."

"What about usable evidence at the crime scene?" Sandrine turned to Jean-Claude Mazet.

"Much too much. In contrast to the first victim's apartment, the guy's apartment hadn't been cleaned in a long time. The apartment is teeming with fingerprints and DNA of different origins. This will take a while. I hope you didn't sit on this guy's couch because under UV-light, it looked really, really disgusting. I put on two pairs of gloves before examining it more closely."

Adel wiped his hands on his trousers and Sandrine was sure he would take them to the cleaners after work.

"The cable ties with which he was tied to the bed posts are identical to those used in the first crime. I bet they came from the same package."

Sandrine pinned Aimée Vilette and Dominique Petitjean's photos side by side.

"I'm assuming the murders were committed by the same person. Both knew something about the perpetrator that wasn't allowed to be made public under any circumstances. Either he was afraid of the police or of losing his reputation," Adel said.

"Mademoiselle Vilette had a special Sunday evening broadcast planned during which she wanted to make her story public. But why was Petitjean silenced? If he was aware of the abuse, he would have made himself liable to prosecution. He couldn't have had any interest in Chardon having to answer in court. He would have had to sit next to him on the prisoner's bench," Dubois said.

"Perhaps he found out who was behind the first murder," Matisse suggested. "After everything we've learned about this guy, I believe he was dumb enough to blackmail the wrong person."

"That would in turn point to our psychiatrist," replied Dubois. "The two have been friends since their youth. He knew the man's financial circumstances and could not have imagined that he would kill him. Chardon waved money at him, they met and drank a sip or two to their deal. Petitjean had way too much and that was it for the guy."

"The question is: what did Dominique Petitjean find out

that we're overlooking?" Sandrine looked around but all she got were shrugs. "I don't understand the role of the VHS tape," she said, breaking the silence. "We found it in the apartment on Rue de la Cloche and Aimée Vilette went to great lengths to view and digitise it. Unfortunately her encryption is too difficult for us to unlock. Petitjean claimed that she stole it from him."

"It's probably just a lie, like the title that we couldn't find," said Dubois, who had helped her search for the film.

"The man owned a lot of these old tapes and one was in Aimée's apartment. Why shouldn't we believe him?" Sandrine asked Dubois.

"Because he obviously lied to us," said Inès. "I wasted half a day looking for *Hot Desire Beyond Walls* without success. The film doesn't exist."

"Inès could be right," said Sandrine. "He didn't attach much importance to the theft until he mentioned it to us. He may have noticed something at that moment and made the decision to lie to us, in order to feather his own nest. The man was chronically broke. I guess money was more important to him than helping the police. And he must have had an idea how to make money with the video. Blackmail, perhaps."

"Did we find a cassette in Chardon's house?" asked Matisse.

"There was a dusty box in the basement. We haven't been able to sift through it yet. But Brigadier Azarou found something even better," said Sandrine. "The gag that was stuck in Petitjean's mouth matches the items hidden in Chardon's wardrobe."

Adel took out his cell phone and sent a photo of the black leather mask and short-handled leather whip to the projector. "These things are all the same brand and are usually sold in a set. BDSM Starter Set, so to speak. However, a leather collar with a metal chain is missing. We were able to find traces of an identical leather care product on all items which leads me to conclude that they were purchased together."

"Where do you get something like that around here?" Poutin grimaced in disgust. "Certainly not in Saint-Malo."

"Mostly on the internet or mail order. The closest shop specialising in these toys is in Rennes. I asked our colleagues to drop by and they texted me a few minutes ago." Adel swiped the display but couldn't seem to find the message.

"And?" Sandrine probed.

"Take it easy now. Ah. Here it is," he said. "The store in Rennes was the brand's leader. Those things are no longer manufactured. The company went bankrupt three years ago. Didn't sell so well."

"So those things couldn't have been bought very recently." Matisse nodded. "This is how we'll nail Chardon. No lawyer will be able to get him out of this."

"Add to that the fight with Aimée Vilette and a great motive. The man would have gone to prison for years if she'd talked," Adel agreed.

"There are still a few discrepancies," said Sandrine. "We must clear them up before we can close the investigation."

"And they would be?" Commissaire Matisse asked, clearly thinking they had enough evidence. She understood only too well that he wanted to close the case as soon as possible. Deborah Binet's talk about a serial killer in Saint-Malo had hit him in the gut.

"We can't prove that the photos were taken by Petitjean," said Sandrine.

"I was just about to get to that point. We discovered his partial print on the backside. Whether he sent them I can't say but that he held them in his hand, is certain," said Jean-Claude Mazet.

"Good work." Commissaire Matisse looked absolutely satisfied.

"Why did Dominique Petitjean send the photos to Aimée's boyfriend? He wanted to make money, not send Chardon to prison," Poutin wondered.

"Maybe he was planning on increasing the pressure on his old friend. The psychiatrist was not recognizable in the photos. Any lawyer could have easily saved him from an indictment, after all there was an identical accusation against François Deloir and neither of them could be proven," said Adel.

"Then there was no reason for Chardon to go underground," she said. "He could have calmly removed the evidence from his home."

"Maybe he didn't know which photos Petitjean had sent and panicked that he was recognizable," Matisse concluded.

"That may be so," said Sandrine thoughtfully. "I wish we had his laptop or at least the hard drive where he stored the photos. I don't believe Aimée Vilette was his only victim. He also meticulously recorded the murders. The recordings are most certainly on his laptop, too, if he hasn't deleted them yet."

"We're trying to get the server from his practice. However, this could take some time. It's all sensitive medical data, but it's like playing with fire – it's easy to get burned. But that would be an ideal hiding place. It would be enough to invent a patient and hide the photos behind it. He could look at the stuff any time he wanted without being noticed," said Adel.

"I will pass this on to the public prosecutor," Matisse decided. "Any objections?"

"The VHS tape is such a pain in the neck," said Sandrine. "I would like to ..."

"Forget about that thing. I'm sure it was a red herring that Chardon used to send us off in the wrong direction. We have enough evidence against the man, that his lawyers will not be able to save him. He'll spend the rest of his life in prison. And that would be really gratifying for me," Matisse said, decisively. The case seemed to be closed in his opinion, so now they just had to arrest Chardon.

"As you wish," said Sandrine. She knew her boss was right. They had enough evidence to convict him.

"How's the manhunt going?"

"A patrol car is posted outside his house, his family and his colleagues have been questioned, nobody has seen or heard from him since yesterday," said Dubois. "Maybe he's already fled from the area. He could be anywhere by now, even abroad. As a precaution, we dragged his boat into the harbour so he won't be able to sail across the channel to England."

"Well done. You and Poutin continue the search for the man while the rest of us take care of the paperwork," Sandrine decided.

Matisse nodded in agreement. Dubois was a very meticulous police officer who was predestined for such an assignment.

"I'll inform the prosecution. The sooner we can stop the talk about a serial killer, the better." The commissaire stood up and left, the remaining members of the team following him out.

Sandrine's cell phone vibrated and she pulled it out of her jacket pocket. It was Léon.

"I hope you're not standing right next to a corpse."

"I am on duty but there are no dead bodies in sight right now. What can I do for you?"

"By chance I'm in town and I was hoping to invite you to a nice long lunch."

Across the desk the keyboard fell silent as Adel tried inconspicuously to crane his neck and prick his ears without realising that he'd failed miserably.

"It's the Équinoxe Club owner and he's inviting me to lunch," she whispered conspiratorially.

"It's okay, it's not like I was listening," he said, defensively.

"It sure seemed that way."

"Nonsense. Anyway, I need the transcripts of Bergier's interrogation." He stood up and went into Inès' office.

"You seem to have some nosy colleagues?" She could vividly imagine Léon grinning.

"That's an occupational hazard among police officers, or an essential quality, depending on how you look at it."

"How about a well-deserved lunch break? Only if you're not presently tied up with the case."

"It's pretty quiet right now." She couldn't do much more than wait to hear from her colleagues regarding the manhunt, pathology and forensics while typing up reports, the thought of which bored her to death before she even started. "I can't do a long meal but coffee and a snack along the beach would be fine, if that works for you."

"Where?"

"I'll meet you in a half hour at Plage du Sillon."

"Agreed," he said and ended the conversation.

Sandrine lay her phone on the table and stored her pistol in her desk's lockable drawer. A walk by the sea was exactly what she needed and in good company at that.

* * *

Léon was sitting on a bench near the Brasserie du Sillon. It was nearing noon and the tide had reached its peak, pushing back the beach to a narrow strip and washing over the sandcastles of the children. The giant vertical logs which were sunk in the sand as breakwaters, stretched beyond the water's edge. Most tourists had packed their things and taken seats in restaurants and snack bars on the beach promenade.

"Great to see you." Léon stood up and gave her a welcoming kiss on the cheek. It seemed almost normal to her, even though she barely knew the man.

"How nice, you've already got our coffee."

"And two sandwiches." He held up a bag from Mullière, her favourite bakery. "*Paté de campagne* with butter, cornichons and a dab of dijon mustard."

"How do you know what kind of baguette I like?"

"I happened to run into Rosalie this morning at the Cancale oyster market."

"And she's got nothing better to do than tell you where I like to get my food from?" *Has it actually gotten to the stage where she gives men tips on how to score points with me?*

"You know how it goes, we're chatting innocently enough and unexpectedly end up talking about you. Pure coincidence. Besides, Rosalie and I have hardly any mutual friends that we can gossip about."

She stifled an ironic remark, actually flattered that he had bothered to track down Rosalie to elicit some advice. Although *elicit* was probably the wrong term. It felt more like a conspiracy. Rosalie made no secret that she thought it would do Sandrine good to fall in love again. From the looks of it, Léon seemed just right for her. She smiled at the thought. After all, her best friend had good taste in men.

"So now I get to enjoy a delicious baguette instead of a rubbery hot dog on the promenade." She sat down on the bench and took her shoes off. She rolled her socks up and stuck them deep in her shoes and tied them together with the laces.

"Would you like take a walk on the beach?"

"I want to feel the water and sand," she said as she rolled her trouser legs up.

"And when will that be?"

"As soon as the murderer sits in a cell and confesses."

"The serial killer running loose in Saint-Malo?" he asked.

Sandrine moaned softly. "There is no serial killer. This is nonsense, only conjured up to increase newspaper circulation."

"Are you sure?"

"One only speaks about a serial killer after a third victim is found. To my knowledge we only have two."

"One more victim could emerge," he replied as he took off his shoes, too. "Just be careful that he doesn't get you next."

"He'd better not."

"So the odds are against you coming to the barbecue on Friday night?"

"I think I can make it." They had as good as convicted Chardon. With each result that came in from forensics, the noose tightened around the man's neck.

"So you're hot on the man's heels?"

"You're not trying to pry confidential information from me, are you? If you are, then we'd sadly have to end our meeting."

"Nonsense. The less I know about murder and manslaughter, the more I like it."

"Then let's go." She picked up her paper coffee cup and the bag containing her baguette. From the promenade, stone steps led down the wall to the beach. She slung her shoes over her left shoulder. A wave of icy water ran over her bare feet and washed the sand away under her soles. Goosebumps ran up and down her legs and the soft hair on her arms stood up. She embraced the warm coffee cup and took a sip.

"It's really beautiful here," said Léon. "I love the sea."

She nodded and looked out over the water. Sea and sky merged on the horizon.

"Do you miss the big city?" he asked in a tone that sounded a little too casual.

"Paris?" Except for a couple of summer holidays in Cancale with her Aunt Celine or with her parents in the Côte d'Azur, she had spent her entire life in the capital. "Strangely, not as much as I had feared." She knew what he was getting at. "It's much easier to get a parking place here," she tried to joke, but Léon didn't laugh.

"I would be happy if you decided to stay here."

"Until I show up and raid your club for the first time, then you'd wish that I had moved on."

"I'm an honest business man, with a clean club and accurate bookkeeping," he exclaimed with mock indignation. "I look forward to a visit from you and your colleagues." He smiled at her. "I would have let you put a pair of handcuffs on me, too."

She took his arm and pulled him closer. It felt pleasant and somehow familiar to feel him so near to her.

"I don't know what I'll decide. Do I really want to spend the rest of my life dealing with criminals or being pushed around by politicians?"

"I can't imagine anyone pushing you around." His confidence in her felt good. "You've found friends here."

"You're talking about Rosalie and you, right?"

"We're at the top of the list I hope. And don't forget Lilou. I'm pretty sure she's starting to like you, too."

Sandrine's eyebrows shot up in amazement. If that was the case, the woman was incomparably adept at hiding it.

"You also have nice colleagues at work who appreciate you very much."

"How do you know that? Can you read minds?"

"I have many sterling qualities but not that. I don't have to. Inès Boni is one of the club's regulars. She likes to sit at the bar, watch me mix cocktails and has nothing against a little chit chat now and then. I got the impression that she somehow found out that I once slept on your sofa, which by the way, was way too small. In any case, she likes to tell me how likable and incredibly good at your job you are. If I remember correctly, she casually mentioned that you are single."

"She and my brigadiers are little chatterboxes, don't believe a word that they say." She decided to have a little chat with Inès. She had an office to run, not a dating agency.

"Don't get upset. They like you and are trying to convince you to stay in Saint-Malo." He turned his head to her. "Which I can totally understand, by the way."

"I'm a terrible person that you'll probably regret inviting to a romantic dinner. When I start talking about my job, all romance goes out the window."

"We'll start with our barbecue on Friday. If you don't feel romantic, you can gut the fish and get all bloody."

Sandrine laughed loudly. A larger wave slapped against her calves and soaked her trousers. Startled, she clutched Léon's arm to stay on her feet.

"You are welcome to hold onto me."

"I'll keep that in mind. But I'm not yet ready to make a decision. Multi-tasking doesn't work for me. As long as I'm on a case, I don't have room for anything else in my head."

"Then make an effort to catch this guy soon."

She just nodded. She hoped she would, even though her gut told her that she was missing something.

They stood for a while with their feet in the water, and Sandrine tried to imagine what it would be like to choose a life in Saint-Malo. But she didn't know if she was ready for that yet.

* * *

Her cell phone vibrated. Sandrine cursed and turned on her side. It was already past midnight and she was sleepy.

"What the hell ..."

She pulled the phone towards her and tapped the fingerprint sensor. The display lit up. Someone had sent her a text message. She didn't recognize the number.

I'll wait for you in Saint-Malo, by the tide pool at Bons Secours. I'll give you twenty minutes. Come alone. After that, no one will be able to reach me. Philippe Chardon.

"You son of a bitch." She jumped out of the bed, all fatigue gone and a load of adrenaline shooting through her body. Getting to Saint-Malo in twenty minutes would be extremely tight. The duckling with its 29 hp engine was out of the question, she wouldn't make it in that. She ran downstairs and grabbed the leather trousers that lay over the back of the armchair. She gave up searching for socks and put on her boots. As she walked out, she picked up her leather jacket and her helmet which hung on the wardrobe.

"Answer it already," she hissed into her phone, while she turned the key to the garage.

"Yes?" The brigadier sounded sleepy.

"Chardon is in Saint-Malo at that tide pool on the beach in front of the deceased's home."

"I'm on my way."

"Don't let him see you. No police presence. If he wants to turn himself in, just the two of us will do fine. Come quietly." She didn't give him the opportunity to answer, instead ending the phone call and putting the phone away.

A few seconds later, she raced her motorcycle out of the garage up the gravel-strewn driveway. The whole neighbourhood were probably cursing her but she couldn't take that into consideration right now. The last houses of Cancale were behind her and she stepped hard on the gas pedal. The machine jumped forward and the landscape raced past her.

The nocturnal country road in front of her was lonely and she drove her motorcycle to the limit. She had to brake hard at a sharp curve but now a long straight road lay in front of her and the speed gauge shot up. Marc Bergier's farm showed up on the side of the road in the glare of the headlights. She thought about the geese briefly, which she'd probably startled for a moment. *Someone else being chased out of their bed.*

Soon she reached the first houses within the city limits. A traffic camera flashed and she hoped that no overzealous police officers would give chase. Within sight of the city wall, she ignored the street and the roundabouts, instead shooting over the pedestrian area, past the children's carousel and the tourist office, directly through the Porte de Saint-Vincent in the old town. The facades of the narrow houses seemed to reflect and multiply the motorcycle's noise. She tried to suppress the idea of how many complaints the police would get tonight. The rear wheel spun under the damp pavement but Sandrine was able to get the machine under control and continued to race farther.

Instead of parking in front of the building on Rue de la Cloche, she decided to drive to Porte de Saint-Pierre. She drove through the city gate and onto the wide dock and stopped. At this point, it was fourteen or fifteen feet above the sea. The beach was covered in darkness. She switched on the motorcycle's high beams and directed the head light onto the beach. Low tide had begun and only the upper edge of the tidal pool broke through the surface of the water. No sign of Philippe Chardon. *He's playing with me again,* was her first thought. She took a look at her watch. She had just made it in the time limit the man had given her. So where was he?

At walking pace, she carefully drove her motorbike on the long, paved ramp down to the beach. On the right edge were the sail school's sport boats and catamarans. She kept an eye on them as she drove by in case Chardon was hiding in between them. At the end of the ramp, she stopped the machine and directed the headlight onto the beach. Suddenly, she stopped. Something seemed to be floating in the tidal pool. She shone the light over the water's surface. It looked like a human leg, floating on the surface.

"*Merde!*" she cursed loudly. Her helmet fell into the sand, her jacket and boots following. Sandrine ran over the beach toward the tide pool. Icy water splashed onto her bare feet and began to seep into her leather trousers. "Damn you, you bastard, you can't do this to me," she yelled. The first wave hit her hip. She hoped she could reach the man without losing her footing. The closer she got, the clearer the human outline became just below the water's surface. Had he not worn a light-coloured suit, he would have been invisible in the darkness. *Why are only the legs floating?* She grabbed his calf and tugged but the rest of the body moved sluggishly. He must have gotten caught somewhere, maybe on a rock.

Sandrine held her breath and dove down. It was indeed Philippe Chardon, floating head down in the water in front of her. He wore a leather band around his neck to which a metal chain was attached. She pulled it but something heavy held it to the ground. She fished a pocket knife from her trouser pocket and cut through the collar. The now-freed body moved upwards. Sandrine emerged and gasped for air.

As the man slowly drifted away, she grabbed his leg and pulled him back. She turned the body over onto his back and Philippe Chardon's pale face looked at her with cold eyes.

"You coward!" she yelled and hit the flat of her hand on the water in frustration. He had preferred death over being arrested. *So why did you send the message when you had no intention of waiting?* He wouldn't be able to answer this question anymore.

She dragged him to the beach. Mazet would be mad that she'd cut the leather collar but she had to try everything she could to save him. But she had come too late; he had made his threat and now was no longer available to anyone.

Someone ran down the ramp and the powerful light of a flashlight cut through the night. "Sandrine?" Adel called out.

"I'm down here." Exhausted, she dropped to the ground.

"I came as quickly as ... Is that Chardon?"

"We're both too late. He's dead."

"Suicide?"

"Seems obvious to me but that's up to Dr. Hervé."

Adel grabbed the dead man by the shoulders and dragged him onto the beach until the waves no longer reached the body.

"I'll call Mazet and the forensics team."

"They should close off the entire section of beach," she decided.

"Will do."

The brigadier took a couple of steps aside and phoned his colleagues. With the wind blowing in from the English Channel, Sandrine shivered and rubbed her hands over her forearms.

"They're on their way." Adel squatted next to her and handed her the leather jacket that she'd thrown in the sand.

"Look over there." She pointed towards the sailing school.

"What's that?" he asked and turned to look.

She quickly stripped off her soaking wet T-shirt over her head, dropped it on the ground and threw her bra behind it. She put on her motorcycle jacket and pulled the zipper up to her neck. *Now dry trousers,* she wished.

She wasn't particularly bashful but Adel wouldn't approve of his boss undressing in front of him.

"Didn't he want to speak to you? Why did he kill himself first?"

She handed him the phone with the text message.

"I may have been a minute or two late but from the looks of Chardon's body, he must have gotten in the water shortly after he sent the message."

"Actually he should have floated up in the salt water."

"He wore a collar. I couldn't see it but I'm guessing a weight was connected to the chain that held his head under the water. Have Mazet look for it. It probably matches the rest of the set we found at his home."

"So he was contemplating suicide when he left his house? Why else would he have taken the leather collar and left the other items behind?"

"Must have been," she answered thoughtfully. "We were on his heels. It seems obvious even though he didn't seem like the type of person that would put an end to his own life. Drowning yourself is not a pleasant death."

They left the body and went to the ramp. Sandrine wiped the sand off her feet with the wet T-shirt and put on her boots.

"Too bad they're closed," she said and pointed to the beach bar that was built against the wall of the ramp. "I could use a hot coffee right now."

"I'll fix you one at the station."

She twisted her mouth. Adel's coffee was so thin, you could see through it.

"You get Dubois and Poutin out of their beds and I'll explain to Matisse that we have a third body now," she suggested.

"All right." Adel steered the flashlight along the wall to the beach bar. "Something's there." He went over and knelt on the ground. "A travel bag," he cried. "Looks pretty expensive. Probably Chardon's."

Why would he carry luggage when he was planning to kill himself? That made no sense. She didn't believe in spur-of-the-moment acts and neither did Adel. Who would take a collar from a BDSM set he had previously used for a murder on a nocturnal trip to the beach? The deed was planned, that was certain, but nothing more. In the light of his flashlight she saw Adel digging into the travel bag and taking something out. He stepped toward her then sat next to her.

"It belongs to Chardon. His passport and laptop were in it, as well as this." He handed her two sheets of paper that looked like they came out of an inkjet printer. She lit it up and held her breath for a moment. "These are pictures from the crime scenes." One of them was Aimée Vilette tied on the table and the other Dominique Petitjean with the gag in his mouth.

"We have our murderer," said Adel. "Who else would carry these photos?"

"Why would he print them then put them in his travel bag?"

"Instead of a farewell letter? I call this a confession."

"It's possible."

"He killed himself because he sees no other way out, and leaves behind evidence we need for his conviction. So we would be sure to find them and they wouldn't be stolen by anybody, he sent you a text and ordered you here. Everything fits perfectly. He saved us and the court system a heck of a lot of work."

"So it seems," she said thoughtfully. She didn't like that the man had escaped arrest at all. Somehow, she felt deprived of her victory. He had slipped through her fingers at the last second and would never rot in jail, a fate he so richly deserved. She let the photos fall on the ground and leaned her back against the wall and stretched her legs. It was going to be a long night.

She picked up her phone and called Commissaire Matisse's number. "I'm so sorry to bother you so late, but we found Philippe Chardon's body ... No, we can't say for sure, he needs to be examined first but we're assuming suicide." She listened to her boss for a while and nodded several times. Her wet feet were getting cold and she wished she'd brought a pair of dry socks with her.

"Will do." She ended the conversation and stuck her phone in her jacket pocket.

"What did he say?"

"What can he say? The case appears to be solved and a dead murderer is less work than a live one." She sounded more cynical than she intended to be and she knew she was being unfair to her boss. The sight of the crime scene photos Chardon had taken turned her stomach. As if killing them both wasn't bad enough, filming them humiliated the victims even more.

"He's informing his colleagues and making his way here."

In the distance she heard police sirens quickly approaching. Sandrine looked up at the houses rising above the walls. Was it a coincidence that Chardon had taken his own life in view of Aimée Vilette's living room window? *More like another admission of guilt. The investigations in this case closed almost at the same time. Kind of fitting.*

Adel sat down next to her. All they had to do was wait on their colleagues and, until then, keep the crime scene secure.

On the Way to Rennes

There was a knock on the cell door. Sandrine opened her eyes.

"It's open," she cried.

Commissaire Matisse stepped in. "You've chosen an unusual place to sleep. How long have you been working?"

"No idea, maybe until three or four this morning. After that, it wasn't worth driving home." She yawned widely before she sat up. "I guess Mazet's people worked through the night."

"He sent most of them home this morning. At least the ones who were on site searching for clues. The lab tech is still working. He's on his way here. The rest of the team are waiting upstairs."

"Let me splash some water on my face, then I'll be there." She reached for her leather trousers that she'd hung up to dry. They felt damp and clammy and in some places traces of salt appeared. Even with the most careful waterproofing, they couldn't compete with a dip in the sea. *I'd better take these to the cleaners.* Sweatpants, a black T-shirt and a pair of Crocs that Inès had brought for her had to do for today.

"It's always handy to have spare clothes in the police

station," Matisse said, gazing at the bulging trouser legs that were rolled up to the knees. "You can't go in front of the press like that."

"Chardon wanted to meet me. I didn't have time to put together a suitable outfit."

"Don't do that again. I'd hate to scrape my best detective off a tree because she was driving like a maniac."

"What choice did I have? I had hoped to catch him before he disappeared, but unfortunately I interpreted his last sentence incorrectly. I didn't think the man was suicidal. I would have thought he was more likely to meticulously organise his escape so he could spend the rest of his life on a luxury island in the Caribbean without extradition agreements."

"You were wrong, that's not your fault. Inès spoke with Dr. Hervé on the telephone. Philippe Chardon was probably already in the water before you left your house. For a reason he can't tell us, he wanted you to find him." He opened the cell door and turned one more time towards her. "Good job, Lieutenant."

* * *

Inès Boni lay today's daily newspaper on Sandrine's desk. A report written by Deborah Binet took up most of the front page: 'Serial murder in Saint-Malo.'

"Looks like she got her big story. I suppose people are clamouring for this edition now," said Sandrine.

"The woman is utterly irresponsible, frightening inhabitants unnecessarily. Some of my friends are driving their kids to school and picking them up in the afternoon. I'm glad we were able to solve the case, even if the murderer wasn't brought to justice."

"We'll see as soon as the results of the investigation are in."

"Is there any doubt?" Inès sat down across from her in the brigadiers' work area.

"Suicide always raises questions. I prefer the confession of a living murderer, but even then some of them lie. It's incredible how often people confess to a crime just because they want to be in the limelight or believe that it's important to protect someone they care about." Sandrine ripped off the front page, crumpled it up and stuffed it into her boots sitting next to her desk. Salt water from her trousers had soaked them.

"By the way, Prosecutor Lagarde is already in the conference room. He's contemplating a press conference where he can present the perpetrator and reap the rewards of good press."

"I don't begrudge him that."

"I do. You solved the case and should get the credit."

"The team solved the case," she replied. "And I think we all deserve a strong espresso from your high tech machine after toiling all night."

The office manager laughed and nodded. "Already in the works. There's also breakfast for all."

"From the canteen?"

"No, from Mullière, your favourite, so I heard."

"You are an angel. If it wasn't against the rules, I'd give you a big hug."

"It's sufficient when someone acknowledges me every now and then. But you could do me a favour."

"I knew nothing's for free in this life," Sandrine joked. "Spit it out."

"You might want to consider going on Arianne Briand's show to talk about your work and your career. That would be especially motivating for a lot of young women. Most of them are discouraged from joining the police department and we could use some more really smart women here."

At that moment, Prosecutor Lagarde stepped into the office and marched to the conference without greeting anyone.

"Of all the conceited chauvinists strutting around here," Inès said, ending her little lecture.

"I'll think about it. Arianne Briand is not unpleasant."

"Tough but just. She's one of the few who thinks before she talks."

"All right, once the case is thoroughly resolved, then you can tell her that I'm ready for an interview. But only if you come with me."

"Me?"

"You run the whole place with one hand tied behind your back, that's a real achievement."

Inès Boni nodded joyfully. She had probably talked with the local radio journalist in the last few days and offered her support.

Sandrine stood up and gazed at her feet. She would probably have to walk through the police station in those old Crocs for a little while. *Better than barefoot.*

"Then there's the application you have to sign," the office manager called after her. Sandrine ignored her. She was not yet ready to make a decision. First she had to close the case.

Prosecutor Lagarde and Commissaire Matisse stood in front of the bulletin board talking. Lagarde seemed to be utterly satisfied, at least nodding patronisingly to Sandrine as she entered the room and sat down at the table.

"The promised espresso." Inès put a cup full to the brim with several packets of sugar and a tiny spoon in front of her. Dubois winked as he shoved a basket of croissants and baguettes over the table.

"Our prosecutor is already planning his appearance in front of the press," he whispered to her. She didn't doubt his assessment of the situation and picked up an almond croissant.

"Thank you. How long were you at the crime scene?"

"Poutin and I just got back. He's downstairs smoking. While we were there, the mayor showed up and scolded us for closing off the beach until forensics could do their job. Crime scenes and tourism don't mix very well."

Lagarde ended his conversation and turned to the team. "On behalf of the public prosecutor I would like to thank you for your tireless efforts. Now that we've identified the perpetrator, we'll inform the press as soon as possible, so that the wild speculation about a serial killer can be put to rest."

Sandrine shot Commissaire Matisse a puzzled look. The man just shrugged. Nothing could stop the prosecutor from portraying himself to the press as a city hero. One would be more likely to stop a steamroller with bare hands than keep Lagarde off the front page of the newspaper.

Her boss stood up in front of the bulletin board. "Before the case can be considered resolved, we have to gather the facts and reconstruct as completely as possible the sequence of events." He turned to Lagarde. "The press will ask a lot of hard questions, so we should be prepared for them."

"Of course we should," the man agreed. From the disparaging expression on his face, the situation seemed totally clear to him.

Adel entered the conference room and sat next to Sandrine.

"I've spoken to Dr. Hervé," Matisse continued. "He now has three corpses lying on his tables. He couldn't give me more than a rough assessment of Philippe Chardon. According to him, his death occurred somewhere between midnight and the arrival of Lieutenant Perrot on the scene. He found salt water in his lungs—death by drowning. Chardon was alive when he stepped into the tide pool, which makes foul play rather unlikely. The blood alcohol level was just above one thousand. The man had been drinking but not excessively as was the case with Petitjean. Probably to give himself courage."

"Who wouldn't take a sip before killing themselves," Dubois commented.

"However, traces of an unknown substance were found in his blood. Dr. Hervé wouldn't officially utter the word Oxycodone, but ..." He did not end the sentence.

"Did he take the pills voluntarily or are there any signs of coercion?" Sandrine asked, whereupon the prosecutor gave her a dirty look. Since he wanted to close the case, he probably preferred to ignore critical questions or even doubts.

"There are no external injuries that would indicate he swallowed them under duress," Commissaire Matisse answered. "Which doesn't rule out the possibility that he took them without his knowledge."

"The man was a coward. He undoubtedly knew that he would go to prison for a very long time for two murders and repeated sexual abuse of a minor. He took the pills to make his suicide easier." Lagarde's tone became sharper with every word until he was almost spitting them out.

The door opened and Marie stuck her head in.

The colourful beads in her braided hair rattled together and headphones hung from her neck. "Jean-Claude sent me. He's busy in the lab but for questions that I can't answer, he's available by phone."

Sandrine waved her in. She had no doubt that the competent young woman would need no help from her boss. Jean-Claude Mazet had put together a very efficient team, but what was just as important: his people looked up to him. Otherwise, they would scarcely have pulled an all-nighter.

"We couldn't get more out of our doctor. The toxicological exam will take some time. Until then, we must work with what's available to us right now," Marie continued.

Lagarde sniffed at Marie, as if she was an intern who wasn't really needed in the lab.

"What can forensics do?" he asked her impatiently.

"The collar that the man was wearing came from the same set as the gag which was used in Petitjean's murder and the other things that were found in Chardon's wardrobe."

"He took it with him. That's clear," the prosecutor said, interrupting her.

"I present evidence, the conclusions are up to the investigators," she replied calmly.

"Thank you, Marie, that helps us," said Sandrine.

"How does that help us?" Lagarde asked, emphasising the word *us*. "Chardon packed it when he escaped. We assume he wasn't planning any sex games otherwise he wouldn't have left the mask and the whip behind, so he must have been contemplating suicide that afternoon."

Without replying, Sandrine signalled the technician to proceed.

"A weight was attached to the end of the leash. A twenty-kilo dumbbell to be exact. It's a brand you can buy in most sports stores, so that won't get us anywhere. Anyway, it was enough to keep his head underwater."

"Did the examination of his laptop reveal anything?" Sandrine asked.

"I found a hidden directory. Rather amateurishly laid out, in comparison to Aimée Vilette's computer memory, which we still haven't cracked. She wasn't his only victim. I found nudes of at least two dozen other girls. All minors, I would guess. At the moment, we are still denied access to his office documents, from which we could deduce their identities."

"The public prosecutor will apply for a decision from the examining magistrate," said Matisse, putting pressure on Lagarde.

"The photos that Brigadier Azarou found in the travel bag are authentic. I couldn't detect any photo-manipulation. They were definitely taken at the crime scene. As soon as the search warrant for Chardon's practice comes through, I can determine if he printed them there. I can exclude the printer in his house."

"Then we have all the evidence necessary to convict the man as the murderer of Mademoiselle Vilette and Monsieur Petitjean," Lagarde said, interrupting her once more. "Who else would be in possession of these photos if not the perpetrator? Or does somebody go around and distribute them like flyers across the city?"

"That would be a conclusion that is not in my line of work," Marie answered, which made the man's cheeks glow red. "Despite intensive research, I couldn't find similar crime scene photos on his laptop. I would have expected to find some in his hidden directory, but I couldn't. And I couldn't find the video recordings of the crime scene there either. If they were in his possession, then they must be on another storage medium."

"Maybe we'll find them on his office computer," said Adel.

"How do you imagine the course of events, if we assume that Philippe Chardon committed them?" Matisse asked her.

"On the condition ..." Sandrine began.

"That there are no doubts," the prosecutor said, interrupting her. The man was becoming more and more impatient and demanding. Maybe he was under tremendous pressure from his superiors.

"That there is little doubt," she corrected him. "Chardon recently moved from Saint-Brieuc to Saint-Malo to join a group practice. We can't say how he and Aimée Vilette met. What we do know is that they were watched as they fought fiercely and that after the argument she relapsed into a washing compulsion. Shortly thereafter, she announced a special local radio broadcast. In this broadcast, she intended to make the sexual abuse public, at least if we believe her brother. Chardon couldn't let her ruin him and possibly put him in jail. He sought her out then silenced her."

"'The mouth is the root of all misfortune'." Adel quoted the saying that the murderer had written on Aimée's stomach.

"Chardon distracted us with some leads to writer Pierre Salazar and his publisher Grégoire Argent as well as the farmer Marc Bergier."

"Ingenious," Dubois said. "But why Petitjean? The two were friends."

"Petitjean was – at least as an assistant – involved in the abuse. At some point, he probably realised that his buddy, Philippe Chardon, was behind the murder of Mademoiselle Vilette and tried to blackmail him," said Sandrine.

"Why did he send the photos to Sebastian Duval, the victim's boyfriend? It makes no sense." Everyone looked at Inès Boni who usually asked very few questions.

"That's not entirely clear to me either," Sandrine admitted. "I guess he was trying to increase the pressure on Chardon. In themselves, the photos were inconclusive, as the male who we suspected was the psychiatrist could not be identified. A similar accusation was brought against the victim's stepfather. It can be assumed that Petitjean was in possession of other photos, in which the perpetrator was more clearly identifiable. It had to be clear to Chardon that his old buddy would not hesitate to send them if he did not agree to pay."

"The man would have incriminated himself. Assisting in sexual abuse is also a criminal offence," Commissaire Matisse objected.

"He must have assumed that Chardon had much more to lose than he did. Petitjean would have denied everything and it would have been his word against Chardon's. Our photographer had a questionable reputation in Saint-Malo, which would be less damaged unlike that of the psychiatrist."

"The abuse photos had Petitjean's partial prints on them. We can also prove that they were definitely printed on his printer."

"That settles the blackmail," said Lagarde immediately. "Chardon silenced his accomplice as well."

"We're assuming that's the case for now," Sandrine agreed. "After Sébastien Duval attacked the psychiatrist, Chardon made his first crucial mistake and fled. If he had gone home to carefully destroy the evidence, we wouldn't have been able to prove much on him, probably not even enough to get a search warrant." She couldn't help taking a swipe at the prosecutor who had been protecting his golf partner.

"I suspect the collection of photos from years of abuse were too precious for him to simply delete," said Commissaire Matisse thoughtfully.

"Even after his escape, it would have been difficult to prove the murders. Without the discovery of his sex toys, we couldn't have proven a connection between him and the murder of Petitjean. I believe he killed his friend to shut him up, too. Ironically, right now it appears that Monsieur Chardon chose death-by-suffocation for himself, too and in front of Aimée Vilette's living room window," said Sandrine.

"Another clue to his guilt. With the files from his computer and the photos found in his travel bag, the case is watertight. We'll close the case now and this afternoon hold a press conference. Then Saint-Malo residents can calm down," the prosecutor decided.

"I would like to follow up on a few more leads to complete the investigation," proposed Sandrine.

"What leads?"

"I hate it when outstanding questions have yet to be

answered. I would love to solve the mystery of the VHS cassette."

"Which probably has nothing to do with the case," Lagarde insisted. "Leave the damned cassette alone and concentrate on making the charge waterproof. Your job now is not to introduce any more confusion. Do we understand each other?"

"Of course I understand," Sandrine answered. But that didn't mean she agreed with his instructions. Pressure from above only bolstered her resistance.

"Then my office will send out invitations to the press. This afternoon at three o'clock." Lagarde looked at Matisse and waited for his consent.

"We'll be there on time," he replied.

"It will be satisfactory if only you take part. The case is so clear that we don't really need Lieutenant Perrot. She's needed here more," replied the prosecutor.

Her boss threw her an interrogative glance and Sandrine nodded in agreement. She preferred not to play a part in this press conference.

"As you wish, Lagarde," Matisse said in agreement with the prosecutor.

"Then I'll see you at the prosecutor's office." The man stood up, dusted some imaginary lint from his suit and left the room without saying good-bye. His respect for the investigators had quickly vanished.

"Get to work," Sandrine told her team members. "And take the remaining croissants with you."

Shortly thereafter she spent some time alone with Commissaire Matisse.

"It was your investigation, why did you turn it over to this man?" Matisse asked Sandrine.

"Press conferences aren't one of my favourite pastimes. I would prefer to examine the evidence again. Lagarde is right about one thing: we have to ensure the case is absolutely water-tight," said Sandrine.

"Are you dissatisfied?" asked her boss.

"I hate investigations that don't conclude with a confession. Especially with suicides, there's always an element of doubt that nags at me."

"The case seems pretty clear to me."

"The prosecutor would agree with you. It's just ... an irrational gut feeling tells me that somehow I've missed something. I'm sure that feeling will pass soon."

"Have you thought about your future? Inès Boni has the transfer application, which is waiting for your signature."

"As long as I'm working on an unsolved case, I'm not ready to make a decision like that. Even what little private life I have is suffering as well. Now that the investigation is complete, I'll make a decision this weekend."

"Good. Your entire team would be happy to keep you here with us, including me. Our people appreciate you very much."

"Thank you."

"Now I need to prepare for the pack of journalists. I'll see you later."

On the way to her desk, Sandrine saw Marie who was talking with Inès. It appeared that the young female forensics technician had been waiting for her.

"Lieutenant Perrot," Marie addressed her.

"Yes?"

"I understand that we shouldn't be working on this any more but I know the feeling of missing something or forgetting something pretty well." Her bright white teeth flashed between her lips as she laughed. "Before I leave the house in the morning, I often check three times to see if the stove is actually turned off."

"So what are you trying to tell me?"

"The stain on the back of the cardboard sleeve of the cassette. After careful examination, it seems to be the blurred impression of a label. It probably got wet once."

"And how does this help us?"

"It belongs to a second-hand shop in Rennes. I looked around the website which is filled with garbage like those old porno videos. I don't think this is going to get us anywhere, but I at least wanted to tell you." She handed her a piece of paper with a handwritten address on it.

"Do you have any doubts about the man's guilt?" Sandrine asked.

"Me? No way. I think he's guilty. Nevertheless, I think he deserves a thoroughly exhaustive investigation just like anyone else."

"Thank you, Marie. I'll put it in my files."

"Glad to help."

Sandrine said good-bye. Out of the corner of her eye, she noticed Inès giving her friend a prompting glance.

"There's something else," Marie said hesitantly.

"No problem. I'm not in a hurry. Writing up reports is not exactly my favourite thing."

"I like working with you. I just wanted to say that. And Jean-Claude also appreciates you very much."

"Thank you, I'm glad to hear that. I feel the same way about you and your team."

"We would be delighted if you decided to stay in Saint-Malo."

"I'll think about it very seriously. Mademoiselle Boni will probably be the first to know." *And after that it would only be a matter of seconds before the entire police department knew, too,* she thought.

. . .

"You've been sitting at your computer for at least an hour now and haven't typed one word yet." Adel rolled his chair around the desk until he was sitting next to her. "You haven't even opened your software program. What's going on?"

She held the note that Marie had given her between her fingers and tapped the edge of the paper against her lower lip. "It's probably just the long night getting under my skin. I'm getting old."

Adel laughed. When his colleague turned to look at him, he fell silent for a moment.

"That's nonsense," he said gently. "You're up to something and I know I'm not going to like it."

"How much overtime have you accumulated in the last few days?"

"A bunch, why?"

She picked up her motorcycle boots and fished out the crumpled newspaper.

"Dry?"

"Yes. The case is solved, the murderer is dead and this afternoon our bosses will be holding a press conference."

"Correct."

"Then why the hurry?" She balled up the newspaper pages and threw them into a high arc into the trash. "Let's take the afternoon off. You heard the prosecutor, he doesn't need either of us during the press conference."

"You don't really mean that, do you?"

She turned her chair and looked at Inès, who was sitting in her glass-enclosed office. The woman looked up and Sandrine waved to her. The office manager got up and walked over to them.

"What's up?" Inès asked.

"Arianne Briand's weekly show, to which we've both been invited is tonight, right?"

"Correct. Every Thursday, at six p.m."

She looked at the clock which was hanging on the wall. It was approaching three o'clock. The press conference would begin soon.

"Who is today's guest? Odette Marchal, right?"

"Exactly. Her book came out this week."

"I will be off duty for the rest of the day. You should do the same, Adel. The paperwork can wait." She put her shoulder holster on and took the pistol out of her desk drawer.

"Why do you need a gun, if you are off duty?" Adel said, sounding worried.

"I'm going to talk my favourite bartender into giving me some free cocktails." She turned to Inès, who looked at her with an open mouth.

"Just kidding. Don't worry." She got up and pulled her keys out of her trouser pocket.

"See you tomorrow," she said to the office manager.

"What are you up to?" Adel sounded suspicious. He knew it was something he wasn't going to like.

"Nothing special. Have a nice afternoon but keep your phone on."

She picked up her motorcycle gear and left the office. In the restroom, she pulled on her leather trousers which were now halfway dry. On the way to her motorcycle, she tapped in Commissaire Matisse's number.

"We're on our way to the press conference. Did something happen?"

"Not yet."

"What are you doing?" His voice sounded halfway between curious and alarmed.

"Do you know that feeling when you have an itch on your back but you just can't reach it? It drives you crazy." She heard the man take several deep breaths.

"Then maybe just find someone to give you a hand. That shouldn't be too difficult for you. I've heard tales about an attractive club owner."

"Thanks for the advice. I would also like to give you some advice because I appreciate you very much."

"Hurry. Lagarde won't wait very long for me before he makes his opening remarks."

"Be careful about calling Chardon to be strongly suspected of murder, leave the back door open."

"Have you found any new evidence?"

"No. As I said, just a powerful itch."

"And this has nothing at all to do with the fact that you can't stand our public prosecutor?"

"Can you tell?"

"You're joking, right?" In the background she heard Lagarde calling for Matisse.

"Do both of us a favour."

"All right, I trust you but I don't believe I can stop Lagarde."

"I just want to prevent the police from looking incompetent." She ended the call and stuck her phone in her jacket pocket.

* * *

Sandrine took the four-lane road from Saint-Malo to Rennes. The wind blew back the hair that stuck out from underneath her helmet and the landscape flew past her. She was on the move but not going nearly as fast as last night. She didn't have much time, but should be enough. An hour later she stopped in front of the shop whose address Marie had given her. It looked more like a small warehouse; it was located in a commercial area on the outskirts of Rennes. In the shop window there were several loveless-looking dolls dressed in cheap plastic lingerie. A dusty spider web hung between two of them.

When she stepped inside, the doorbell announced her arrival. While waiting for a sales associate, she looked around. Boxes were stacked on shelves. Some had pictures on them, but most of them only had a label to indicate the contents. The shop seemed to specialise exclusively in cheap erotic items.

"Can I help you?"

She hadn't heard the thin, almost completely-tattooed man standing behind the counter come in. He crossed his arms in front of his chest and looked at her curiously.

"Lieutenant Perrot, police," she said, introducing herself.

"You think I was born yesterday?" he replied harshly. "There's a 750 BMW out there and you don't look like a motorcycle cop to me. Also we don't give discounts to police if that's what you're after."

"No discount? With such a wonderful selection? I'm incredibly disappointed." She pulled her police badge out of her back pocket and held it out in front of the man.

"Wow. In my youth the police looked way different. I guess the past wasn't always better."

"Glad to hear it."

"Still no discount," the man affirmed, stroking his bald head. "And this no place for someone like you. We just store cheap junk here."

"I'm guessing there's probably not a lot of walk-in customers in this shop."

"We sell surplus goods, discontinued models and goods from insolvencies. We sell most of this stuff over the Internet. A few people have gotten lost in the shop but I can count them on one hand."

"Do you have VHS cassettes?"

"Oh, yes." He nodded. "It's like vinyl records. I thought I'd have to scrap them all, but hey, they've made a real comeback."

Sandrine pulled out her phone and loaded a photo of the porn video that she'd found at Aimée Vilette's.

"I assume it's yours, or at least, it has your shop label on it."

He took the Smartphone and looked at the picture. "*Sinful Sisters*," he read aloud. "Yup, that's ours. For a little film from the nineties, it wasn't so bad. I really got into it. There's not much going on here in the shop, so you can get bored." He swiped the screen. "Hey, this one's ours, too."

"What?"

"Well, the SM stuff."

"Are you sure?"

"Of course. They went bankrupt and I took their stock in exchange for a sandwich from their bankruptcy administrator. A real bargain. It paid for my new kitchen."

"Somebody purchased these things here last week."

"I'm sorry, but I would have remembered that. During the week I wasn't selling anything and on Thursday I went shopping for new goods. Zuri ran the store alone. She's really good at it and she chats with everyone. I love that woman."

"Can I speak to Zuri then?"

"Not possible. Today she's in college. Examination in literary studies. Something about the influence of Hegel and Kierkegaard on the works of Simone de Beauvoir. But I don't know anything about that stuff."

"More than I do, that's for sure."

"As I said, there's not much going on in the store and she needed someone to foist her lectures on. Bits and pieces just stick with you, whether you like it or not. I'm not into that feminist stuff."

"Too bad she's not here, it's kind of important."

"She'll be back on Monday. It's strange but she really likes to help the police." He rubbed the silver nose ring in his septum thoughtfully. Sandrine decided not to ask the man why he thought it was so strange. She would probably have to come back here again.

"But if you have some time," he said, "maybe I can help you."

"I have time."

The clerk gestured to a corner behind a shelf. The lens of a nondescript camera pointed in their direction.

"A lot of idiots think a sex shop makes a lot of money and then try to steal from us from time to time." He bent down and picked up a baseball bat. "One look and most go away. With all due respect, you can't rely on the police so I live by the motto: if you want it done right, do it on your own." He hesitated, then a wide grin spread across his face. "Well, not in every aspect of life, if you know what I mean." He winked at her then laid the bat across the counter.

She knew all too well that he was alluding to his sexual preferences, where he probably made exceptions to the 'if you want it done right, do it on your own' rule. She wondered why he had gone into raptures about his like for cheap porn movies such as *Sinful Sisters*.

"Where can I see Thursday's footage?"

"In the office." He turned around and opened the door to a nicer storage space. There was a computer on a camping table. "The camera automatically streams to the hard disk. Just choose the day and approximate time, and there you go."

"How do your customers feel about being filmed?"

"What customers? I claim it's a dummy to keep the insurance company happy. So far, everybody's believed it." The man called up the video program. "Thursday, you say? That would be here. There's not much footage since the camera only records when the motion detector turns it on. Zuri claims that this is the newest technology." He stepped aside and offered her the worn-out chair. "I've got some packages I need to put together. The work won't get done by itself."

"I imagine so, since your most diligent worker is missing on top of that."

"Yes. But she'll be back on Monday. With some luck." The man had completely missed her irony. He left her behind and went to the shop that also served as a warehouse. She heard him open a box and the crackle of bubble wrap.

It didn't take long for her to stop the recording.

"There you are."

She leaned over the table and watched the figure standing in front of the sales counter. A woman with a hip-length braid put a cassette in a package that probably also contained the S&M toys. The printer was on and she printed the still image. Then she picked up the phone and called Marie.

"I have a recording from a surveillance camera that needs to be backed up. Can you arrange that? Exactly ... the address in Rennes ... Thank you."

Sandrine took the sheet out of the printer, looked at it for a moment and stuck it in her pocket. The camera was worth its weight in gold. Zuri had given her boss expert advice. The face was recognizable beyond a shadow of a doubt. A glance at her watch told her the press conference had already ended. She hoped Commissaire Matisse had taken her advice to heart and measured his words carefully.

She called Dr. Hervé in forensic medicine.

"The report isn't ready yet. I will contact you when the investigations are complete."

"I only have one question. Do you believe it was a suicide?"

"I will tell you as soon as I have Monsieur Chardon off the table and the results have come back from the lab."

"I just need a rough assessment based on your many years of experience. A gut feeling, so to speak."

"So far, suicide is still on the table. I haven't been able to detect any evidence of violent coercion and it's not uncommon for depressed people to take a sip of liquid courage beforehand or some sedatives. Miosis, narrowing of the pupils suggests the intake of opioids or barbiturates."

"How heavily was he under the influence of alcohol or drugs?"

"Just between us and completely confidential, I would say that he was lucky to have made it to the beach on his own two feet."

"Thank you. That helps a lot."

"Nothing that I've told you can be used in court. Remember that."

"I will. I'm just trying to get a feel for what happened." She ended the conversation, shut down the computer and sent a text message to Adel to meet her at the local radio station. She would make it back to Saint-Malo on time and finally close the case.

* * *

"Madame Briand is waiting for me," she told the man at the reception desk of the local radio station. She walked past him briskly.

"She didn't tell me about it." He jumped up and ran after her. "They're already on the air."

"Good. Then I've arrived on time. Where do I go?"

"Up the stairs to the second floor," he replied.

"Thank you." She left him behind and marched off. It was quarter past six, which meant the show had started fifteen minutes ago. Finding the studio was easy, as all the rooms were encased in glass. Arianne Briand and Odette Marchal sat opposite each other. There was a microphone between them on the table. The two women looked at her briefly. The journalist seemed to be more surprised than the writer, who gave Sandrine a big smile as if she had expected her visit. Rajiv Bhamra and Grégoire Argent sat in the control room, which housed the sound equipment plus other technology. While the young sound engineer and producer sat behind a recording console and several monitors, drinking from a thermos, the publisher listened to the interview with intense concentration. Not surprisingly; this year's balance sheet depended on the success of Odette's book.

"Oh, the woman from the police department. It will be a while before Arianne finishes this broadcast. Afterwards, she'll have some time for you," Rajiv Bharma greeted her.

"May I sit quietly in a corner? I promise not to disturb anyone but this interview is so exciting. I would like to get an impression of what's coming up next."

"Of course. Get yourself a chair."

Sandrine sat next to Grégoire Argent.

"Madame Perrot, what a surprise. Or has someone been murdered again?"

"Not that I've heard of."

"Poor Philippe took his own life, as Madame Briand told me. She was at the press conference and somehow missed you."

"Don't believe everything the press says. Or the police."

"You're right about that."

"Unfortunately, we must now assume that Monsieur Chardon was murdered, just like Aimée Vilette and Dominique Petitjean."

"That's awful," he said, giving Sandrine an irritated look. "That would mean that the killer is still at large."

"So one would assume."

"I hope you catch the guy before he kills more people.

Maybe there's more to the theory of a serial killer than I suspected."

"No one else is going to die now."

"Are you sure of that?"

"We know who committed the murders and will arrest that person sometime in the course of the day."

"Really?"

She took her handcuffs out of her jacket pocket and made eye contact with Odette Marchal. The woman held her gaze and Sandrine held the handcuffs up high. Madame Marchal dropped her shoulders and gazed at the table in front of her. She knew what Sandrine wanted. Arianne noticed Odette's distress and signalled Rajiv to pause for a long commercial break.

"Oh, no. This is a mistake," exclaimed Grégoire Argent. "Odette could never harm anyone. Out of the question. You can't arrest her."

"You love this woman, don't you?"

"Maybe in the past, but today we're just good friends and business partners."

"Your feelings for Odette never changed. You loved her so much that you would kill for her."

"I'm supposed to have killed someone?" he exclaimed.

The sound engineer turned to her and gave her a puzzled look.

"Would you please wait outside for a moment?" Sandrine asked him.

"I have to go to the restroom anyway," he replied. He turned off the sound for the control booth monitors.

"This is absolute nonsense. My life is literature. My only familiarity about violence is from reading and I usually flip past brutal passages," said Grégoire as soon as the sound engineer closed the door behind him.

"That's how you come across to others, or at least that's how you want to appear. For a while I believed the charade though my intuition told me something different."

"There's nothing that connects me to the murders. I hardly knew the young woman, why would I kill her?"

"To protect Odette, the love of your life."

He looked over at the writer and their gazes locked for a few breaths, almost as if they were having a silent conversation. The bond that connected these two people seemed pretty strong. Strong enough to kill for their mutual welfare. She wondered if he really knew Odette as much as he'd assumed.

"To protect her from what? She hardly knew Mademoiselle Vilette."

"You appreciate good stories, correct?" asked Sandrine.

"That's my job."

"A man I know well often claimed that several of his paintings hang in the Louvre, without anybody knowing about it."

"An interesting beginning."

"I always dismissed it as showing off until I came into closer contact with the scene of art forgers and thieves."

"That's what a cop's job entails."

That was before I became a cop.

Her father and Uncle Thomas taught her everything she knew about forgery and art theft.

"There are several types of art thieves. Some recognize an opportunity and decide to steal. With a little luck they'll snag a picture of great value, but that's when the real trouble begins. You can distribute money, cut a diamond, melt gold but how can you sell a picture that everyone knows is stolen? Difficult. Sooner or later, these people get caught by the police."

"And the other type?"

"These are the thieves who have already sold the picture to an interested party before the theft or who steal it on their behalf. They are perfectly prepared to bring a Trojan horse with them."

"I don't understand the connection."

"They exchange the real picture for a fake one. Generally, no one notices the theft and when they do, it's years later, when all evidence has long since been lost."

"This is how counterfeits reach the Louvre? Ingenious."

"That's exactly what our killer did. Mademoiselle Vilette went to great lengths to watch a VHS cassette that she had found at Petitjean's then stole it from him. My gut feeling told me that was the key to solving the case."

"An old film. That seems unlikely to me."

"You went to great lengths to leave clues intended to confuse us: an angry farmer who publicly threatened her, your friend, Pierre Salazar, whom the woman had humiliated, even Philippe Chardon whom she could have sent to prison. And then your Trojan horse."

"I have no idea what you're talking about."

"You needed the tape so badly, you were willing to commit murder. To mislead us, you purchased a substitute cassette, *Sinful Sisters*, in order to switch it with the cassette that Aimée stole from Petitjean, namely *Hot Desire Beyond Walls* featuring Madame Marchal."

"This is not only a very confusing theory but one that is equally unfounded."

She handed him the printout of the surveillance footage.

"Here you are buying the cassette you would ultimately exchange for the other after the murder. Just like the set the gag and collar came from."

Grégoire held the paper in his trembling hands and stared at it. It had not occurred to him that the shabby little shop could have a functioning camera. One of the few mistakes that the man had made.

"The owner could remember the title well. Exactly the same one that my colleagues had to watch. Of course, he wouldn't have seen anything that suggested a motive, how could he?" Grégoire let the paper fall on the floor and laid his hands flat on his thighs. His gaze returned to Odette Marchal. She must have suspected or even known that he was behind the murders as well as the reason for Sandrine's visit to the studio.

"It was a porn film that your dear friend was in, wasn't it? Did Petitjean only record the film? Or did he take a more active part?" *In any case, he claimed to.*

"Odette was doing pretty badly back then. She was a wreck, addicted to alcohol and drugs. She would have done anything to get money for her next fix."

"And did Petitjean take advantage of that?"

"He was a bastard, just like Chardon. They both deserved what happened to them."

"But Aimée Vilette – what did she have to do with it?"

"She happened to see the tape at Petitjean's. Odette was on the cover, so the woman must have noticed. She was curious and had a sharp mind."

"How did you know about the theft?"

"Odette had visited Petitjean and they chatted about old times. He joked that the clean-cut kid had stolen the film. He thought it was funny. Odette didn't think that much about it until she had an interview with another blogger."

"Carine Fortier?"

"I think that's her name. An uninteresting person. However she casually mentioned that her so-called female friend was planning on dropping a bombshell on Sunday. Odette assumed that it could only be about her and panicked. Sometimes she's convinced that the world revolves around her. Anyway, she came to me. Who would buy books from a children's book author who had once been a drug addict and involved in porn? Probably nobody."

"This would have been a huge loss for the publishing house."

"Oh," he waved, "it was all about Odette." He continued quietly, "It was always about her."

"You protected her."

"I tried but I failed. What happened in the past couldn't happen again. It took so much strength to dig her way out of the swamp of drugs and alcohol. I couldn't let her get pulled back in, which would have been inevitable when greedy people, like these bloggers, exploit the story in the media."

"You wanted to silence Aimée."

He turned to her. "What choice did I have?"

"Your planning was perfectly thought out."

"No." He shook his head. "It was a complete failure."

"Do tell."

"The young woman was amazed to see me but still let me in. Probably because I seemed trustworthy. It was easy to knock her down and tie her to the table."

"You recorded everything meticulously."

"Yes. At some point Odette had to know how much effort I had made to protect her. She had to see with her own eyes how much I loved her." He took a sip from the thermos. "The woman denied that the bombshell was about Odette's past. She didn't care, at least that's what she claimed. She wanted Philippe's abuse made public."

"Did you believe her?"

"Not at first. But she had photos of her and Philippe. Naked in his old office. It was obvious. He had several liver spots on his neck, which I recognized without a doubt. I couldn't go back and had to improvise. I hastily drew the Japanese saying with a black marker, not a work that did justice to the occasion."

"Aimée had these photos?"

"Dominique, the idiot, was dumb enough to send them to her so he could blackmail her. She was sick of him and threw him out. He believed that he could force her to employ him again and participate in her business. But he was only making her go on the offensive. The guy always had problems with strong women, just like Philippe."

"So you took both the cassette and the photos with you?"

"I was certain that Dominique, in a sober moment, would find the connection between Odette and this blogger, Aimée Vilette. So he, too, had to be silenced which wasn't difficult."

In that case, Petitijean hadn't been looking for the termination letter in her apartment but the photos that he had used to blackmail Aimée Vilette. That's why forensics found his fingerprints on both the desk and the photos.

"And Philippe Chardon? Why him?"

"I needed a murderer who the police could proudly present to the public. And the man deserved it. He got Odette into drugs. Without him, her life would have been so much happier. No, I'm not sorry about him. You asked me why a man like him would choose a profession to help strangers. All a facade, as you've already found out about for yourself. He was a predator. No, a scavenger. Philippe looked for victims that had been hurt and would show little resistance to his manipulations. It intoxicated him to dominate others, to make them do things they would have never done voluntarily." He shrugged. "The pictures say it all."

"You sent the text message to distract the police?"

"I wasn't afraid of the rest of the police force, but you are different. During our first meeting with Rosalie at the café, I got goosebumps. I knew there and then: if anybody would be able to discover my deception, it would be you."

She let the compliment pass without reacting.

'How did you get him to flee? He couldn't be identified in the photos. We couldn't have proven it was him."

"Not from the photos I sent to Mademoiselle Vilette's boyfriend but from other photos that I found at Petitjean's, yes. Duval's attack on him had shaken his self-confidence. He didn't know which pictures the man possessed and had turned over to the police. No wonder he panicked. What could be better than to call an old friend to ask for help?"

"He was in your home when I visited you?"

"No, in my boat on the Rance. He didn't dare go home, so he gave me his key to pick up a couple of things, which I gladly did."

"And you took the opportunity to hide things in his closet?"

"Of course. I offered to take him out of the country. Philippe was so exhausted that he didn't notice that the little pills that I gave him looked different than the ones I took."

"Where did you get the drugs from?"

"He had them with him. Philippe regularly prescribed opioids for his patients who were in pain, some of which he diverted to himself. What made you conclude that he didn't kill himself? It would be an obvious course of action in his case."

"You love literature and didn't send me a short text message. It had to be extravagant with correct spelling. Your mistake. At that time, Chardon would have been so out of it from the alcohol and drugs you foisted upon him that he couldn't operate the display on the mobile phone. At least that is what the medical examiner claims. Someone must have done that for him and that was the one who put the collar on him and pushed him into the sea."

"An old weakness. I can't keep it short and detest sloppy writing: incorrect punctuation, misspelling and bad grammar."

Someone knocked on the door. It was Adel, accompanied by two police officers in uniform. She waved them in.

271

The sound engineer came back. "It's too crowded in here. I'm sorry, I can't have this many people in my control room."

"Don't worry, we'll be gone soon." She handcuffed Grégoire Argent. "Can you take him to the police station?" she asked Adel.

"I will. What are you going to do?"

"I'll come by later."

Odette Marchal watched the men until they disappeared behind the staircase door. She remained silent as a single tear shone in the hard light of the ceiling fixture.

"I'm ready to continue, Rajiv," she said as she tapped her headphones.

"I'm turning the sound back on again," the young man said, pressing a switch.

Odette Marchal leaned back into her chair and made eye contact with Sandrine. Her deep exhalation could be clearly heard over the loudspeakers. Arianne Briand sensed that something unexpected had happened and held back her questions. Her guest needed to make the next move. Odette's voice filled the control room.

"We talk about strong women, Arianne, but what makes us strong? The career and prosperity we work so hard to achieve? Our status in society? Or are these things just a facade that we use to protect ourselves? The injuries that we have suffered or inflicted upon ourselves and which we have survived are the things that make us strong. The defeats which threw us into the muck and from which we arose again. Strength does not manifest itself through victories but in how we deal with defeat. I have often been ashamed of my past and kept it a secret but this must come to an end." With a pensive voice she began to explain. From her youth, the insatiable urge to not miss out on any given opportunity: the wild parties, the drugs, the wrong men who exploited her and her first film roles in cheap sex films.

Many bad decisions that ended up in attempted suicide. But also her painfully slow way back to life. Arianne Brand asked hardly any questions but let her speak freely.

"We are about to turn to the first callers," declared Rajiv Bhamra. "I don't know if she just buried her career as an author."

"I have to go," Sandrine announced. "Please see that someone brings Madame Marchal home, as she has just lost her driver and best friend."

"Don't worry, I'll do it myself."

"Thank you." She looked over at Odette Marchal one last time, who looked sad, but also relieved. Sandrine left the radio station.

At Home

Sandrine stopped next to the small, green transport vehicle which belonged to Alain Thibaud who delivered vegetables from his farm. She took her helmet off. The smell of charcoal was in the air and she could hear voices.

"I thought I heard a motorcycle." Léon walked up to her. "You caught your killer?"

"Just in time for the barbecue." She dismounted and jacked up the motorcycle with a flourish.

"Satisfied now?" he asked her.

"I would have preferred that the victims were still alive and that my job would have been redundant."

"But they're not and the people of Saint-Malo are lucky to have you."

"Very sweet of you." She hung her helmet on the left side view mirror, walked toward him and kissed him on the cheek. "Enough with the compliments, I'm starving to death."

"The first fish are already on the grill, shouldn't take long." He put his arm around Sandrine's shoulder and they went behind the old farmhouse. About a dozen people sat at a rustic, wooden table, chatting loudly.

"Here comes our lieutenant, everybody make room and slide closer together," yelled Alain who stood at the barbecue. Dark smoke escaped from a narrow chimney. She went to him.

"Thank you so much for the invitation, despite what happened to the barn."

"No problem. Actually, that old thing belonged to the Morvan family and I never used it. I'm glad to have someone new around here." He turned to the people at the table. "I know all their stories by heart and most of them are fake anyway," he called out to his friends.

"What can I offer you?" Léon pulled her in front of the brick barbecue. "We have pollock, redfish, some trout ..."

"Since when is anybody able to catch trout from the sea?" she asked in amazement.

Alain laughed aloud. "You start by going to the fish counter at Carrefour. If we only had his catch, we'd all have to share one measly mackerel."

Léon raised his hands apologetically. "There are good days and bad days, today was a particularly bad day."

"Good thing the closest supermarket isn't far away."

"I'd wait a little longer," Alain added. "There's been a salt marsh lamb in the smoker since this morning and it will be ready soon. You can't miss that. Simone conjured up some orange-pomegranate-syrup, which goes very well with it." He waved at a woman who must be the one who had brought it.

"In the last few days, I've hardly had a bite to eat. I'll have some of both, as well as the veggies, which look really delicious."

Sandrine leaned back in her camping chair, stretched her legs out and watched the flames rising from an open fire. She nibbled on a stalk of green asparagus, which was wrapped in a strip of bacon. Her phone rang: it was Arianne Briand. She was off duty and didn't want to be asked about the case. But her curiosity won her over and she answered the call.

"Can I speak with you briefly?" the journalist asked.

"I'm at a private party. If it's about the case, I'll be available on Monday."

"Kind of, but I think this will be of interest to you."

"Go ahead and shoot."

"Today we received a video and audio file from Aimée Vilette."

"What?"

"From her personally. She must have uploaded it to the Internet and dated it to be sent automatically for today's broadcast."

"Have you already seen it?"

"It was addressed to me, so yes."

"Did she talk about the abuse?"

"Exactly as you suspected. She accused Philippe Chardon."

"She must have known she was in danger or she wouldn't have taken such precautions," said Sandrine.

"I think so, too."

"What are you going to do with the footage?"

"Aimée's show, the 'Midnight Chat's, is on in two hours. I would like to broadcast it – she would have wanted that – otherwise it would have made no sense for her to send it to me. It's an incredible story. The dead speaking from the grave. Who would want to miss it?"

"I hear a slight hesitation."

"We talked about it and decided to leave the decision up to her boyfriend and her parents. If they agree, we'll broadcast it tonight otherwise ..."

Sandrine's respect for the woman grew. She had a fantastic story and was ready to give it up out of consideration for the victim's family. She regretted thinking that Arianne Briand was so much like Deborah Binet that they could have been twins.

Nothing would have stopped the latter from putting this breaking story on the front page.

"I don't think her parents will have any objection. They'll be happy to hear her voice again. Hopefully this would put an end to the idle chatter that has gone on for too long."

"I hope so. In any case, the files are ready for you here. It's probably evidence so I don't want to send via email."

"Thank you. I'll send somebody to pick it up."

Arianne Briand ended the conversation and Sandrine sent a text message to Adel and Inès. The two would certainly not want to miss the show. Léon came over and sat next to her.

"Is everything all right or is work calling you again?"

"No. I'm off duty the whole weekend." She stuck the rest of the asparagus in her mouth. "Delicious."

"What can I get you?" asked Léon and pointed to the grill.

"Not an easy choice." She smiled at him. "I was convinced you were just going to show off but the salmon fillet with curry sauce looks exquisite and I'd like to taste barbecue oysters for the first time in my life."

"It's fun to grill for someone who appreciates it."

"Maybe I should get a grill myself. Not such a big one, but a small one for one or two people."

Léon sat up in his chair and leaned toward her. "You only need something like that if you want to make your house into a home."

"I have an interesting job, a house close to the sea and people I like." She lay her hand on his and squeezed it tightly. "Which are all excellent reasons to stay."

"So, have you decided?"

"I will sign it on Monday." She didn't expect how easy the decision would be for her. She already felt at home here.

"Lieutenant Perrot is staying with us. How wonderful," said Léon and smiled at her.

"Capitaine, to be exact." Along with her disciplinary hearing, her demotion would also go in the trash.

"I'm so happy."

"I feel the same way," she said and meant it quite sincerely. Life in Brittany seemed very promising at the moment and she decided to enjoy it to the fullest.

Directory of persons

- Sandrine Perrot: Unorthodox investigator in Saint-Malo
- Adel Azarou: Brigadier with a penchant for fashionable clothing
- Jean Matisse: Career-conscious head of the Commissariat
- Jean-Claude Mazet: Forensic scientist often underestimated at first glance
- Inès Boni: Office manager and invaluable source of information
- Doktor Hervé: Meticulous coroner
- Renard Dubois and Luc Poutin: Police Brigadiers
- Gerard Lagarde: Public prosecutor who likes to claim the successes of others
- Aimée Vilette: Influencer from Saint-Malo
- Dominique Petitjean: Third rate photographer with a dubious background
- Suzanne Leriche: Psychologist and Aimée Vilette's friend
- Rajiv Bhamra: Sound Engineer and producer

- Arianne Briand: Program director and clever journalist on local radio
- Philippe Chardon: Psychiatrist and avid sailor
- Rosalie Simonas: Successful crime writer and friend of Sandrine
- Odette Marchal: Author with a turbulent past
- Pierre Salazar: Writer of predictable crime fiction
- Grégoire Argent: Publisher with an unrequited love
- Deborah Binet: Ambitious journalist who's always hoping for tips
- Marc Bergier: Goose breeder who easily loses his temper
- Léon Martinau: Club owner and ambitious angler
- Lilou Lanvers: Martial arts fighter who often surprises

Thanks

I am delighted that you joined Sandrine Perrot and Adel Azarou in their investigation in Brittany. Feedback from my readers is very important to me. Critique, praise and ideas are always welcome, and I am happy to answer any questions.

My email address is: Author@Christophe-Villain.com

Newsletter: To not miss any new publications you can sign up to the newsletter and get the free novella: Death in Paris - The prequel to the Brittany Mystery Series.

Free Novella

Subscribe to the newsletter and receive a free eBook: Death in Paris.
Sandrine Perrot's back story, her last case in Paris.

Sandrine held the warm coffee cup in her hands and looked out through the café window. The gusty wind drove dark clouds across the sky and swirled leaves along the boulevard. Pedestrians zipped up their jackets and scrambled to keep dry before the impending rain. She wasn't particularly excited about the prospect of having to take her motorbike on the road. Sandrine forgot to shop most of the time and hated to cook. Café Central was her salvation so she wouldn't turn up at work with her stomach growling.

"Would you like anything else to drink?" asked the waitress, who regularly saw Sandrine during her morning shift. She bet the young girl was a student who worked here to earn a few euros. Judging by her distinct accent, she was probably from Provence.

"Thank you but I have to get on the road pretty soon."

"Not a nice day." The young woman took a peek outside and picked up the used plate on

which the remains of scrambled eggs and baguette crumbs lay.

"That's why I hold on to my coffee cup for a while and enjoy the warmth in the café before I have to go to work." A bad feeling swept over her that she couldn't pin down to any specific event, but it nagged at her, as if the day could only get worse. The case she was investigating was stuck in her head and she couldn't shake it, which she usually could.

"No hurry," said the waitress, looking around the half-empty café. "It doesn't get crowded again until lunchtime, so until then I don't have much to do."

Sandrine's cell phone, which was lying on the table in front of her, vibrated and she glanced at the display.

"I'm afraid I have to take this call."

The waitress took the hint and took the dirty dishes into the kitchen. "Hello, Martin, what's up?"

She listened to her colleague in silence for a while.

"On the Richard Lenoir Boulevard? I'll be there in fifteen minutes."

Sandrine ended the call and cursed under her breath. Her gut feeling had proved to be right; the day lived up to its promise. She put money on the table, pulled on the waterproof motorcycle jacket and picked up the helmet that was lying on a chair.

She quickly drank the rest of the coffee. The waitress gave her a friendly wave as she left.

Her motorcycle was parked on the wide sidewalk between two trees. She wiped the wet seat with her sleeve before climbing on and pulling on her gloves. She took a deep breath and started the engine. Shortly thereafter, she merged into traffic.

Half a dozen patrol cars and an ambulance were parked by the Saint-Martin Canal. The paramedics were hunkered down in the car and puffs of smoke rose through their slightly ajar windows. They were more comfortable than their police colleagues, who had to go out to cordon off the area. The first onlookers were already gathering on one of the narrow bridges that spanned the watercourse. Sandrine drove through a gap in the metal fence separating the canal from the boulevard and parked the motorcycle on the wide pedestrian promenade. Bollards – stocky

vertical posts – were set at regular intervals, but today no boats were moored here and the lock gate was closed.

"Good morning, Sandrine," a grey-haired man with angular features greeted her. His badge identified him as Major de Police. "Kind of shitty weather to be out on a motorcycle."

"Hello, Martin. It's still a lot quicker than driving a car. Not to mention parking." She stuffed her gloves and scarf into her helmet and stuffed it into one of the panniers. "Is it our guy?"

"The Necktie Killer? Looks like it."

"Is that what they call him now?" She shook her head in disgust. "Far too friendly sounding. He's a sadistic murderer and should be considered and referred to as such."

"I didn't invent it. We owe that to the journalists who needed punchy headlines." He held up his hands defensively.

"I'm sorry. I was thinking of the victims."

"That's all right. Whenever things like that don't get to you anymore, it's time to change careers."

"In there?" she asked, looking toward the entrance to the Saint-Martin Canal, which ran underground for the next few miles. Even on sunny days, this gloomy place seemed ominous to her. "Who from our team is here?"

"Brossault, the medical examiner with the forensic guys and some cops cordoning off the area. The big boys are on their way, it was probably too early in the morning for them."

Sandrine laughed softly. The chief of homicide and the juge d'instruction, the prosecutor in charge of the investigation, would not be long in coming. They were forced to demonstrate that

the police were doing everything they could to take the perpetrator off the street since the series of murders was dominating the front pages of the newspapers. However, they hadn't even come an inch closer to him since they'd found the first victim in the summer. It was now February and two more dead women had joined the list of victims.

"Let's go then," she said, walking towards the scene of the crime.

The rain started, pattering on the dark water of the canal. Major Martin Alary pulled up the collar of his raincoat and walked faster across the slippery pavement. A uniformed cop stepped aside and waved them through the barricade.

"Was it closed?" Sandrine asked, looking at the lock where the water was damming up. The Saint-Martin Canal was just under two-and-a-half-miles long, and connected the Bassin de la Villette in the north with the Seine in the south. It had a total of five locks – enclosures with gates at each end where the water level could be raised or lowered.

"Most people only use the exposed area: a few tourist boats, but mostly paddle boats and small motorboats used for family outings in the Bassin de la Villette. Hardly more than a dozen boats a day traverse the entire length of the canal."

"The less water traffic, the more noticeable things are. Let's hope someone noticed something."

They entered the tunnel through an open metal door guarded by another police officer. Martin Alary wiped raindrops from his shoulders and adjusted his gun holster. A brick path, on which two people could comfortably walk side by side, ran along the length of the canal. The dim light of the rainy day reached only a few feet deep into the tunnel, and the antique-looking lamps that hung at regular intervals on the wall allowed one to see the way, but were useless for forensic

work. The forensics team had already set up blazingly bright spotlights so they wouldn't miss a thing.

A thin man with a pointed beard and a bald head walked towards them.

"Ah. Capitaine Perrot and Major Alary. Already here?" Marcel Carron, the forensics manager, patted Sandrine's companion on the shoulder and gave him a wink before turning to face her. He refrained from giving her a chummy pat on the back.

"How far along are you with securing the crime scene?"

"Almost done. However, there was hardly anything to secure."

"What can you tell me?"

"An employee of the city building department discovered the body during a routine examination. She was floating in the water. He informed us immediately and left the site. Very prudent."

"Is this also the scene of the crime?" the major asked.

"There's no evidence thus far," Carron replied. "We've searched the path for evidence of a struggle, but to no avail. The corpse is unclothed, but we couldn't find clothes anywhere."

"Not surprising."

"I concur."

"Any idea how the body got here?" Alary asked.

"There aren't many options left. There is no current in the canal sufficient enough to move a human body. She would have been spotted within one of the locks."

"Then she was put here," said Sandrine.

"The question is how." The forensic scientist pointed to the metal door at the entrance to the tunnel. "Entry is forbidden and the door is normally locked. However, there's no problem climbing over the door but dragging a corpse of an adult person up and over would be almost impossible without risking being discovered."

"Then there's only one option left," Sandrine said, stepping up to the railing that was too dirty to touch. "The perpetrator threw her off a boat at this point."

"An ideal location," the major agreed. "Nobody would notice since people seldom come in here."

"I'm assuming there's no security camera in the tunnel." Despite saying this, Sandrine looked around.

"Maybe the doctor can tell us more." She wasn't particularly hopeful. So far, the killer had left no usable evidence.

"Good luck."

Sandrine pulled a pair of disposable gloves and shoe covers out of her jacket pocket and put them on. Even though the forensic scientist assumed there wouldn't be anything of interest here, she played it safe.

A few feet away, she found Doctor Brossault standing next to the victim, a blue blanket spread over it.

"Bonjour," she greeted the older man in a dark suit, bow tie and handkerchief in his breast pocket. He turned to face her and used his forefinger to push his rimless glasses up the bridge of his nose. "An ideal place to dump a body, isn't it?"

"Absolutely." He nodded enthusiastically. "The murderer has a soft spot for historical places. You have to give him that."

"The canal dates back from the early 19th century, from what I remember from my history class." "1825 if you want to be exact, but who cares about that anyway?"

Sandrine suppressed a grin. The medical examiner was the type of person who always wanted to be as precise as possible and didn't withhold his knowledge.

"The canal, anyway. The structure built over the canal did not take place until much later: in 1860. At first, it was designed by Haussmann to improve traffic in the city."

"At first?" Sandrine asked. The man loved sharing his knowledge of history and enlightening those around him. It made him happy, so she let him have his fun.

"Naturally. Napoleon III was not exactly a popular head of state. Resistance to his rule simmered particularly in the revolutionary neighbourhoods such as Faubourg-Montmartre and Ménilmontant. So the plan to build over the canal came in handy. A wide swath through the city along which to send cavalry to maintain law and order."

"Interesting," said Major Alary, who Sandrine heard come up behind her. "But it didn't do him any good in the end."

"Fortunately," the doctor agreed.

Sandrine knelt down next to the body and looked inquisitively at the medical examiner. Only when he nodded did she lift the blanket under which the victim lay. A young woman's bloodless face stared at her with lifeless blue eyes. Blonde hair clung damply to pale skin. She wore a silk tie around her neck, where strangulation marks could be seen.

"She was strangled," Sandrine murmured, more to herself than to Doctor Brossault. "Just like the previous two victims," he confirmed.

"What can you tell me?"

"I'd put the woman in her mid-twenties, blonde and attractive like the other victims. She was strangled with the necktie. There are cuts on her wrists. Without wanting to commit myself, I would conclude that plastic restraints were used. The police use those things, too."

"Any other signs that she fought back?"

"I can't imagine that she didn't, but she had no chance of surviving. Not with her hands tied. Of course we are also looking for narcotics."

"Maybe the tie will get us further."

"A silk tie. Quite expensive and downright exclusive. Forensics will confirm that, although I can't imagine Monsieur Carron being an expert on the subject."

She looked up at him probingly.

"Have you ever seen the man properly dressed before?" His brow furrowed as if surprised at her lack of awareness.

"What's so special about these ties?"

"The quality of the silk is impeccable. In terms of design, I would guess mid-century. In addition, our killer is able to tie a perfect Windsor knot, something that is becoming increasingly rare these days. People either forgo a tie completely or fasten it sloppily. I would narrow the circle of perpetrators down to people with style and money."

He finished the sentence and straightened his bow tie.

Sandrine put the blanket back over the woman's face. She would see her again in the medical examiner's office. She'd seen enough for now.

To subscribe to the newsletter, please use the QR code.

Other Books

Emerald Coast Murder

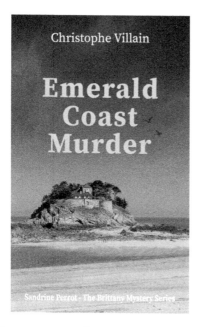

Sandrine Perrot's investigation takes her from the picturesque fishing towns to the rural hinterland of Brittany's Emerald Coast.

Police Lieutenant Sandrine Perrot is on leave from her post in Paris and has settled in Cancale, the oyster capital of Brittany. She is temporarily assigned to the Saint-Malo police station for this case. The body of an unidentified woman is discovered on the Brittany coast path along the bay of Mont- Saint-Michel.

With her new assistant, Adel Azarou, she takes on the investigation, which leads them to a cold case from Paris, but also deep into the tragic history of a venerable hotelier family.

Deadly Tides at Mont-Saint-Michel

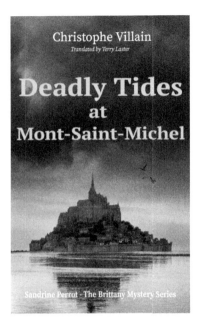

A dead woman loved by all.

Instead of spending a pleasant day with Léon on the coast and at Le
Mont-Saint-Michel, Sandrine Perrot is called to a fatal accident in the
Saint-Malo marina. The driver's death touches her personally, as she
had just met the woman. In the course of the forensic investigation, she
discovers that there is more to the alleged accident than she first
suspected.

Her investigation leads her into the world of a well-known family in Le
Mont-Saint-Michel, a family marked by antiquated traditions but also
by conflicts between siblings.

Another person soon disappears without a trace. Was he trying to
evade interrogation, or was an unwelcome witness being silenced?

Printed in Great Britain
by Amazon